Shingo

Shuichi   son

Yasuko   Shingo's wife

Kikuko   Shuichi's "

Fusako   daughter of Shingo

Kuriko   "   " Fusako

Satoko

Tanizaki   ? Shingo's secretary
Shingo

by Yasunari Kawabata

SNOW COUNTRY

THOUSAND CRANES

SNOW COUNTRY
and THOUSAND CRANES
Nobel Prize Edition 1969

The Sound of the Mountain

Shingo   Yasuko

Shuichi — Kikuko   Fusako

Satoko   Kuniko

Yasunari Kawabata

The Sound of
the Mountain

Translated from the Japanese
by Edward G. Seidensticker

Charles E. Tuttle Company: Publishers
Suido 1-chome, 2-6, Bunkyo-ku, Tokyo

UNESCO COLLECTION OF
REPRESENTATIVE WORKS
Japanese Series
This book has been accepted in the Japanese Series of the
Translations Collection of the United Nations Educational,
Scientific and Cultural Organization (UNESCO).

Originally published in Japanese as *Yama no Oto*

Published by the Charles E. Tuttle Company, Inc., of Rutland,
Vermont and Tokyo, Japan, with editorial offices at Suido
1-chome, 2-6, Bunkyo-ku, Tokyo, Japan, by special arrangement with Alfred A. Knopf, Inc., New York.

First Tuttle edition published 1971
Tenth printing, 1990

PRINTED IN JAPAN

Contents

Contents

Note on the Pronunciation of Japanese Names

Consonants are pronounced approximately as in English, except that "g" is always hard, as in Gilbert. Vowels are pronounced as in Italian. Also as in Italian, the final *e* is always sounded. Thus the name Kaname is pronounced Kah-nah-meh. There is no heavy penultimate accent as in English; it is adequate to accent each syllable equally.

The Japanese name order has been followed throughout this translation, with the family name first.

The Sound of the Mountain

The Sound of the Mountain

Ogata Shingo, his brow slightly furrowed, his lips slightly parted, wore an air of thought. Perhaps to a stranger it would not have appeared so. It might have seemed rather that something had saddened him.

His son Shuichi knew what was happening. It happened so frequently that he gave it little thought.

Indeed, more was apparent to him than the simple fact that his father was thinking. He knew that his father was trying to remember something.

Shingo took off his hat and, absently holding it in his right hand, set it on his knee. Shuichi put it on the rack above them.

"Let me see. What was it, I wonder?" At such times Shingo found speech difficult. "What was the name of the maid that left the other day?"

"You mean Kayo?"

"Kayo. That was it. And when was it that she left?"

"Last Thursday. That would make it five days ago."

"Five days ago? Just five days ago she quit, and I can't remember anything about her."

To Shuichi his father's performance seemed a trifle exaggerated.

"That Kayo—I think it must have been two or three days before she quit. When I went out for a walk I had a blister on my foot, and I said I thought I had picked up ringworm. 'Footsore,' she said. I liked that. It had a gentle, old-fashioned ring to it. I liked it very much. But now that I think about it I'm sure she said I had a boot sore. There was something wrong with the way she said it. Say 'footsore.' "

"Footsore."

"And now say 'boot sore.' "

"Boot sore."

"I thought so. Her accent was wrong."

Of provincial origins, Shingo was never very confident about standard Tokyo pronunciation. Shuichi had grown up in Tokyo.

"It had a very pleasant sound to it, very gentle and elegant, when I thought she said 'footsore.' She was there in the hallway. And now it occurs to me what she really said, and I can't even think of her name. I can't remember her clothes or her face. I imagine she was with us six months or so?"

"Something of the sort." Used to these problems, Shuichi offered his father no sympathy.

Shingo was accustomed enough to them himself, and yet he felt a twinge of something like fear. However hard he tried to remember the girl, he could not summon her up. There were times when such futile searchings were leavened by sentimentality.

So it was now. It had seemed to him that Kayo, leaning slightly forward there in the hallway, was consoling him for being footsore.

She had been with them six months, and he could call up only the memory of that single word. He felt that a life was being lost.

2

Yasuko, Shingo's wife, was sixty-three, a year older than he.

They had a son, a daughter, and two grandchildren, daughters of the girl, Fusako.

Yasuko was young for her age. One would not have taken her to be older than her husband. Not that Shingo himself seemed particularly old. They seemed natural together, he just enough older than she to make them a most ordinary couple. Though diminutive, she was in robust health.

Yasuko was no beauty. In their younger years she had looked older than he, and had disliked being seen in public with him.

Shingo could not have said at what age she had begun to look the younger of the two. Probably it had been somewhere toward their mid-fifties. Women generally age faster than men, but in their case the reverse had been true.

The year before, the year he had entered his second cycle of sixty years, Shingo had spat up blood—from his lungs, it had seemed. He had not had a medical examination, however, and presently the affliction had gone away. It had not come back.

Nor had it meant that he grew suddenly older. His skin had seemed firmer since, and in the two weeks or so that he had been in bed the color of his eyes and lips had improved.

Shingo had not detected symptoms of tuberculosis in himself, and to spit blood at his age gave him the darkest forebodings. Partly because of them he refused to be examined. To Shuichi such behavior was no more than the stubborn refusal of the aged to face facts. Shingo was not able to agree.

Yasuko was a good sleeper. Sometimes, in the middle of the night, Shingo would be tempted to blame her snoring for having awakened him. She had snored, it seemed, as a girl of fifteen or sixteen, and her parents had been at great pains to correct the habit; it had stopped when she married. Then, when she passed fifty, it had begun again.

When she snored Shingo would twist her nose in an effort to stop her. If the twisting had no effect, he would take her by the throat and shake her. On nights when he was not in good spirits he would be repelled by the sight of the aged flesh with which he had lived for so long.

Tonight he was not in good spirits. Turning on the light, he looked at her profile and took her by the throat. She was a little sweaty.

Only when she snored did he reach out to touch her. The fact seemed to him infinitely saddening.

He took up a magazine lying at his pillow. Then, the room being sultry, he got up, opened a shutter, and sat down beside it.

The moon was bright.

One of his daughter-in-law's dresses was hanging outside, unpleasantly gray. Perhaps she had forgotten to take in her laundry, or perhaps she had left a sweat-soaked garment to take the dew of night.

A screeching of insects came from the garden. There were locusts on the trunk of the cherry tree to the left. He had not known that locusts could make such a rasping sound; but locusts indeed they were.

He wondered if locusts might sometimes be troubled with nightmares.

A locust flew in and lit on the skirt of the mosquito net. It made no sound as he picked it up.

"A mute." It would not be one of the locusts he had heard at the tree.

Lest it fly back in, attracted by the light, he threw it with all his strength toward the top of the tree. He felt nothing against his hand as he released it.

Gripping the shutter, he looked toward the tree. He could not tell whether the locust had lodged there or flown on. There was a vast depth to the moonlit night, stretching far on either side.

Though August had only begun, autumn insects were already singing.

He thought he could detect a dripping of dew from leaf to leaf.

Then he heard the sound of the mountain.

It was a windless night. The moon was near full, but in the moist, sultry air the fringe of trees that outlined the mountain was blurred. They were motionless, however.

Not a leaf on the fern by the veranda was stirring.

In these mountain recesses of Kamakura the sea could sometimes be heard at night. Shingo wondered if he might have heard the sound of the sea. But no—it was the mountain.

It was like wind, far away, but with a depth like a rumbling of the earth. Thinking that it might be in himself, a ringing in his ears, Shingo shook his head.

The sound stopped, and he was suddenly afraid. A chill passed over him, as if he had been notified that death was approaching. He wanted to question himself, calmly and deliberately, to ask whether it had been the sound of the wind, the sound of the sea, or a sound in his ears. But he had heard no such sound, he was sure. He had heard the mountain.

It was as if a demon had passed, making the mountain sound out.

The steep slope, wrapped in the damp shades of night, was like a dark wall. So small a mound of a mountain, that it was all in Shingo's garden; it was like an egg cut in half.

There were other mountains behind it and around it, but the sound did seem to have come from that particular mountain to the rear of Shingo's house.

Stars were shining through the trees at its crest.

As he closed the shutter, a strange memory came to him.

Some ten days before, he had been awaiting a guest at a newly built restaurant. A single geisha was with him. The guest was late, and so were the other geisha.

"Why don't you take off your tie?" she said. "You must be warm."

Shingo nodded, and let her take it off for him.

She was not a geisha with whom he was particularly familiar, but when she had folded the tie and put it into the pocket of his coat, which lay beside the alcove, the conversation moved on to personal matters.

Some two months before, she said, she had been on the point of committing suicide with the carpenter who had built the restaurant. But as they had prepared to take poison, doubts had overtaken her. Were the portions in fact lethal?

"He said there was plenty. The doses were all measured out, his and mine, he said, and that proved it."

But she could not believe him. Her doubts only grew.

"I asked him who did the measuring. Someone might have measured out just enough to make us sick and teach us a lesson. I asked him who the druggist or doctor was that gave it to him, but he wouldn't say. Isn't that strange? There we were, going to die together. Why wouldn't he answer me? After all, who was to know afterwards?"

"A good yarn," Shingo had wanted to say.

And so she had insisted, she went on, that they try again after *she* had found someone to do the measuring.

"I have it here with me."

Shingo thought the story an odd one. All that had really stayed with him was the fact that the man was a carpenter and had built the restaurant.

The geisha had taken two packets from her purse and opened them for him.

He had only glanced at them. He had had no way of knowing whether or not they were poison.

As he closed the shutter, he thought of the geisha.

He went back to bed. He did not wake his wife to tell her of the fear that had come over him on hearing the sound of the mountain.

3

Shuichi and Shingo worked for the same firm. The son served as a sort of prompter for the father.

There were other prompters too, Yasuko and Kikuko, Shuichi's wife. The three of them worked together, a team supplementing Shingo's powers of memory. The girl in the office was yet another prompter.

Coming into Shingo's office, Shuichi took a book from the small stand in one corner and began leafing through it.

"Well, well," he said. He went over to the girl's desk and pointed to an open page.

"What is it?" asked Shingo, smiling. Shuichi brought the book to him.

"One is not to understand that the sense of chastity has here been lost," said the passage in question. "We have but a device for loving longer. A man unable to bear the pain of loving a woman, a woman unable to bear the pain of loving a man—they should go happily out in search of other partners, and so find a way to make their hearts more steadfast."

"Where is 'here'?"

"Paris. It's a novelist's account of his trip to Europe."

Shingo's mind was no longer as alive as it had once been to aphorism and paradox. This seemed to him, however, neither of the two. It seemed, more simply, penetrating insight.

Shuichi had probably not been moved by the passage. He had found a way, on the spur of the moment, for signaling to the girl that he wanted her to go out with him after work.

As he got off the train in Kamakura, Shingo found himself wishing that he had come home with Shuichi, or perhaps later.

The bus was crowded with commuters. He decided to walk.

The fishmonger nodded a greeting as Shingo stood outside the shop. He went in. The water in the tub of prawns was a cloudy white. He prodded a lobster. It should have been alive, but it did not move. He decided on whelks, of which there was a good supply.

When asked how many he wanted, however, he was perplexed.

"Well, make it three. Three of the biggest ones."

"Shall I dress them for you, sir?"

The fishmonger and his son dug out the meat with butcher knives. Shingo disliked the sound of scraping against the shell.

As the man washed and cut the meat, two girls stopped in front of the shop.

"What will you have?" he asked, going on with the dicing.

"Herring."

"How many?"

"One."

"One?"

"Yes."

"Just one?"

The herring were not the smallest possible, but they were little larger than minnows. The girl did not seem to be especially put off by this show of disapproval, however.

The man took up the herring in a bit of paper and handed it to her.

"But we didn't need any fish," said the second girl, hanging over the other and prodding her elbow.

"I wonder if they'll still be here on Saturday," said the other. She was looking at the lobsters. "My boy friend sort of likes them."

The second girl did not answer.

Startled, Shingo ventured a glance.

Prostitutes of the new sort, they had bare backs, cloth shoes, and good figures.

The fishmonger collected the diced meat at the center of his board and, dividing it in three parts, began to put it back into the shells.

"We're getting more and more of their kind. Even here in Kamakura."

His asperity struck Shingo as most odd. "But I thought they were behaving rather well," he said, protesting against he hardly knew what.

Casually, the man was putting the meat back into the

shells, so mixed together, thought Shingo, that it was unlikely to be reassembled in the particular shells from which it had come. He was aware of very small niceties.

Today was Thursday. Two more days until Saturday—but then, he told himself, there were plenty of lobsters to be had these days. He wondered how the uncouth maiden would prepare lobster for her American friend. A lobster made a simple, uncouth dish, however, fried or boiled or roasted.

Shingo had felt well disposed toward the girls, and yet afterwards he was taken with vague feelings of despondency.

There were four in his family, but he had bought only three whelks. He had not acted precisely out of consideration for Kikuko, although he had of course known that Shuichi would not be home for dinner. He had simply deleted Shuichi.

At a grocery farther on he bought gingko nuts.

4

It was unusual for Shingo to buy food on his way home, but neither Yasuko nor Kikuko showed surprise.

Perhaps they wished to hide their thoughts about the fact that Shuichi, who should have been with him, was not.

Handing his purchases to Kikuko, he followed her into the kitchen.

"Some water please, with a little sugar in it." He went to the faucet himself.

In the sink were prawns and lobsters. He was struck

by the coincidence. He had seen both at the fishmonger's, but had not thought of buying both.

"A good color," he said. The prawns had a fresh luster.

Kikuko cracked a gingko nut with the back of a knife.

"It was a nice thought, but I'm afraid they're no good."

"Oh? I did think they were a little out of season."

"I'll call the grocery and tell them."

"Don't bother. But all these shellfish—my contribution doesn't add much."

"We might open a seaside restaurant." Kikuko showed the tip of her tongue, in mild derision. "Let's see, now. We can boil these, shell and all. So maybe we should roast the lobsters and fry the prawns. I'll go buy some mushrooms. While I'm at it would you mind going out to get eggplant from the garden?"

"I'd be delighted."

"Little ones. And bring in some sage, too. I wonder if the prawns might be enough by themselves."

Kikuko brought only two whelks to the table.

"But there should be another," said Shingo, a little puzzled.

"Oh, dear. But the two of you have such bad teeth, Grandpa—I thought you might want to share one nicely between you."

"I don't see any grandchildren around."

Yasuko looked down and snickered.

"I'm sorry." Kikuko got up lightly and went to the kitchen for the third.

"We should do as Kikuko says," said Yasuko. "Share one nicely between us."

Shingo thought Kikuko's words beautifully apt. It was

as though his own problem, whether to buy three or four, had thus been brushed away. Her tact and skill were not to be underestimated.

She might have been expected to say that she would leave one for Shuichi, or that she and Yasuko would share one. Perhaps she had considered these possibilities.

"But were there only three in the store?" asked Yasuko, not alive to such subtleties. "You only brought three, and there are four of us."

"We didn't need another. Shuichi didn't come home."

Yasuko smiled what should have been a wry smile, but, perhaps because of her age, it ended up as something less than that.

No trace of a shadow passed over Kikuko's face, nor did she ask what might have happened to Shuichi.

She was the youngest of eight children.

The other seven were also married, and all had numerous progeny. Shingo sometimes thought of the fecundity she had inherited from her parents.

She would complain that he had not yet learned the names of her brothers and sisters. He was even further from remembering the names of her nieces and nephews. She had been born at a time when her mother no longer wanted children or thought herself capable of having them. Indeed, her mother had felt rather ashamed, at her age, and had considered abortion. It had been a difficult birth. Forceps had been applied to Kikuko's head.

Kikuko had told Shingo of having heard these facts from her mother.

It was difficult for him to understand a mother who

would speak of such things to her daughter, or a girl who would reveal them to her father-in-law.

Kikuko had held back her hair to show a faint scar on her forehead.

The scar, whenever he chanced to glimpse it afterwards, somehow drew him to her.

Still, Kikuko had been reared as the pet of the family, it seemed. She was not spoiled, precisely, but she seemed to expect affection. And there was something a little weak about her.

When she had first come as a bride, Shingo had noted the slight but beautiful way she had of moving her shoulders. In it, for him, there was a bright, fresh coquetry.

Something about the delicate figure made him think of Yasuko's sister.

Shingo had as a boy been strongly attracted to the sister. After her death Yasuko had gone to take care of the children. Yasuko had quite immersed herself in the work, as if wishing to supplant her sister. It was true that she had been fond of the brother-in-law, a handsome man, but she had also been in love with her sister, so beautiful a woman as to make it difficult to believe that the two could have had the same mother. To Yasuko her sister and brother-in-law had been like inhabitants of a dream world.

She worked hard for her brother-in-law and the children, but the man behaved as if he were quite indifferent to her feelings. He lost himself in pleasure, and for Yasuko self-immolation became a career.

And so Shingo had married her.

Now more than thirty years had passed, and Shingo

did not think the marriage a mistake. A long marriage was not necessarily governed by its origins.

Yet the image of the sister remained with both of them. Neither spoke of her, and neither had forgotten her.

There was nothing especially unhealthy about the fact that, after Kikuko came into the house, Shingo's memories were pierced by moments of brightness, like flashes of lightning.

Married to her less than two years, Shuichi had already found another woman, a source of some surprise for Shingo.

Unlike Shingo himself, reared in the provinces, Shuichi showed no evidence of deprivation in matters of love and desire. Shingo could not have said when his son had had his first woman.

Shingo was certain that whoever now held Shuichi's attention was a business woman, perhaps a prostitute of sorts.

He suspected that affairs with women in the office meant no more than dancing after work, and might be only for purposes of distracting his father's attention.

She would not in any case be a sheltered girl like the one before him. Somehow Shingo had sensed as much from Kikuko herself. Since the beginning of the affair there had been a ripening in the relations between Kikuko and Shuichi. There had been a change in Kikuko's body.

Waking in the night—it was the night they had had the shellfish—Shingo heard Kikuko's voice as he had not heard it before.

He suspected that she knew nothing of Shuichi's mistress.

"And so Father has made the apologies, with a shell-fish," he muttered to himself.

How was it that, although she knew nothing of the other woman, she should feel emanations come drifting toward her?

Shingo drowsed off, and suddenly it was dawn. He went for the paper. The moon was still high. After glancing over the news he fell asleep once more.

5

Shuichi pushed his way aboard the train and surrendered his seat to Shingo when the latter followed after.

He then handed over the evening paper and took Shingo's bifocals from his pocket. Shingo had a pair of his own, but he was much given to forgetting them. Shuichi was entrusted with a spare set.

Shuichi leaned over the paper. "Tanizaki said today that a classmate of hers was looking for work. We do need a maid, you know. So I said we'd take her."

"Don't you think it might be a little dangerous, having a friend of Tanizaki's around?"

"Dangerous?"

"She might hear things from Tanizaki and pass them on to Kikuko."

"What would she have to pass on?"

"Well, I suppose it will be good to have a maid with proper introductions." Shingo turned back to the paper.

"Has Tanizaki been talking about me?" asked Shuichi as they got off in Kamakura.

"She hasn't said a thing. I would have imagined that you had silenced her."

"Oh, fine. Suppose something actually were going on between me and your secretary. You'd be the joke of the office."

"Of course. But make sure, if you don't mind, that Kikuko doesn't find out."

Shuichi did not seem inclined toward secretiveness. "So Tanizaki *has* been talking."

"She knows you have a girl friend. And so I imagine she wants to go out with you herself."

"Maybe. Half of it might be jealousy."

"Splendid."

"I'm going to break it off. I'm trying to break it off."

"I don't understand you. Well, let me hear all about it some time."

"After I've broken it off."

"Don't let Kikuko know."

"She may already know."

Shingo lapsed into disgruntled silence.

It continued through dinner. He got up abruptly from the table and went to his room.

Kikuko brought him watermelon.

"You forgot the salt," said Yasuko, coming after her. The two sat down on the veranda. "Kikuko kept calling and calling. Didn't you hear her?"

"No. I did know that there was watermelon in the icebox."

"He didn't hear you," said Yasuko. "And you called and called."

"It's because he's annoyed about something." Kikuko turned to her mother-in-law.

Shingo was silent for a moment. "There's been something wrong with my ears these last few days, I think.

The other night I opened the shutter to let in a little air, and I heard the mountain rumbling. And you were snoring away."

Yasuko and Kikuko both looked toward the mountain.

"Do mountains roar?" asked Kikuko. "But you did say something once, Mother—remember? You said that just before your sister died Father heard the mountain roar."

Shingo was startled. He could not forgive himself for not remembering. He had heard the sound of the mountain, and why had the memory not come to him?

Apparently Kikuko regretted having made the remark. Her beautiful shoulders were motionless.

The Wings of the Locust

❁

Fusako, the daughter, came home with her two children.

"Might another be on the way?" asked Shingo casually, although he knew that with the older girl four and the younger barely past her first birthday the spacing would not call for another quite yet.

"You asked the same question just the other day." She laid the younger child on its back and started to unswaddle it. "And what about Kikuko?"

Her question was also a casual one, but Kikuko's face, as she looked down at the baby, was suddenly tense.

"Leave it as it is for a while," said Shingo.

"Her name is Kuniko, not 'it'. Didn't you name her yourself?"

Only Shingo, it seemed, was aware of the expression on Kikuko's face. He did not let it worry him, however. He was much taken with the movements of the emancipated little legs.

"Yes, leave her," said Yasuko. "She looks very happy. It must have been warm." She half tickled, half slapped the baby's stomach and thighs. "Why don't we send your mother and sister off, now, to freshen themselves up a bit?"

"Shall I get towels?" Kikuko started for the door.

"We've brought our own," said Fusako. It appeared that she meant to stay for some time.

Fusako took towels and clothes from a kerchief. The older child, Satoko, stood behind her, clinging sullenly to her. Satoko had not said a word since their arrival. Her thick black hair caught the eye.

Shingo had seen the kerchief before, but all he remembered was that it had been in the house. He did not know when.

Fusako had walked from the station with Kuniko on her back, Satoko tugging on one hand, the kerchief in the other. It must have been a pleasing sight, thought Shingo.

Satoko was not an easy child to lead. She had a way of being particularly difficult when matters were already complicated enough for her mother.

Did it trouble Yasuko, Shingo wondered, that of the two young women it was Kikuko who kept herself in good trim?

Yasuko sat rubbing a reddish spot on the inside of the baby's thigh. Fusako had gone to bathe. "I don't know, she somehow seems more manageable than Satoko."

"She was born after things started going bad with her father," said Shingo. "It all happened after Satoko was born, and it had an effect on her."

"Would a four-year-old child understand?"

"She would indeed. And it would influence her."

"I think she was born the way she is."

After elaborate contortions the baby turned over on its stomach, crawled off, and, catching hold of the door, stood up.

"Let's go have a walk, just the two of us," said Kikuko, taking the child by the hands and walking it to the next room.

Yasuko promptly went over to the purse beside Fusako's belongings and opened it.

"And what the devil do you think you're doing?" Shingo kept his voice low, but he was almost quivering with annoyance. "Stop it. Stop it, I tell you."

"And why should I?" Yasuko was calm.

"I told you to stop. What do you think you're up to?" His hands were trembling.

"I don't intend to steal anything."

"It's worse than stealing."

Yasuko replaced the purse. She was still sitting beside it, however. "And what is wrong with being interested in the affairs of your own daughter? Maybe she's come to us without enough money to buy the children candy. I want to know how things are with her. That's all."

Shingo glared at her.

Fusako came back from the bath.

"I looked inside your purse, Fusako," said Yasuko the moment her daughter stepped into the room, "and so I got a scolding from your father. If it was wrong I apologize."

"If it was wrong!" snorted Shingo.

This way of taking Fusako into her confidence only irritated him more.

He asked himself whether it might be true, as Yasuko's manner suggested, that such incidents were routine between mother and daughter. He was shaking with anger, and the fatigue of his years came flooding over him.

Fusako looked at him. It was possible that she was less surprised at her mother's behavior than at her father's.

"Please. Go ahead and look! Help yourself!" she said, half flinging the words out and slapping the purse down at her mother's knee.

Her manner did nothing to lessen his irritation.

Yasuko did not take up the purse.

"Without any money I wouldn't be able to run away, Aihara thought. I couldn't run away if I didn't have any money. So of course there's nothing in it. Go ahead and look."

Kuniko, her hands still in Kikuko's, suddenly collapsed. Kikuko picked her up.

Fusako lifted her blouse and presented her breast. She was not a beautiful woman, but she had a good figure. Her carriage was erect and the milk-swollen breast was firm.

"Is Shuichi away somewhere?" she asked. "Even on Sunday?"

She seemed to feel that she must do something to relieve the tension.

2

Almost home, Shingo looked up at the sunflowers blooming beside a neighboring house.

He was directly beneath the blossoms, which hung down over the gate.

The daughter of the house paused behind him. She could have pushed past him and gone into the house, but because she knew him, she waited there.

"What big flowers," he said, noticing her. "Remarkable flowers."

She smiled, a little shyly. "We pinched them back to one flower for each plant."

"Oh? That's why they're so big, then. Have they been blooming long?"

"Yes."

"How many days now?"

The girl—she was perhaps twelve or thirteen—did not answer. Apparently lost in silent calculation, she looked at Shingo, and then, with him, at the flowers again. Her face was round and sunburned, but her arms and legs were thin.

Thinking to make way for her, Shingo looked down the street. Two or three doors further on there were more sunflowers, three to each plant. The blossoms were only half the size of these.

As he started off he looked up again.

Kikuko was calling him. Indeed, she was standing

right behind him. Stalks of green soybeans protruded from her market bag.

"You've been admiring the sunflowers?"

Of more concern to her, no doubt, than the fact that he admired the sunflowers, was the fact that he had come home without Shuichi. Almost home, he was viewing sunflowers by himself.

"They're fine specimens," he said. "Like heads of famous people."

Kikuko nodded, her manner casual.

Shingo had put no thought into the words. The comparison had simply occurred to him. He had not been searching for one.

With the remark, however, he felt in all its immediacy the strength of the great, heavy, flowering heads. He felt the regularity and order with which they were put together. The petals were like crowns, and the greater part of the central discs was taken up by stamens, clusters of them, which seemed to thrust their way up by main strength. There was no suggestion that they were fighting one another, however. They were quietly systematic, and strength seemed to flow from them.

The flowers were larger in circumference than a human head. It was perhaps the formal arrangement of volume that had made Shingo think of a brain.

The power of nature within them made him think of a giant symbol of masculinity. He did not know whether they were male or not, but somehow he thought them so.

The summer sun was fading, and the evening air was calm.

The petals were golden, like women.

He walked away from the sunflowers, wondering

whether it was Kikuko's coming that had set him to thinking strange thoughts.

"My head hasn't been very clear these last few days. I suppose that's why sunflowers made me think of heads. I wish mine could be as clean as they are. I was thinking on the train—if only there were some way to get your head cleaned and refinished. Just chop it off— well, maybe that would be a little violent. Just detach it and hand it over to some university hospital as if you were handing over a bundle of laundry. 'Do this up for me, please,' you'd say. And the rest of you would be quietly asleep for three or four days or a week while the hospital was busy cleaning your head and getting rid of the garbage. No tossing and no dreaming."

"You must be tired," said Kikuko, a shadow passing over her face.

"I am. Today someone came to see me in the office. I took a puff on a cigarette and laid it down and lighted another and laid it down, and I saw that there were three of them, lighted and almost unsmoked. It was very embarrassing."

He had thought on the train of sending his head to a laundry, it was true, but he had been drawn not so much to the idea of the laundered head as to that of the sleeping body. A very pleasant sleep, with head detached. There could be no doubt of it: he was tired.

He had had two dreams toward dawn this morning and the dead had figured in both.

"Aren't you taking a vacation this summer?"

"I'd thought of going to Kamikochi. There's no one I can leave my head with, and so I think I'd like to go have a look at the mountains."

"Oh, go, by all means," said Kikuko, a little too gaily.

"But we have Fusako with us now. She's come for a rest too. What do you think? Would it be better for her with me in the house, or away?"

"I envy her, having such a good father." Kikuko did not seem wholly at ease.

Had he hoped, he wondered, to badger her, throw her off the scent, distract her from the image of his own solitary figure, coming home without his son? Such had not been his conscious intention; and yet he wondered.

"Are you being sarcastic?" he asked.

He spoke lightly, but Kikuko seemed surprised.

"Take a look at Fusako and then tell me whether I've been a good father."

She flushed to the ears. "It wasn't your fault about Fusako," she said, and he felt consolation in her voice.

3

Shingo disliked cold drinks even in hot weather. Yasuko did not give them to him, and the habit of not taking them had formed over the years.

In the morning when he got up and in the evening when he came home he would have a brimming cup of tea. Kikuko always saw to supplying it.

When they got home from viewing the sunflowers she hurried for his tea. He drank about half of it, changed to a cotton kimono, and took his cup out to the veranda, sipping as he went. Kikuko came after him with a cold towel and cigarettes and poured more tea. Then she went for his glasses and the evening paper.

He looked out at the garden. It seemed too much of an effort, when he had wiped his face, to put on his glasses.

The grass was rough and untended. On the far side was a clump of bush clover and pampas grass, so tall that it almost looked wild.

There were butterflies beyond. Shingo could see them flickering past gaps in the leaves, more than one butterfly, surely. He waited to see whether they would alight on the bush clover or come out from behind it. They went on fluttering through the leaves, however.

He began to feel that there was some sort of special little world apart over behind the shrubbery. The butterfly wings beyond the leaves of bush clover seemed to him extraordinarily beautiful.

He thought of the stars he had seen through the trees on the hilltop, that night a month earlier, when the moon had been near full.

Yasuko came out and sat down beside him.

"Shuichi will be late again?" she asked, fanning herself.

Shingo nodded and continued to look at the garden. "There are butterflies behind the shrubbery."

But as if they disliked being seen by Yasuko, the butterflies flew up over the bush clover. There were three of them.

"Swallowtails."

For swallowtails they were small, and their color was somehow muddy.

They cut a line diagonally across the board fence and emerged against the pine next door. Forming a vertical column, they proceeded, without breaking the column or changing the distance that separated them, up the middle of the tree to the top. It had grown untended, and did not have the shaped look of a garden tree.

A moment later another swallowtail butterfly appeared from an unexpected quarter and, describing a horizontal line across the garden, skimmed the top of the bush clover.

"This morning I had two dreams about dead people. The old man at the Tatsumiya treated me to noodles."

"You didn't eat them, did you?"

"Shouldn't I have?" Shingo wondered if eating food offered in a dream by a dead person meant that the dreamer himself would die. "I don't really remember. I don't think I did. I do remember that they were cold." He thought he must have awakened before eating.

He could remember even the color of the noodles, laid on bamboo, in a frame lacquered black on the outside and red on the inside.

He did not know, however, whether he had seen the color in the dream or assigned it upon awakening. In any case, the noodles were clear in his mind, though everything else was blurred.

One helping of noodles had been laid on the floor, and it seemed that Shingo had been standing beside it. The shopkeeper and his family, it seemed, had been sitting down. It seemed that no one had had a cushion to sit on. It seemed, strangely, that Shingo alone had been standing. So much he could remember, but only vaguely.

Awakening from the dream, he had remembered it clearly. After going back to sleep and getting up in the morning, he had remembered it even more clearly. Now, however, it was almost gone. The picture centering on the noodles had stayed in his mind, but he could not remember the plot, what had gone before and followed after.

The man in the dream was a cabinetmaker who had died in his seventies some three or four years before. Because he was an artisan of the old school, Shingo had taken a great liking to him and given him considerable work. Yet he had not been such a close friend as to figure in a dream so long after his death.

It seemed to Shingo that the noodles had appeared in the family quarters, at the back of the shop. Even though he might on occasion have stood outside talking to the old man, he could not remember having gone into the back rooms. He was puzzled to know why he should have had a dream in which noodles figured.

The old man had had six children, all daughters.

Shingo had slept with a girl in the dream, but now, in the evening, he could not remember whether or not it had been one of the daughters.

He remembered clearly having touched someone, but he had no notion who she might have been. He could remember nothing that even gave him a hint.

He felt that he had known who it was when he woke, and when, after going to sleep again, he had again awakened, he had perhaps still known. But now, in the evening, he could remember nothing at all.

Since the dream was a continuation of the one about the old cabinetmaker, he tried to decide whether the girl he had slept with might have been one of the man's daughters. No sort of awareness came to him. He could not even call up the faces of the Tatsumi daughters.

It was a continuation, that much was clear; but he did not know what had gone before and come after the noodles. It now seemed likely that they had been the clearest image in his mind when he woke. Yet would it not be true to the laws of dreams if he had awakened at the shock of contact with the girl?

Not, of course, that it had been a sharp enough sensation to wake him.

Here, too, nothing definite of the dream remained. The figure had gone, and he could not bring it back; all that remained was a sense of physical disparity, a failure of physical contact.

Shingo had not, in actuality, experienced such a woman. He had not recognized her, but because she had been a mere girl, the meeting could not have happened in real life.

At sixty-two, an absence of sensual dreams would not be unusual, but what puzzled him now was the positive insipidity of it all.

He had promptly gone back to sleep and had another dream.

Fat old Aida had come around, a half-gallon bottle of sake in his hand. He had, it seemed, drunk a good bit already. The pores on his red face were agape.

Shingo could remember no more of the dream. He did not know whether the house had been this one or a house he had lived in earlier.

Aida had, until ten years or so before, been a director of Shingo's company. He had died of apoplexy toward the end of the previous year. In his last years he had grown thin.

"And then I had another dream. This time Aida came around to the house with a bottle."

"Mr. Aida? But that's strange. Mr. Aida didn't drink."

"That's true. He had asthma, and when he had his stroke it was the mucus that killed him. But he didn't drink. He was always wandering around with a medicine bottle in his hand."

And yet he had strode into the dream like a brave roisterer. The image floated up vividly in Shingo's mind.

"And did you and Mr. Aida have a drinking party?"

"I didn't have a drop. Aida was walking toward me, but I woke up before he had a chance to sit down."

"It's not very pleasant, dreaming of dead people."

"Maybe they've come for me."

He had reached an age when most of his friends were dead. It was perhaps natural that he should dream of the dead.

Neither the old cabinetmaker nor Aida had appeared to him as dead, however. They had come into his dreams as living people.

And the figures of both, as they had come into the dreams, were still vivid in his mind. They were much clearer than his usual memories of the two men. Aida's face, red from drink, was of a sort that the living Aida had never presented; and yet Shingo remembered such details as the distended pores.

Why should it be that, remembering the other two so clearly, he could not call up the face of the girl who had touched him, could not remember who she might be?

He asked whether, from feelings of guilt, he had managed to forget. But such did not seem to be the case. He had not been awake long enough for more than a certain sensual disappointment.

He was not especially interested in the fact that it had come to him in a dream.

He did not describe this part of the dream to Yasuko. Kikuko and Fusako were getting dinner. He could hear their voices in the kitchen. They seemed a trifle too loud.

4

Every night locusts would come flying in from the cherry tree.

Shingo walked over to the trunk of the tree.

Engulfed by the sound of whirring wings, he looked up. He was astonished at the number of locusts, and astonished too at the noise of their wings. It was as if a flock of sparrows had started up.

Locusts were flying off as he looked into the great tree.

All the clouds in the sky were racing toward the east. The weather forecast had said that that most ominous of days, the two-hundred-tenth after the beginning of spring,* was likely to pass without incident, but Shingo suspected that there would be winds and showers to bring down the temperature.

"Has something happened?" Kikuko came up. "I heard locusts and wondered."

"They do make you think there might have been an accident, don't they? You hear about the wings of ducks and geese, but these are just as impressive."

Kikuko was holding a needle and red thread. "It wasn't the wings. It was the screeching all of a sudden, as if something might be threatening them."

"I hadn't noticed that so much."

* *Early in September.*

He looked into the room from which she had come. Spread out in it were the makings of a child's dress, the cloth from an ancient singlet of Yasuko's. "Does Satoko still play with locusts?"

Kikuko nodded. A faint motion of her lips seemed to shape the word "yes."

Locusts were strange and interesting creatures to Satoko, a child of the city; and there was something in her nature that responded to the sport. At first she had been afraid when Fusako had given her one to play with. Then Fusako had cut off the wings, and afterwards whenever the child caught a locust she would come running up to anyone nearby, Kikuko or Yasuko or whomever, to have the wings clipped.

Yasuko hated the practice.

Fusako had not always been that sort of girl, she grumbled. Her husband had ruined her.

Yasuko had blanched when she found a swarm of red ants dragging off a wingless locust.

She was not, on the whole, a person to be moved by such matters. Shingo was both amused and disturbed.

Her recoil, as from a poisonous vapor, was perhaps a sign of some evil foreboding. Shingo suspected that locusts were not the problem.

Satoko was an obdurate child, and when the adult in question had surrendered and cut the wings she would still be dawdling about. Then, with somber, shadowy eyes, she would throw the insect, its wings freshly cut, out into the garden, as if to hide it. She knew that adults would be watching her.

Fusako apparently poured forth her complaints to Yasuko every day, but it seemed, from the fact that she never touched upon the question of when she would be leaving, that she had not yet brought herself to the heart of the matter.

When they were in bed Yasuko would pass the day's complaints on to Shingo. Though he did not pay a great deal of attention, he would feel that something had been left out.

He knew that as her father he should step forward to give Fusako advice; but she was thirty and married, and matters are not simple for fathers in such cases. It would not be easy to accommodate a woman with two children. A decision was postponed from day to day, as if the principals were all waiting for nature to take its course.

"Isn't Father nice to Kikuko," said Fusako.

Kikuko and Shuichi were both at the dinner table.

"Yes, of course," said Yasuko. "I try to be good to her myself."

Fusako's manner had not suggested that she required an answer. There was laughter in the tone of Yasuko's gratuitous answer, but it was meant to quell Fusako all the same.

"After all, she's good to us."

Kikuko turned crimson.

Yasuko's second remark was uncomplicated enough. It contained something like a thrust at her daughter, however.

It seemed to suggest that she liked her happy daughter-in-law and disliked her unhappy daughter. One might have suspected cruelty and malice. Shingo sensed something like self-loathing too. He detected a similar vein in himself. Yet it seemed strange to him that Yasuko, .

woman and aging mother, should have given way to it in the presence of her daughter.

"I don't agree that she's all that kind," said Shuichi. "She's not to her husband." The joke was not successful.

It should have been clear to all of them, to Shuichi and Yasuko as well as to Kikuko herself, that Shingo was particularly gentle toward Kikuko. The fact scarcely needed mentioning, and somehow mention of it saddened him.

Kikuko was for him a window looking out of a gloomy house. His blood kin were not as he would wish them to be, and if they were not able to live as they themselves wished to live, then the impact of the blood relation became leaden and oppressive. His daughter-in-law brought relief.

Kindness toward her was a beam lighting isolation. It was a way of pampering himself, of bringing a touch of mellowness into his life.

For her part, Kikuko did not indulge in dark conjectures on the psychology of the aged, nor did she seem afraid of him.

Fusako's remark, he felt, brushed against his secret.

It had been made at dinner some three or four evenings before.

Under the cherry tree, Shingo thought of it, and of Satoko and the locust wings.

"Is Fusako having a nap?"

"Yes." Kikuko looked into his face. "She's giving Kuniko hers."

"She's a funny child, Satoko. Whenever Fusako gives the baby its nap she goes along and lies there clinging to her mother's back. That's when she behaves."

"It's sweet, really."

"Yasuko can't stand the child. But when she gets to be fourteen or fifteen she'll be snoring away, the image of her grandmother."

Kikuko did not seem to understand.

She called after Shingo as he turned to go off.

"You went dancing?"

"What?" Shingo looked around. "You know about it, do you?"

Two nights earlier he had gone to a dance hall with the girl from his office.

Today was Sunday; so it would appear that the girl, Tanizaki Eiko, had told Shuichi the day before, and Shuichi had passed the news on to Kikuko.

Shingo had not been dancing in years. The girl had clearly been surprised at his invitation. She had said that if she went out with him troublesome rumors would spread through the office, and he had said that she only needed to keep quiet. And it seemed that she had promptly told Shuichi.

Shuichi, for his part, had neither yesterday nor today given Shingo a hint that he knew.

Eiko evidently went dancing with Shuichi from time to time. Shingo had asked her out because he had thought he might see Shuichi's mistress at the hall the two frequented.

He had not, however, been able to find a likely girl, and he had not been up to asking Eiko for an identification.

Apparently the surprise had made the girl a bit giddy. The note of discord struck Shingo as dangerous and touching.

Although in her early twenties, she had tiny breasts, barely enough to fill one's cupped hands. Shingo was put in mind of an erotic print by Harunobu.

Given the noisy surroundings, he was somehow amused by the association.

"Next time let me take *you*," he said to Kikuko.

"Yes. Please do."

She had been blushing from the time she called him back.

Had she guessed that he had gone in the hope of seeing Shuichi's mistress?

He had no particular reason to keep the incident a secret, but the thought of the other women left him a little flustered.

He went from the front door to Shuichi's room. "Tanizaki told you?" He did not sit down.

"Ah, yes. That she did. Important news having to do with our household."

"I wouldn't have thought it all that newsworthy. But when you take her dancing next time, buy her a decent summer dress."

"You were ashamed of her, were you?"

"The blouse and skirt didn't seem to match very well."

"Oh, she has clothes enough. It's your fault for not warning her. Just make your dates in advance, and she'll come dressed for the occasion." He turned away.

Skirting the room where Fusako and the two children were sleeping, Shingo looked up at the clock.

"Five," he muttered, as if to confirm an important fact.

A Blaze of Clouds

Although the newspaper had predicted that the two-hundred-tenth day would pass uneventfully that year, there was a typhoon the night before.

Shingo could not remember how many days earlier he had seen the article, and so it could not perhaps have been called a weather forecast. There were of course forecasts and warnings as the day approached.

"I suppose you'll be coming home early tonight?" said Shingo to Shuichi. It was more a suggestion than a query.

Having helped Shingo with his preparations for departing, the girl Eiko hurried to go home herself. Through the transparent white raincoat, her breasts seemed even smaller.

He had taken greater notice of them since, on the night he had gone dancing with her, he had noticed how meager they were.

Eiko came running down the stairs after them and stood with them in the entrance. Because of the down-pour, she had apparently not taken time to repowder her face.

"And where is it you live?" But Shingo did not finish the question. He must have asked it twenty times already, and he did not remember the answer.

At Kamakura Station passengers stood under the eaves trying to judge the violence of the wind and rain.

As Shingo and Shuichi passed the house with sunflowers at the gate, the theme song from *Quatorze Juillet* came through the wind and rain.

"She doesn't seem very worried," said Shuichi.

They knew that it would be Kikuko playing the Lys Gauty record.

When it was over she started it again.

Midway through they heard shutters being closed.

And they heard Kikuko singing to the record as she closed them.

Through the storm and the music, she did not hear the two come in from the gate.

"My shoes are flooded." Shuichi took off his stockings in the doorway.

Shingo went in, wet stockings and all.

"So you're back." Kikuko came toward them, her face glowing with pleasure.

Shuichi handed her his stockings.

"Father's must be wet too," said Kikuko. Starting the record again, she went off with their wet clothes.

"They can hear you all over town, Kikuko," said Shuichi as he wound an obi around his waist. "You might try to seem a little more worried."

"But I was playing it *because* I was worried. I couldn't sit still, thinking about the two of you."

But her frolicsome manner suggested that she found the storm exhilarating.

She was still humming to herself as she went off for Shingo's tea.

Shuichi, fond of the Parisian *chanson*, had bought the collection for her.

He knew French. Kikuko did not, but, with lessons in pronunciation, she had become fairly proficient at imitating the record. Not, of course, that she could give, as could Gauty, a sense of having struggled and somehow lived on. All the same, her delicate, hesitant delivery was most pleasing.

Kikuko's wedding present from her seminary classmates had been a collection of nursery songs from the world over. In the early months of her marriage she had been very fond of it. When she was alone, she would quietly join in the singing; it gave Shingo a sense of warm repose.

A most womanly kind of observance, thought Shingo. And he felt that, listening to the nursery songs, she was sunk in memories of her girlhood.

"Shall I ask you to play them at my funeral?" Shingo had once said to her. "Then I won't need any prayers." He had not been serious, but then suddenly he was on the edge of tears.

But Kikuko was still childless, and it seemed, since he had not heard it recently, that she had tired of the collection.

As the *chanson* was nearing its end, it suddenly faded away.

"The electricity has gone off," said Yasuko from the breakfast room.

"It won't go back on tonight," said Kikuko, switching off the phonograph. "Let's have dinner early, Mother."

At dinner, the thin candles went out three or four times as the wind blew through cracks in the shutters.

The ocean seemed to be shouting above the wind. It was as if the sea were doing more than the wind to heighten the terror.

2

The scent of the candle that he had just blown out was still in Shingo's nostrils.

Each time the house would shake, Yasuko would reach for the matchbox on the bed and rattle it, as if to reassure herself and to let Shingo know.

And she would reach for his hand, and gently touch it.

"Will we be all right?"

"Of course. And if something does blow over the fence, we can't very well go out and look."

"Will it be all right at Fusako's?"

"At Fusako's?" He had not thought of Fusako. "I imagine so. On a night like this they ought to go off to sleep early like a good married couple, whatever they do on other nights."

"How could they sleep?" Turning away his remark, she fell silent.

They heard Shuichi's voice and Kikuko's. There was a soft coaxing quality in Kikuko's.

"She has two small children," said Yasuko after a time. "Things are not as easy as they are with us."

"And he has a crippled mother. How is her arthritis?"

"There's that too. If they were to run away Aihara would have to carry the old lady on his back."

"Can't she walk?"

"She can move around, I believe. But in this storm? Gives you the blues, doesn't it."

"Gives you the blues?" The word "blues" from the sixty-three-year-old Yasuko struck Shingo as comical.

"It said in the paper that a woman changes her hair style any number of times in the course of her life. I liked that."

"What was it in?"

It was, according to Yasuko, in the opening words of the eulogy of a painter in the old style, a specialist in portraits of women, to a recently deceased woman painter, also of old-style beauties.

But in the eulogy proper it came out that with the woman artist the case had been the opposite. For a good fifty years, from her twenties to her death at seventy-five, she had worn her hair straight back and held in place by a comb.

Yasuko apparently found it admirable that a woman could make her way through life with her hair pulled straight back; but the thought that through her life a woman wore her hair in many ways also seemed to appeal to her.

Yasuko was in the habit of saving the newspapers she read every day and looking again through several days' accumulation. One could not be sure how old an article she would suddenly come up with. And since she always listened carefully to the nine-o'clock news commentary as well, she would launch forth on the most improbable topics.

"And so you mean that Fusako will do her hair all sorts of ways?"

"She's a woman, after all. But there won't be as many changes with her as there were with us who did it the old way. And it would be more fun if she were as good-looking as Kikuko."

"You weren't kind to her when she came home. She was desperate."

"Don't you suppose I was under your influence? You only care about Kikuko."

"That's not true. An invention of yours."

"It is true. You never liked Fusako—Shuichi was always your favorite. That's the way you are. Even now that he has another woman you can't say anything to him. And you really show too much affection for Kikuko. It amounts to cruelty. She can't give a sign of her jealousy because she's afraid of what it might do to you. It really gives me the blues. I hope the typhoon blows us all away."

Shingo was startled. "A typhoon," he said, thinking of the rising fury of his wife's observations.

"Yes, it is a typhoon. And Fusako, trying to have her parents get a divorce for her, at her age, in this day and age. It's cowardly."

"Not really. But has there been talk of a separation?"

"More important is what I can see right ahead of me, your scowling face when she comes back and you have to take care of her and those two children."

"You've been outspoken enough yourself."

"That is because we have Kikuko, whom Father is so fond of. But Kikuko aside, I have to admit I don't like it. Sometimes Kikuko says or does something that takes a load off my mind, but when Fusako says something the load only gets heavier. It wasn't so bad before she got married. I know perfectly well that it's my own daughter and grandchildren I'm talking about, and I can still feel that way? Frightening, that's what it is. It's your influence."

"You're more of a coward than Fusako."

"I was joking. You couldn't see me stick out my tongue."

"The old woman is good with her tongue. Remarkably."

"But I do feel sorry for her. Don't you?"

"We can take her in if you want." Then, as if he remembered something: "The kerchief she brought with her."

"The kerchief?"

"The kerchief. I've seen it before, but can't remember where. Is it ours?"

"The big cotton one? She took her mirror in it when she got married. It was a very big mirror."

"So that was it."

"I didn't like that bundle. She could perfectly well have put her things in the suitcase she took on her honeymoon."

"A suitcase would have been heavy, and she had those

two children. And I don't suppose she cared very much at that point how she looked."

"But we have Kikuko to think of. That kerchief—I brought something wrapped in it when we were married."

"Oh?"

"It's even older. It was my sister's. When she died they sent it home with a dwarf tree tied up in it. A fine maple."

"Oh?" said Shingo again, softly. His head was full of the red glow of that remarkable maple.

Back in the country, his father-in-law's chief extravagance had been dwarf trees. He gave particular attention, it seemed, to maples. Yasuko's elder sister was his assistant.

In bed with the storm roaring about him, Shingo could see her among the shelves of dwarf trees.

Probably her father had given her one when she married. Perhaps she had asked for it. And when she died her husband's family had sent it back, because it was so important to her father, and because they had no one to look after it. Or possibly her father had gone for it.

The maple that now filled Shingo's head had been on the family altar.

Had her sister died in autumn then? Autumn came early to Shinano.

But would they have sent it back immediately upon her death? That it should have been red and on the altar made everything seem a little too neatly arranged. Was not a nostalgic syndrome working upon his imagination? He had no confidence.

Shingo could not remember the anniversary of his sister-in-law's death. Yet he did not ask Yasuko.

That was because Yasuko had once said: "Father never let me help him with his trees. I suppose it had something to do with my nature, but he felt much closer to my sister. I couldn't stand up to her myself. I wasn't just jealous, I was ashamed. She did everything so much better than I did."

That was the sort of remark she could make when the talk touched upon Shingo's preference for Shuichi, and she would add: "I suppose I was rather like Fusako myself."

Shingo was surprised to learn that the kerchief was a memento of Yasuko's sister. He fell silent, now that the sister had come into the conversation.

"Suppose we go to sleep," said Yasuko. "They'll think we old ones have trouble sleeping too. Kikuko laughed away through the storm, and she put on one record after another. I *am* sorry for her."

"There was a contradiction even in those few words."

"There always is."

"That was for me to say. I go to bed early for a change, and see what happens to me."

The dwarf maple was still with Shingo.

And in another part of his mind he asked whether, even now that he had been married to Yasuko for more than thirty years, his boyhood yearning for her sister was still with him, an old wound.

He went to sleep an hour or so after Yasuko. A violent crash awoke him.

"What is it?"

He heard Kikuko groping her way along the veranda.

"Are you awake? They say a sheet of tin from the shrine blew over onto our roof."

3

The tin roof of the *mikoshi* * shed had quite blown away.

The caretaker came early in the morning to collect seven or eight sheets from Shingo's roof and garden.

The Yokosuka line was running. Shingo left for work.

"How was it? Could you sleep?" Shingo asked Eiko as she brought tea.

"Not a wink." Eiko described the wake of the storm as she had seen it from the train window.

"I don't suppose we can go dancing today," said Shingo after he had had a cigarette or two.

Eiko looked up smiling.

"The morning after the other time, my hips were stiff. It's my age."

She smiled mischievously, from her eyes down toward her nose. "Don't you suppose it's because of the way you arch your back?"

"Arch my back? Do I? Do I bend from the hips?"

"You arch your back and keep your distance. As if it might be against the law to touch me."

"That can't be true."

"Oh, but it is."

"Was I trying to make myself look good? I wasn't aware of it."

---

* *The portable shrine used in Shinto festivals.*

"No?"

"You young people hang on to each other so when you dance. It's all in very bad taste."

"That's not kind of you."

Shingo had thought, the time before, that Eiko had been a little off balance, a little giddy perhaps; and that had been too sanguine a view. The point was rather that he had been stiff and clumsy himself.

"Well, let's go again. This time I'll lean forward and hang on to you."

She looked down and laughed. "I'd be delighted. But not tonight. Not in this dress."

"No, not tonight."

She was wearing a white blouse and had a white ribbon in her hair.

It was not unusual for her to wear a white blouse. Possibly the white ribbon, a fairly broad one, made it look whiter. Her hair was knotted tightly at the back. She was, one might say, dressed for a storm.

The hairline was fresh and clean, tracing a curve behind her ears. The hair stood out cleanly against the fair skin it normally covered.

She had on a thin wool skirt of navy blue. It was somewhat worn.

When she was so dressed, the smallness of her breasts did not matter.

"Has Shuichi asked you out again?"

"No."

"What a pity. The young man keeps his distance because you go dancing with his father."

"I'll have to ask *him* to go out."

"And so I needn't worry?"

"If you insist on making fun of me, I'll have to refuse to go dancing with you."

"I'm not making fun of you. But I haven't been able to look you in the eye since you began noticing him."

She reacted with silence.

"I suppose you know Shuichi's woman."

This time she registered confusion.

"A dancer?"

There was no reply.

"Is she older?"

"Older? She's older than his wife."

"And good-looking?"

"Yes, very good-looking." She stumbled over the words, but continued: "She has a husky voice. No, not so much husky as broken, you might say. In two parts. He finds it very erotic."

"Well!"

She seemed about to go on. He did not want to listen.

He felt ashamed for himself, and he felt a revulsion, as if the true nature of Shuichi's woman and of Eiko herself were about to emerge.

He was taken aback by this initial observation, about the eroticism in the woman's voice. There had been bad taste on Shuichi's part, of course, but what about Eiko herself?

Noting the displeasure on his face, Eiko fell silent.

That night too Shuichi went home with Shingo. When they had closed the shutters the four of them went out to see a movie version of the Kabuki play *Kanjincho*.

As Shuichi took off his undershirt, changing to go to the movie, Shingo saw red marks high on his chest and shoulder. Had Kikuko left them there during the storm?

The principal actors in the film, Koshiro and Uzaemon and Kikugoro, were all dead.

Shingo's feelings were different from those of Kikuko and Shuichi.

"I wonder how many times we saw Koshiro do Benkei," said Yasuko.

"I forget."

"Yes, you always forget."

The town was bright in the moonlight. Shingo looked up at the sky.

The moon was in a blaze. Or so, just then, it seemed to Shingo.

The clouds around the moon made him think of the flames behind Acala in a painting, or a painting of a fox-spirit. They were coiling, twisted clouds.

But the clouds, and the moon too, were cold and faintly white. Shingo felt autumn come over him.

The moon, high in the east, was almost full. It lay in a blaze of clouds, it was dimmed by them.

There were no other clouds near the blaze in which the moon lay. In a single night after the storm the sky had turned a deep black.

The shops were shuttered. The town too had taken on a melancholy aspect in the course of the night. People were on their way home from the movie through silent, deserted streets.

"I couldn't sleep last night. I'm going to bed early." Shingo felt a lonely chill pass over him, and a yearning for human warmth.

And it was as if a crucial moment had come, as if a decision were forcing itself upon him.

The Chestnuts

❁

The gingko is sending out shoots again," said Kikuko.

"You've only just noticed?" said Shingo. "I've been watching it for some time now."

"But you always sit facing it, Father."

Kikuko, who sat so that Shingo saw her in profile, was looking at the gingko behind her.

The places of the four as they took their meals had in the course of time become fixed.

Shingo sat facing east. On his left was Yasuko, facing

south, and on his right Shuichi, who faced north. Kikuko, facing west, sat opposite Shingo.

Since the garden was to the south and east, it might be said that the old people occupied the better places. And the women's places were the convenient ones for serving.

At times other than meals, they had come to occupy the same fixed places.

So it was that Kikuko always had the gingko behind her.

Yet Shingo was troubled: that she had not noticed unseasonal buds on the great tree suggested a certain emptiness.

"But you ought to notice when you open the shutters or go out to clean the veranda," he said.

"I suppose that's true."

"Of course it is. And you're facing it when you come in the gate. You have to look at it whether you want to or not. Do you have so much on your mind that you come in looking at the ground?"

"This will never do." Kikuko gave her shoulders that slight, beautiful shrug. "I'll be very careful from now on to notice everything you do and imitate it."

For Shingo, there was a touch of sadness in the remark. "This won't do either."

In all his life no woman had so loved him as to want him to notice everything she did.

Kikuko continued to gaze in the direction of the gingko. "And some of the trees up the mountain are putting out new leaves."

"So they are. I wonder if they lost their leaves in the typhoon."

The mountain in Shingo's garden was cut off by the shrine precincts, a level stretch just above. The gingko lay at the boundary, but from Shingo's breakfast room it looked as if it were yet higher.

It had been stripped bare on the night of the storm.

The gingko and the cherry were the trees left bare by the wind.

Since they were the larger of the trees around the house, they were perhaps good targets for the storm. Or was it that their leaves were especially vulnerable?

The cherry had had a few drooping leaves even after the storm, but it had shed them since, and now stood quite naked.

The leaves of the bamboo up the mountain had withered, perhaps because, with the ocean so near, the wind had brought in salt spray. Stalks of bamboo had broken off and blown into the garden.

The great gingko was again sending out buds.

Shingo faced it as he turned up the lane from the main street, and every day on his way home he looked at it. He also saw it from the breakfast room.

"The gingko has a sort of strength that the cherry doesn't," he said. "I've been thinking the ones that live long are different from the others. It must take a great deal of strength for an old tree like that to put out leaves in the fall."

"But there's something sad about them."

"I've been wondering whether they'd be as big as the leaves that came out in the spring, but they refuse to grow."

Besides being small, the leaves were scattered, too few to hide the branches. They seemed thin, and they were a pale yellowish color, insufficiently green.

It was as if the autumn sun fell on a gingko that was, after all, naked.

The trees in the shrine precincts were mostly evergreen. They seemed to be strong against wind and rain, and were quite undamaged. Above the luxuriant evergreens was the pale green of new leaves. Kikuko had just discovered them.

Yasuko had come in through the back gate. He heard running water. She said something, but, over the sound of water, he could not make out what.

"What did you say?" he shouted.

Kikuko helped him. "She says that the bush clover is blooming very nicely."

"Oh?"

Kikuko passed on another message. "And she says that the pampas grass is putting out plumes."

"Oh?"

Yasuko had something more to say.

"Oh, be quiet. I can't hear you."

"I'll be happy to interpret." On the edge of laughter, Kikuko looked down.

"Interpret? It's just an old woman talking to herself."

"She says she dreamed last night that the house in Shinano was going to pieces."

"Oh?"

"And what is your answer?"

"I said 'Oh,' and that's all I have to say."

The sound of water stopped. Yasuko called Kikuko.

"Put these in water, please, Kikuko. They were so beautiful that I had to break some off. But you take care of them, please."

"Let me show them to Father first."

She came in with an armful of bush clover and pampas grass.

Yasuko had evidently washed her hands and then moistened a Shigaraki vase, which she brought in.

"The amaranth next door is a beautiful color too," she said as she sat down.

"There is amaranth by the house with the sunflowers," said Shingo, remembering that those remarkable sunflowers had been knocked down in the storm.

Blossoms had lain in the street, broken off with six inches or so of stem. They had been there for several days, like severed human heads.

First the petals withered, and then the stems dried and turned dirty and gray.

Shingo had to step over them on his way to and from work. He did not like to look at them.

The bases of the stems stood leafless by the gate.

Beside them, five or six stalks of amaranth were taking on color.

"But there aren't any around here like the ones next door," said Yasuko.

2

It was her family house that Yasuko had dreamed of.

It had been unoccupied for several years now, since her parents' death.

Apparently meaning Yasuko to succeed to the family name,* her father had sent his older daughter out in

---

* It is common for a husband to take his wife's name when her family is without male heirs.

marriage. It should have been the opposite for a father who favored his older daughter, but, with so many men asking for the hand of her beautiful sister, he had probably felt sorry for Yasuko.

Perhaps, therefore, he gave up hope for Yasuko when, after her sister's death, she went to work in the house into which the sister had married, and seemed intent upon taking her place. Perhaps he felt a certain guilt because parents and family had made her feel so inclined.

Yasuko's marriage to Shingo seemed to please him.

He decided to live out his years with no family heir.

Shingo was now older than the father had been when he gave Yasuko in marriage.

Yasuko's mother had died first, and the fields had all been sold when the father died, leaving only the house and a modest amount of forest land. There were no heirlooms of any importance.

The remaining property was in Yasuko's name, but the management had been turned over to a country relative. The forests had probably been cut down to pay taxes. It had been many years since Yasuko had last had either income or expenses related to the country place.

There was a prospective buyer when, during the war, the countryside was crowded with refugees, but Yasuko felt nostalgic about the house, and Shingo did not press her.

It was in that house that they had been married. In return for giving his only surviving daughter in marriage, the father had asked that the ceremony be held in his house.

A chestnut fell as they were exchanging marriage

cups. It struck a large stone in the garden, and, because of the angle, rebounded a very long way and fell into a brook. The rebound was so extraordinary that Shingo was on the point of calling out in surprise. He looked around the room.

No one else seemed to have noticed.

The next day Shingo went down to hunt for it. He found several chestnuts at the edge of the water. He could not be sure he had the one that had fallen during the ceremony; but he picked one up, thinking to tell Yasuko of it.

But then he decided that he was being childish. And would Yasuko, and others to whom he might speak of it, believe him?

He threw it into a clump of grass by the water.

It was less fear that Yasuko would not believe him than shyness before her brother-in-law that kept him from speaking.

Had the brother-in-law not been present, Shingo might have spoken of it at the ceremony the day before. In the presence of her brother-in-law, he felt a constraint very like shame.

He had certain feelings of guilt for having continued to be drawn to the sister even after she was married, and the sister's death and Yasuko's marriage had disturbed her brother-in-law.

For Yasuko, the feelings of shame must have been even stronger. One might say that, pretending not to know her real feelings, her sister's widower had used her as a convenient substitute for a maid.

It was natural that, as a relative, he should be invited to Yasuko's wedding. Very uncomfortable all the same. Shingo found it difficult to look at him.

The brother-in-law was a handsome man who quite outshone the bride. It seemed to Shingo that there was a peculiar radiance in his part of the room.

To Yasuko, her sister and brother-in-law were inhabitants of a dream world. In marrying her, Shingo had tacitly descended to her own lower rank.

He felt as if her brother-in-law were coldly looking down on the wedding from an elevation.

And the blank left by his failure to speak of so small a thing as the falling chestnut probably stayed on in their marriage.

When Fusako was born, Shingo secretly hoped that she might be a beauty like her aunt. He could not speak of this hope to his wife. But Fusako proved to be even homelier than Yasuko.

As Shingo would have put it, the blood of the older sister had failed to flow through the younger. He was disappointed in Yasuko.

Three or four days after Yasuko dreamed of the house in the country, a telegram came from a relative saying that Fusako had arrived with her two children.

Kikuko signed for the telegram and passed it on to Yasuko, who waited for Shingo to come home from the office.

"Was something warning me in that dream?" She was remarkably calm as she watched Shingo read the telegram.

"Back to the country, is it?"

So she won't kill herself—that was the first thought that came to him.

"But why didn't she come here?"

"She probably thought Aihara would find out and be after her."

"Has anything come from Aihara?"

"No."

"I suppose it's finished, then, with Fusako taking the children, and not a word from him."

"But she came home the other time, and maybe she told him she was coming home again for a while. It wouldn't be easy for him to show his face."

"It's all over, whatever you say."

"I'm surprised that she should have had the nerve to go back to the country."

"Couldn't she just as well have come here?"

"Couldn't she just as well—that's not a very warm way to put it. We have to feel sorry for her, when she can't come back to her own home. We're parents and child, and this is what we've come to. I've been very unhappy."

Frowning, Shingo raised his chin to untie his necktie.

"Where's my kimono?"

Kikuko brought a kimono, and went off silently with his suit.

Yasuko sat with bowed head while he was changing. "It's not at all impossible that Kikuko will run out on us," she muttered, looking at the door Kikuko had closed behind her.

"Do parents have to be responsible forever for their children's marriages?"

"You don't understand women. It's different when women are sad."

"And do you think a woman can understand everything about every other woman?"

"Shuichi is away again tonight. Why can't the two of you come home together? You come home by yourself and here is Kikuko to take care of your clothes. Is that right?"

Shingo did not answer.

"Won't we want to talk to him about Fusako?"

"Shall we send him off to the country? We'll probably have to send him for her."

"She might not want him to come for her. He's always made a fool of her."

"There's no point in talking about that now. We'll send him on Saturday."

"We look good before the rest of the family, I must say. And here we stay away as if we never meant to have another thing to do with them. It's strange that she should pick them to run off to, when they've meant so little to her."

"Who is taking care of her?"

"Maybe she means to stay in the old house. She can't stay on forever with my aunt."

Yasuko's aunt would be in her eighties. Yasuko had had very little to do with her or with her son, the present head of the family. Shingo could not even remember how many brothers and sisters there were.

It was unsettling to think that Fusako had fled to the house seen ruined in his dream.

3

On Saturday morning, Shingo and Shuichi left the house together. There was still some time before Shuichi's train.

Shuichi came into Shingo's office. "I'll leave this with you," he said, handing his umbrella to Eiko.

She cocked her head inquiringly. "You're off on a business trip?"

"Yes."

Putting down his bag, Shuichi took a seat by Shingo's desk.

Eiko's eye followed him. "Take care of yourself. It will probably be cold."

"Oh, yes." Shuichi spoke to Shingo, though he was looking at Eiko. "I was supposed to go dancing with the young lady this evening."

"Oh?"

"Get the old man to take you."

Eiko flushed.

Shingo did not feel inclined to comment.

Eiko picked up the bag as if she were going to see Shuichi off.

"Please. That's not for a lady to do." He snatched the bag and disappeared through the door.

Eiko made an unobtrusive little motion toward the door, and returned disconsolately to her desk. Shingo could not tell whether the gesture had been from confusion or calculation; but it had had in it a touch of the feminine that pleased him.

"What a shame, when he promised you."

"I don't put much stock in his promises these days."

"Shall I be a substitute?"

"If you like."

"Are there complications?"

"What?" She looked up, startled.

"Does Shuichi's woman come to the dance hall?"

"No!"

Shingo had learned from Eiko that the woman's husky voice was erotic. He had not asked for further details.

It was not perhaps remarkable that his secretary should be acquainted with the woman when his own family was not; but he found that fact hard to accept.

It was particularly hard to accept when he had Eiko here before him.

One knew that she was a person of no consequence, and yet on such occasions she seemed to hang heavily before him, like the curtain of life itself. He could not guess what was passing through her mind.

"Did you meet her when he took you dancing?" he asked lightly.

"Yes."

"Many times?"

"No."

"Did he introduce you?"

"It wasn't an introduction, really."

"I don't understand. He took you to meet her—he wanted to make her jealous?"

"I'm no one to be jealous of." Eiko shrugged her shoulders very slightly.

Shingo could see that she was drawn to Shuichi, and that she was jealous.

"Then be someone to be jealous of."

"Really!" She looked down and laughed. "There were two of them too."

"What? She had a man with her?"

"Not a man. A woman."

"I was worried."

"Worried?" She looked at him. "The woman she lives with."

"They have a room together?"

"A house. It's small, but very nice."

"You mean you've been to the house?"

"Yes." Eiko half swallowed the word.

Once more Shingo was surprised. "Where is it?" he asked, somewhat abruptly.

"I shouldn't tell you," she said softly, a shadow crossing her face.

Shingo fell silent.

"In Hongo, near the University."

"Oh?"

She continued as if the pressure had been relieved, "It's up a dark narrow lane, but the house itself is nice. And the other lady is beautiful. I'm very fond of her."

"You mean the one that's not Shuichi's?"

"Yes. She's a very pleasant person."

"Oh? And what do they do? Are they both single?"

"Yes—I don't know, really."

"Two women living together."

Eiko nodded. "I've never known a pleasanter person. I'd like to see her every day." There was a certain coyness in her manner. She spoke as if the pleasantness of the woman made it possible for her to be forgiven something in herself.

All very strange, thought Shingo.

It did occur to him that, in praising the other woman, she might be indirectly reprimanding Shuichi's woman; but he had trouble guessing her real intentions.

Eiko looked out of the window. "It's clearing."

"Suppose you open it a little."

"I was a little worried when he left his umbrella. It's nice that he has good weather for his trip."

She stood for a time with her hand at the open window. Her skirt was askew, higher on one side than the other. Her stance suggested confusion.

She went back to her desk, head bowed.

A boy brought in three or four letters. Eiko put them on Shingo's desk.

"Another funeral," muttered Shingo. "Too many of them. Toriyama this time? At two this afternoon. I wonder what's happened to that wife of his."

Used to the way he talked to himself, Eiko only looked at him.

"I can't go dancing tonight. There's a funeral." His mouth slightly open, he was staring absently before him. "He was persecuted. She really tormented him when she was going through the change of life. She wouldn't feed him. She really wouldn't feed him. He would manage to have breakfast at home somehow, but she would get nothing at all ready for him. There would be food for the children, and he would have some of it when she wasn't watching. He was so afraid of her that he couldn't go home at night. Every night he would wander around or go to a movie or a variety show or something, and stay away until they were all safe in bed. The children all sided with her and helped persecute him."

"I wonder why."

"That's the way it was. The change is a terrible thing."

Eiko seemed to think that she was being made fun of. "Might it have been his fault?"

"He was important in the government, and then he joined a private firm. They've rented a temple for the funeral, so I suppose he did fairly well. He had only good habits when he was in the government."

"I suppose he took care of his family?"

"Naturally."

"It's not easy to understand."

"No, I don't suppose it is. But there are plenty of fine gentlemen in their fifties and sixties who spend their nights wandering around because they're afraid of their wives."

Shingo tried to remember Toriyama's face, but it refused to come to him. They had not met in ten years.

He wondered whether Toriyama had died at home.

4

Shingo thought he might meet university classmates at the funeral. He stood by the temple gate after he had offered incense, but he saw no one he knew.

There was no one his age at the funeral. Perhaps he had come too late.

He looked inside. The line by the door of the main hall was beginning to break up and move away.

The family seemed to be inside.

The widow survived, as Shingo had supposed she would. The thin woman directly in front of the coffin would be she.

She evidently dyed her hair, but had not dyed it in some time. It was white at the roots.

He thought, as he bowed to her, that she had not been

able to dye it because Toriyama's long illness had kept her busy. But then as he turned to light incense before the coffin he felt like muttering to himself that a person could never be sure.

As he had come up the stairs and paid his respects to the family, he had quite forgotten how the dead man had been persecuted; and then as he turned to pay his respects to the dead man, he remembered again. He was astonished at himself.

Making his way out, he turned so as not to have to look at the widow.

He had been startled not by the widow but by his own strange forgetfulness. He felt somehow repelled as he made his way back down the flagstone walk.

And as he walked away, he felt as if forgetfulness and loss lay pressing against the nape of his neck.

There were no longer many people who knew about Toriyama and his wife. Even though a few might survive, the relationship had been lost. It had been left to the wife, to remember as she pleased. There were no third parties to look back upon it intently.

At a gathering of six or seven classmates, including Shingo, there had been no one to give it serious thought when Toriyama's name came up. They only laughed. The man who mentioned it coated his remarks with derision and exaggeration.

Two of the men at the gathering had died before Toriyama.

It was now possible for Shingo to think that not even Toriyama and his wife had known why the wife had persecuted him, or why he had come to be persecuted.

Toriyama was being taken to the grave, not knowing.

For the wife, left behind, it was all in the past. Without Toriyama, it had gone into the past. Probably she too would go to the grave unknowing.

The man who, at the gathering of classmates, had mentioned Toriyama, had as family heirlooms four or five old Nō masks. Toriyama had come calling, he said, and had stayed on and on when the masks were brought out. Since they could hardly have been of such great interest to someone seeing them for the first time, the man went on, he had probably been killing time until his wife would be safely in bed.

But it seemed to Shingo today that a man in his fifties, the head of a household, walking the streets each night, would be sunk in thoughts so deep they could not be shared.

The photograph at the funeral had evidently been taken on New Year's Day or some other holiday before Toriyama left the government. He was in formal dress, his face round and tranquil. The photographer had touched away the shadows.

The quiet face in the picture was too young for the widow by the coffin. One was made to think that she was the persecuted one, old before her time.

She was a short woman, and Shingo looked down at her hair and the white at its roots. One shoulder drooped a little, giving an impression of weariness and emaciation.

The sons and daughters and people who seemed to be their spouses were ranged beside the widow, but Shingo did not really look at them.

"And how are things with you?" he meant to ask if he met an old acquaintance. He waited at the temple gate.

He thought he would reply, if asked the same question, "I've managed somehow to come through; but there's been trouble in my son's family and my daughter's." And it seemed to him that he meant to tell of his problems.

To make such revelations would be of no help to either of them, nor would there be any thought of intercession. They would but walk to the street-car stop and say good-bye.

That much Shingo wanted to do.

"Now that Toriyama is dead, nothing is left of his torment."

"Are Toriyama and his wife to be called successes if their children's families are happy?"

"How much responsibility must a parent take these days for his children's marriages?"

Such mutterings came to Shingo one after another as the sort of things he would like to say were he to meet an old friend.

Sparrows were chirping away on the roof of the temple gate.

They cut arcs along the eaves, and then cut the same arcs again.

5

Two callers were awaiting him when he got back to his office. He had whiskey brought from the cabinet behind him and poured it into black tea. It was a small help to his memory.

As he received the callers, he remembered the sparrows he had seen in the garden the morning before.

At the foot of the mountain, they were pecking at plumes of pampas grass. Were they after the seeds, or after insects? Then he saw that in what he had taken to be a flock of sparrows there were also buntings. He looked more carefully.

Six or seven birds jumped from plume to plume. The plumes waved violently.

There were three buntings, quieter than the sparrows. They did not have the nervous energy of the sparrows, and they were less given to jumping.

The glow of their wings and the fresh color of their breasts made them seem like birds new this year. The sparrows seemed coated with dust.

Shingo of course preferred the buntings. Their call was unlike that of the sparrows, and there was a similar difference in their motions.

He gazed on for a time, wondering whether the sparrows and buntings would quarrel.

But sparrows called to and flew with sparrows, and buntings flocked together.

When occasionally they mingled, there was no sign of a quarrel.

At his morning ablutions, Shingo looked on with admiration.

It was probably because of the sparrows on the temple gate that the scene had come back to him.

When he had seen the callers out, he turned and said to Eiko: "Show me where Shuichi's woman lives."

He had been thinking the possibility over as he talked to the callers. Eiko was taken by surprise.

With a gesture as of resistance, she frowned briefly;

then she seemed to wilt. Yet she answered coolly, her voice restrained and distant. "And what will you do if I take you there?"

"Nothing that will embarrass you."

"Do you mean to see her?"

Shingo had not gone so far as to think of seeing her today.

"Can't you wait and have Shuichi take you?" Still she spoke calmly.

Shingo felt a certain contempt in her voice.

She remained silent even after they were in the cab.

He was unhappy with himself for having imposed upon her, and he felt that he was shaming both himself and his son.

He had imagined himself settling matters while Shuichi was away; but he suspected that he would stop at imagining.

"I think that if you are to talk to someone it should be the other lady."

"The one you say is so pleasant?"

"Yes. Shall I have her come to the office?"

"I wonder."

"He has much too much to drink at their house, and he gets violent and orders the other lady to sing. She has a very good voice. And then Kinu * starts crying. If it makes so much difference to her, then I imagine she listens to what the other lady says."

It was a somewhat confused way of expressing herself. Kinu must be Shuichi's woman.

* Translator's note: The name is Kinuko in the original. It has here been shortened, with Mr. Kawabata's permission, to avoid confusion with Kikuko.

Shingo had not known that Shuichi had taken to drink.

They got out by the University and turned up a narrow lane.

"If Shuichi hears about this, I'll have to leave the office," said Eiko softly. "I'll have to ask to be let go."

A chill passed over Shingo.

Eiko had stopped. "You turn by the stone fence there, and it's the fourth house. You'll see the name Ikeda on the gate. They'll see me. I can't go any farther."

"Let's give it up, then, if it embarrasses you so."

"Why, when you've come this far? You have to go ahead. It means peace in your family."

He felt a certain malice in this defiance.

Eiko had called it a stone fence, but it was actually concrete. He turned past a large maple. There was nothing remarkable about the house, small and old, that carried the name Ikeda. The entrance faced north and was dark. The glass doors upstairs were closed. The house was silent.

There was nothing further to catch his eye.

Disconsolately, he walked on.

What sort of life did his son live behind that door? He was not ready to put in an unannounced appearance.

He turned up another street.

Eiko was not where he had left her. Nor was she to be seen on the main street from which they had turned up the lane.

Back at home, he avoided Kikuko's eye. "Shuichi came by the office for a few minutes and then left," he said. "I'm glad he has good weather."

Exhausted, he went to bed early.

"How many days did he take off?" Yasuko was in the breakfast room.

"I didn't ask," he answered from bed. "But all he has to do is bring Fusako back. I imagine it will be two or three days."

"I helped Kikuko change the wadding in the quilts today."

Fusako would be coming home with two children. Shingo thought how difficult things would be now for Kikuko.

Shuichi should take a separate house, he said to himself. He thought of the house in Hongo.

And he thought of the defiant Eiko. He was with her every day, and he had not until today witnessed such an outburst.

He had never seen Kikuko give vent to her emotions. Yasuko had said that she controlled her jealousy out of consideration for Shingo himself.

He was soon asleep. Awakened by Yasuko's snoring, took her nose between his fingers.

"Do you suppose Fusako will have that kerchief again?" said Yasuko, as if she had been awake all the time.

"I wouldn't be surprised."

They had nothing more to say to each other.

A Dream of Islands

❁

A stray bitch dropped puppies under the floor of Shingo's house.

"Dropped puppies" is a somewhat brusque way of putting the matter; but for Shingo and his family it was just so: suddenly, there was a litter under the veranda.

"We didn't see Teru yesterday, Mother," Kikuko had remarked in the kitchen a week or so before, "and she isn't here today either. Do you suppose she's having puppies?"

"She hasn't been around, now that you mention it," said Yasuko, with no great show of interest.

Shingo was in the *kotatsu* * making tea. He had since autumn been in the habit of having the most expensive of teas in the morning, and he made it for himself.

Kikuko had mentioned Teru while she was getting breakfast. Nothing more had been said.

"Have a cup," said Shingo, pouring tea, as Kikuko brought him his breakfast.

"Thank you very much." This had not happened before. Kikuko's manner was most ceremonious.

There were chrysanthemums on her obi and cloak. "And the season for chrysanthemums is past. With all the stir over Fusako, we forgot about your birthday."

"The pattern on the obi is 'The Four Princes.' You can wear it the year round."

" 'The Four Princes'?"

"Orchid and bamboo and plum and chrysanthemum," said Kikuko briskly. "You must have seen it somewhere. It's always being used in paintings and on kimonos."

"A greedy sort of pattern."

"It was delicious," said Kikuko, putting down the tea bowl.

"Who was it that gave us the *gyokuro?* † In return for a funeral offering, I think. That was when we started drinking it again. We used to drink it all the time, and never *bancha.*"

Shuichi had already left for the office.

As he put on his shoes in the doorway, Shingo was still trying to remember the name of the friend because of whom they had had the *gyokuro.* He could have asked

---

* *A quilt-covered frame over a sunken brazier for warming the extremities.*
† *With* bancha, *three lines below:*
Two varieties of tea. Shingo and Kikuko are drinking the former.

Kikuko, but did not. The friend had taken a young girl to a hot-spring resort and died there suddenly.

"It's true that we don't see Teru," said Shingo.

"Not yesterday, and not today either," said Kikuko.

Sometimes Teru, hearing Shingo prepare for his departure, would come around to the doorway and follow him out the gate.

He had recently seen Kikuko in the doorway feeling Teru's belly.

"All puffy and bloated," said Kikuko, frowning. But she went on feeling for the puppies all the same.

"How many are there?"

Teru looked up quizzically at Kikuko, showing the whites of her eyes. Then she rolled over, belly up.

It was not so swollen as to be repulsive. Toward the tail, where the skin seemed thinner, it was a faint pink. There was dirt around the nipples.

"Ten of them?" said Kikuko. Shingo counted with his eyes. The pair farthest forward was small, as if withered.

Teru had a master and a license, but it appeared that the master did not often feed her. She had become a stray. She made the rounds of the kitchens in the neighborhood. She had been spending more time at Shingo's since Kikuko had taken to giving her leftovers morning and evening, with something special added for Teru herself. Frequently, at night, they heard her barking in the garden. It seemed that she had attached herself to them, but not even Kikuko had come to think her their own.

Teru always went home to have puppies.

Her absence yesterday and today, Kikuko had intended to say, meant that she had again gone home to have puppies.

It seemed sad that she should go home for that purpose.

But this time the puppies had been born under the floor of Shingo's house. It was ten days or so before anyone noticed.

"Teru has had her puppies here, Father," said Kikuko when Shingo and Shuichi came home from the office.

"Oh? Where?"

"Under the maid's room."

"Oh?"

Since they had no maid, the maid's room, small and narrow, was used as a storeroom.

"Teru is always going in under the maid's room. So I looked, and there do seem to be puppies."

"How many?"

"It's too dark to tell. They're back in under."

"So she had them here."

"Mother said that Teru was behaving very strangely, going around and around the tool-shed and pawing at the ground. She was looking for a place to have puppies. I imagine if we had put out straw she would have had them in the shed."

"They'll be one fine problem when they grow up," said Shuichi.

Shingo was pleased that Teru had had her puppies here; but the unpleasant thought also came to him of the day when, unable otherwise to dispose of mongrel puppies, they would have to abandon them.

"I'm told that Teru had puppies here," said Yasuko.

"So I'm told."

"I'm told that she had them under the maid's room. The only room in the house with no one in it. Teru thought things out nicely."

Still in the *kotatsu*, Yasuko frowned slightly as she looked up at Shingo.

Shingo too got into the *kotatsu*. When he had had his cup of tea, he said to Shuichi: "What happened to the maid Tanizaki was to get for us?" He poured a second cup.

"That's an ashtray, Father."

He had poured his second cup into the ashtray.

2

"I am an aged man, and I have not yet climbed Mount Fuji." Shingo was in his office.

They were words that came out of nothing, but they seemed to him somehow significant. He muttered them over again.

Last night he had dreamed of Matsushima Bay and its islands. That was perhaps why the words had come to him.

This morning it had seemed odd to him that he should have dreamed of Matsushima, since he had never been there.

And it occurred to him that at his age he had been to only one of the "three great sights of Japan." He had seen neither Matsushima nor the strand at Amanohashi-date. Once, on his return from a business trip to Kyushu, he had had a look at the Miyajima Shrine. It had been winter, not the proper season.

In the morning, he could remember only fragments of the dream; but the color of the pines on the islands and of the water remained clear and fresh, and he was certain that the dream had been of Matsushima.

On a grassy meadow in the shade of the pines, he had a woman in his arms. They were hiding, in fear. They seemed to have left their companions. The woman was very young, a mere girl. He did not know how old he himself was. He must have been young, however, to judge from the vigor with which they ran among the pines. He did not seem to feel a difference in their ages as he held her in his arms. He embraced her as a young man would. Yet he did not think of himself as rejuvenated, nor did it seem to be a dream of long ago. It was as if, at sixty-two, he were still in his twenties. In that fact lay the strangeness.

The motorboat in which they had come went off across the sea. A woman stood in the boat, waving and waving her handkerchief. The white handkerchief against the sea was vivid in his mind even after he woke. The two were left alone on the island, but there was none of the apprehension that they should have felt. He just told himself that they could see the boat out at sea, and that their hiding place would not be discovered.

Watching the white of the handkerchief, he woke.

He did not know, after he woke, who the woman had been. He could remember neither face nor figure. Nor did any tactile impression remain. Only the colors of the landscape were clear. He knew neither why he was sure that it had been Matsushima nor why he should have dreamed of Matsushima.

He had not been to Matsushima, nor had he crossed by boat to an uninhabited island.

He thought of asking someone in the house whether to see colors in a dream was a sign of nervous exhaustion, but in the end remained silent. He did not find it pleasing to think that he had dreamed of embracing a woman. It seemed altogether reasonable that, at his present age, he should have been his young self.

The contradiction was somehow a comfort to him.

He felt that the strangeness would vanish were he to know who the woman was. As he sat smoking, there was a tap on the door.

"Good morning."

Suzumoto came in. "I thought you wouldn't be here yet."

Suzumoto hung up his hat. Tanizaki came up in some haste to take his coat, but he sat down without removing it. His bald head seemed comical to Shingo. The discoloration of age was to be seen above his ears. The aged skin was muddy.

"What brings you here so early?" Restraining a laugh, Shingo looked at his own hands. A faint discoloration would appear from the back of his hand down over the wrist, and then go away again.

"Mizuta. He had such a pleasant death."

"Ah, yes, Mizuta." Shingo remembered. "They sent *gyokuro* after the funeral, and I got into the habit of drinking it again. Very good it was, too."

"I don't know about the *gyokuro*, but I envy him the way he died. I've heard about such things. But Mizuta of all people."

Shingo snorted.

"Don't you envy him?"

"You're bald and fat, and there's hope for you."

"But I don't have all that much blood pressure. I've been told that Mizuta was so afraid of a stroke that he refused to spend a night alone."

Mizuta had died in a hot-spring hotel. At the funeral his old friends whispered of what Suzumoto called his pleasant death. It seemed a little strange afterwards to have concluded that, by virtue of the fact that he had had a young woman with him, it had been such a death. They were curious to know whether the woman might be at the funeral. There were those who said that she would carry unpleasant memories through her life, and those who said that, if she loved him, she would be grateful for what had happened.

To Shingo, the fact that because they were university classmates these men in their sixties should toss out student jargon seemed another of the ugly marks of old age. They still addressed one another by the nicknames and affectionate diminutives of their student days. They had known all about one another when they were young, and the knowledge brought intimacy and nostalgia; but the moss-grown shell of the ego resented it. The death of Mizuta, who had made a joke of Toriyama's death, had now become a joke.

Suzumoto had insisted, at the funeral, upon speaking of the pleasant death; but the thought of it brought a wave of revulsion over Shingo.

"It's not very good form for an old man," he said.

"No. We don't even dream of women anymore." Suzumoto's tone too was dispassionate.

"Have you ever climbed Fuji?"

"Fuji?" Suzumoto seemed puzzled. "Why Fuji? No, I haven't. Why do you ask?"

"Neither have I. I am an aged man, and I have not yet climbed Mount Fuji."

"What? Is that some sort of dirty joke?"

Shingo let out a guffaw.

At work over an abacus near the door, Eiko snickered.

"When you think about it, there must be a surprising number of people who go to their graves without climbing Fuji or seeing the three great sights. What percentage of Japanese do you suppose climb Fuji?"

"Not one per cent, I'd say." Suzumoto returned to the earlier subject. "I doubt if one person in tens of thousands, in hundreds of thousands, has the good luck of Mizuta."

"He won a lottery? But it must not be pleasant for his family."

"Yes, the family. As a matter of fact his wife came," said Suzumoto, with an air as of entering upon his real business, "and asked me about this." He put a cloth-wrapped parcel on the table. "Masks. No masks. She asked me to buy them. I thought I'd ask you to look them over."

"I know nothing about masks. They're like the three great sights. I know they're in Japan, but I've never been to see them."

There were two boxes. Suzumoto took the masks from their pouches.

"This one is the *jido* mask, I'm told, and this the *kasshiki*. They're both children."

"This one is a child?" Shingo took up the *kasshiki* mask by the paper cord that passed from ear to ear.

"It has hair painted on it. See? In the shape of a gingko leaf. That's the mark of a boy who hasn't come of age. And there are dimples."

"Oh?" Shingo held the mask at arm's length. "Tanizaki. My glasses, there, please."

"No, you have it right as it is. They say you're supposed to hold a Nō mask a little above eye level with your arms stretched out. It's actually better for old men like us. And turn it down a little to cloud it."

"It looks like someone I know. Very realistic."

Turning a Nō mask slightly downward is known as "clouding," explained Suzumoto, because the mask takes on a melancholy aspect; and turning it up is known as "shining" because the expression becomes bright and happy. Turning it to the left or the right, he added, is known as "using" or "cutting" or something of the sort.

"It looks like someone I know," said Shingo again. "It's hard to think of it as a child. More like a young man."

"Children were precocious in those days. And a real child's face would be wrong for the Nō. But look at it carefully. It's a boy. I'm told that the *jido* is a sprite of some sort. Probably a symbol of eternal youth."

Shingo turned the *jido* mask this way and that as Suzumoto directed. The hair was in childish bangs.

"Why not keep them company?" said Suzumoto.

Shingo put the mask on the table. "You buy them. You were the one she asked."

"She actually had five. I bought two women's masks, and forced one on Unno. I thought you might take the others."

"So I get the leftovers? You took good care of yourself, buying the women's masks first."

"You'd rather have the women's?"

"What does it matter, now that they're gone?"

"I can bring them if you want. I'll save money if you take them. It's just that I felt sorry for her because of the way Mizuta died, and couldn't refuse. But she said that these are better made than the women's masks. And don't you like the idea of eternal youth?"

"Mizuta is dead, and Toriyama—he looked at them for such a long time at Mizuta's—Toriyama is dead too. Your masks don't make a person feel very comfortable."

"But the *jido* mask is a symbol of eternal youth. Don't you like the idea?"

"Did you go to Toriyama's funeral?"

"I don't remember why, but I couldn't." Suzumoto stood up. "Well, I'll leave them with you. Take a good look at them. If you don't like them, find someone who does."

"Whether I like them or not is beside the point. They are nothing to me. I don't doubt that they're good masks, and doesn't it mean that if I cut them off from the No, I'll be killing them when I die?"

"You needn't worry."

"Are they expensive?" Shingo asked, as if chasing after him.

"Yes. I was afraid I might forget, and had her write it down. There on the cord. It seems to be about what they're worth, but I'm sure you can bargain."

Shingo put on his glasses and started to untwist the cord; and the moment he could see them clearly the hair and lips of the *jido* mask struck him as so beautiful that he wanted to cry out in surprise.

When Suzumoto had left, Eiko came to his desk.

"Isn't it beautiful."

Eiko nodded silently.

"Put it on for a minute."

"But that would be all wrong. Here I am in foreign

clothes." When Shingo handed her the mask, however, she put it on and tied the cord.

"Move your head, very gently."

Standing before him. Eiko moved her head this way and that.

"Good. Very good." The words came of their own accord. Even with so little movement, the mask quite came to life. Eiko had on a russet dress, and her hair sent waves cascading at the sides of the mask, but she had taken on a charm that held him captive.

"Is that enough?"

"Yes." Shingo immediately sent Eiko out to buy a reference work on No masks.

3

The masks carried the names of the makers. The reference book reported that they did not fall into the category of "old masks," from the Muromachi Period, but they were the work of masters of the next age. Even a novice like Shingo sensed, as he took them in his hands, that they were not forgeries.

"Give you the creeps," said Yasuko, putting on his bifocals.

Kikuko laughed softly. "Can you see with Father's glasses?"

"Bifocals are very promiscuous," Shingo answered for his wife. "Almost anyone's will work for almost anyone."

She was using the glasses he had taken from his pocket.

"In most houses the husband wears them sooner, but in this one the old woman is a year older." In high spirits, Shingo had sat down in the *kotatsu* without taking off his coat. "The chief trouble is that you can't see when you're eating. You can't see the food set before you. If it's in fine pieces, there are times when you can't even make out what it is. You first start wearing them, and take up a bowl of rice like this, and the kernels all blur into one another, and you can't separate them. It's very inconvenient at first." Shingo was gazing at the masks.

But then it came to him that Kikuko, a kimono in front of her, was waiting for him to change. And it came to him that this evening again Shuichi was away from home.

He continued to look at the *kotatsu* as he stood up to change. In part he was avoiding Kikuko's face.

He felt a heaviness in his chest. Probably it was because Shuichi had not come home that Kikuko had come to look at the masks. She set about putting away his clothes as if nothing of importance had happened.

"Like heads from the chopping block. They really give you the creeps," said Yasuko.

Shingo came back to the *kotatsu*. "Which do you like best?"

"This." Yasuko answered without hesitation, taking up the *kasshiki* mask.

"Oh?" Shingo was somewhat intimidated by Yasuko's decisiveness. "They're by different makers, but from the same period. About the time of Toyotomi Hideyoshi." He brought his face to the *jido* mask from directly above.

The *kasshiki* was masculine, the eyebrows those of a man; but the *jido* was neuter. There was a wide space between eyebrows and eyes, and the gently arched eyebrows were those of a girl.

As he brought his face toward it from above, the skin, smooth and lustrous as that of a girl, softened in his aging eyes, and the mask came to life, warm and smiling.

He caught his breath. Three or four inches before his eyes, a live girl was smiling at him, cleanly, beautifully.

The eyes and the mouth were truly alive. In the empty sockets were black pupils. The red lips were sensuously moist. Holding his breath, he came so close as almost to touch his nose to that of the mask, and the blackish pupils came floating up at him, and the flesh of the lower lip swelled. He was on the point of kissing it. Heaving a sigh, he pulled away.

He felt, from a distance, as if it had lied to him. He breathed heavily for a time.

Glumly, he put the *jido* mask back into its pouch of gold brocade on a red ground. He handed the pouch for the *kasshiki* mask to Yasuko.

"Put it away."

He felt as if he had looked behind the lower lip of the *jido*, to where the antique red faded away inside the mouth. The mouth was slightly open, but there were no teeth ranged behind the lower lip. It was like a flower in bud upon a bank of snow.

To bring one's face so near as to touch it was probably, for a No mask, an inexcusable perversion. It was probably a way of viewing the mask not intended by the maker. Shingo felt the secret of the maker's own love in the fact that the mask, most alive when viewed at a proper distance from the No stage, should all the same be most alive when, as now, viewed from no distance at all.

For Shingo had felt a pulsing as of heaven's own perverse love. Yet he sought to laugh at it, telling himself that his ancient eyes had made the skin more alluring than that of a real woman.

He wondered whether this sequence of strange occurrences—he had embraced a girl in a dream, he had thought Eiko quite captivating in the mask, he had almost kissed the *jido*—meant that something was about to shake the foundations of his house.

He had not brought his face to that of a young girl since he had begun wearing bifocals. Would such a face, in his aged eyes, be faintly softer?

"They belonged to Mizuta. You know, the one we got the *gyokuro* from. The one who died at a hot spring."

"Give you the creeps," said Yasuko again.

Shingo put whiskey in his tea. In the kitchen, Kikuko was dicing onions for a fish chowder.

4

On the morning of the twenty-ninth of December, as he was washing his face, Shingo saw Teru out sunning herself with all her puppies.

Even when the puppies had begun to come out from under the maid's room, he had not known whether there were four or five of them. Kikuko would pounce upon a puppy and bring it into the house. In her arms the puppies were docile enough, but they would flee back under the house when they saw someone approaching.

At no one time had they all been out together. Kikuko had said that there were four, and at another time that there were five.

He saw that there were five puppies out in the morning sunlight.

They were at the foot of the mountain, where he had seen the buntings mixed in among the sparrows. It was where earth was piled up from a cave they had dug as an air-raid shelter, and where, during the war, they had had a vegetable patch. It now seemed to be a place where animals sunned themselves.

The pampas grass at which the sparrows and buntings had been so busy had withered, but the powerful stalks, still upright, covered the side of the mound. The earth above was covered with soft weeds. Shingo was filled with admiration at Teru's sagacity in having chosen it.

Teru had taken her puppies out to a good place before people were up, or while their attention was on getting breakfast, and she lay nursing them and letting them warm themselves in the morning sun. They were quietly enjoying a moment when there was no one to bother them. So he thought at first, and smiled at the scene that presented itself in the warm sunlight. It was late December, but in Kamakura the sun was as warm as in autumn.

But as he looked more closely he saw that the five were shoving and jostling one another in a competition for nipples. Their front paws pumped at Teru's belly like pistons, and they were giving free rein to their young animal strength; and Teru, perhaps because they were now strong enough to climb the slope, seemed reluctant to let them nurse. She twisted and turned, and lay on her belly. It was red from the threshing paws.

Finally she got up and shook the puppies away, and

came running down the slope. A black puppy that had clung to a nipple with particular stubbornness was sent tumbling from the mound.

It was a three-foot drop. Shingo caught his breath in alarm. The puppy got up as if nothing had happened, and, after standing there blockishly for a second or two, walked off sniffing at the earth.

"What is it?" He felt that he was seeing the pose for the first time, and that he had seen exactly that pose before. He thought for a moment.

"That's it. The Sotatsu painting," he muttered. "Remarkable."

Shingo had glanced at Sotatsu's ink painting of a puppy, and had thought it altogether stylized, like a toy; and now he was astonished to see it reproduced in life. The dignity and elegance of the black puppy were exactly like the Sotatsu.

He thought again of how realistic the *kasshiki* mask was, and of how it had reminded him of someone.

Sotatsu and the mask-maker were of the same period.

Sotatsu had painted what would today be called a mongrel puppy.

"Come and look. All the puppies are out."

Hugging the ground in fright, the other four puppies came down the slope.

He watched expectantly, but none of the other four struck the Sotatsu pose.

He had seen the puppy become the Sotatsu picture, and the *jido* mask had become a living woman; and had he also had a fleeting glimpse of the two in reverse?

He had hung the *kasshiki* mask on a wall, but he had put the *jido* mask far back in a drawer, like some esoteric object.

Yasuko and Kikuko came to the wash stand to see the puppies.

"You didn't notice while you were washing?"

Kikuko, looking out from behind them, put her hand lightly on Yasuko's shoulder. "A woman is too rushed in the morning. Isn't that so, Mother?"

"It is. And Teru?"

"Where will she have gone? She's left them to wander around like strays," said Shingo. "I hate to think of throwing them away."

"I've already married off two of them," said Kikuko.

"You've found someone to take them?"

"Yes. Teru's owner wants one. He says he wants a female."

"Really? He wants to change her for a puppy now that she's gone astray?"

"So it would seem." Kikuko turned to Yasuko: "Teru has gone off to eat somewhere." Then, leaving her earlier answer to speak for itself, she amplified upon this last remark for Shingo: "Everyone in the neighborhood is amazed at how clever Teru is. She knows when everyone eats, and shows up exactly on time."

"Really?" Shingo was a little disappointed. He had thought that, taking her morning and evening meals here, Teru had made this her home; was she still walking the neighborhood with an eye on all the leftovers?

"To be more precise," added Kikuko, "it's not the mealtimes she knows but the times when people are cleaning up afterwards. Everyone in the neighborhood is talking about how Teru had puppies here, and I get all sorts of reports on her activities. And when you're away, Father, children come and ask to see the puppies."

"She seems very popular."

"Oh, yes," said Yasuko. "One lady said something interesting. She said that now that Teru had had puppies here we would be having a baby. She said that Teru was urging us on. Aren't we to be congratulated?"

"Really, Mother." Kikuko flushed, and took her hand from Yasuko's shoulder.

"I'm just reporting what a lady in the neighborhood said."

"You mean there is someone who puts people and dogs in the same category?" It came to Shingo that the remark had not been very tactful.

But Kikuko looked up. "Grandfather Amamiya is very worried about Teru. He came and asked if we wouldn't take her in. He spoke of her as if she were a child, and I didn't know what to say."

"Why not take her in?" said Shingo. "She's here all the time anyway."

Amamiya had lived next door to Teru's master, but, failing in business, he had sold his house and moved to Tokyo. His old mother and father had lived with him and done odd jobs around the house, and, the Tokyo place being small, they had been left behind in a rented room. The old man was known in the neighborhood as "Grandfather Amamiya."

He was the one Teru was fondest of. Even after he moved into the rented room, he came inquiring after her.

"I'll run and tell him so," said Kikuko, going back into the house. "He'll be very relieved."

His eye on the black puppy, Shingo noticed a broken thistle under the window. The flower had fallen, but the stem, bent from its base, was still a fresh green.

"Thistles are very strong plants," said Shingo.

The Cherry in the Winter

It began raining on New Year's Eve, and New Year's Day was rainy.

On New Year's Day the occidental way of reckoning ages became official. Shingo was therefore sixty-one, Yasuko sixty-two.

New Year's Day was a day for late sleepers; but Shingo was aroused early by Satoko. The child was scampering up and down the veranda.

"Come here, Satoko." Kikuko also seemed to be up. "I've got a New Year's pudding for you. You can help me heat it."

Apparently she wanted to lure the child to the kitchen, away from Shingo's room. Satoko seemed indifferent, however. The scampering went on.

"Satoko," Fusako called from bed. "Come here, Satoko." Satoko was no swifter to answer her mother.

"A rainy New Year," said Yasuko, also awake.

Shingo grunted.

"With Satoko up, Kikuko has to be up and around. Fusako manages to stay in bed, I see." She stumbled over the last words. Shingo was amused. "It's been a long time since I last had a child to wake me up on New Year's morning."

"You'll have plenty of other mornings, too."

"Oh, I don't think so, really. It's just that there aren't any verandas in Aihara's house. Once she gets used to them she'll stop running around."

"I wonder. Don't most children her age like running up and down verandas? Why do her feet sound as if they were sticking to the floor?"

"Because they're so soft." Yasuko listened. "It gives you a strange feeling, doesn't it? She should be five this year, and all of a sudden she's three. It doesn't make all that much difference for me, shifting from sixty-four to sixty-two."

"But there's something you haven't thought of. My birthday comes before yours, and for a while then we'll be the same age. From my birthday to yours."

Yasuko seemed aware of the fact for the first time.

"Quite a discovery. Once in a lifetime."

"Maybe so," muttered Yasuko. "But it doesn't do much good to start being the same age this late in life."

"Satoko," Fusako called again. "Satoko." Apparently

tired of running, Satoko went to her mother. "Just feel how cold your feet are."

Shingo closed his eyes.

"It would be good if she'd do all that running while we're there to see it," said Yasuko after a time. "But when we are she starts sulking and hanging onto her mother."

Perhaps each of them was trying to detect in the other signs of affection for the child.

It seemed to Shingo, in any case, that he was being probed by Yasuko.

Or perhaps he was probing himself.

The sound of the feet clinging to the floor had not been pleasant, for he had not had enough sleep; but, on the other hand, it had not particularly irritated him.

Yet he had not felt the tenderness the footsteps of a grandchild ought to bring. There was no doubt that he was wanting in affection.

No sense of the darkness, out there on the veranda with the shutters still closed, came to him. It had apparently come to Yasuko immediately. In such ways the child was capable of arousing her compassion.

2

Fusako's unhappy marriage had left a scar on Satoko. It aroused a certain compassion in Shingo too, but more frequently it was a source of irritation. For nothing could be done about it.

He was astonished at the extent of his helplessness.

No parent could do a great deal about the married life of his children, of course; but what was truly striking, now that matters had reached a point where divorce seemed the only solution, was the helplessness of the daughter herself.

For her parents to take her and the children in after the divorce would solve nothing. It would be no cure, and it would bring her no life of her own.

Was there then no answer at all for a woman whose marriage had failed?

When, in the autumn, Fusako had left her husband, she had gone not to her parents' house but rather to the family seat in Shinano. It was from there that she had let them know by telegram of her departure.

Shuichi had gone to bring her back.

She had then left again, after a month in Kamakura, saying that she was going to make a clean and final break with Aihara.

Perhaps it would be better for Shingo or Shuichi to go have a talk with him, they had said; but she had not listened. She must go herself.

"But that's exactly the point, what to do with the children," she said when Yasuko suggested that she leave at least them behind. She leaped on Yasuko in a manner almost hysterical. "I don't know whether I'm to have them or Aihara is." And so she had gone out and not come back.

It was after all a matter between husband and wife, and Shingo and his family were worried, not knowing how long they should wait in silence. And so the uneasy days passed.

There came no word from Fusako.

Had she settled down with Aihara again?

"Things are just going to drag on?" said Yasuko.

"Well, it's we who are letting them," replied Shingo. Both faces were clouded.

Then, suddenly, on New Year's Eve, Fusako had come back.

"What's happened?" Yasuko seemed frightened as she looked down at her daughter and grandchildren.

Her hands trembling, Fusako tried to close her umbrella. One or two of the ribs seemed to be broken.

"Is it raining?" asked Yasuko.

Kikuko stepped down into the doorway and took Satoko in her arms.

She had been helping Yasuko with the New Year's food.

Fusako had come in through the kitchen.

Shingo suspected that she had come for money, but such did not seem to be the case.

Yasuko wiped her hands and went into the living room. "A fine thing, sending you away on New Year's Eve!" She stood gazing at her daughter.

Fusako was weeping silently.

"It's better this way," said Shingo. "A clean break."

"Oh? But I wouldn't have thought it possible for anyone to be turned out of the house on New Year's Eve."

"I came of my own accord." Fusako was choked with tears.

"Oh? Well, that's different, I suppose. You've just come to spend the New Year with your family. I shouldn't have put it the way I did. I apologize. But let's not talk about it now. We'll have a good talk during the holiday." Yasuko went to the kitchen.

Shingo was taken somewhat aback by his wife's tone; but it had in it a certain echo of maternal affection.

Yasuko was moved, naturally enough, both by the

sight of her daughter coming home through the kitchen door on New Year's Eve, and by the sound of the child's footsteps on the dark veranda; but Shingo sensed an element of deference toward himself.

Fusako slept later than the others on New Year's morning.

They could hear her gargling as they sat at the table. Her ablutions went on and on.

"Let's have one while we're waiting," said Shuichi, pouring sake for his father. "You're getting a good number of gray hairs these days."

"Of course. At my age you get more of them every day. Every day—sometimes you see them turn gray right in front of your eyes."

"Ridiculous."

"No. Just watch." Shingo leaned forward. Yasuko and Shuichi looked at his head, and Kikuko was gazing intently.

She had Fusako's younger child on her lap.

3

A second *kotatsu* had been brought out for Fusako and the children. Kikuko joined them in another room.

Yasuko sat to one side as Shingo and Shuichi faced each other over wine cups.

Shuichi seldom drank at home; but today, perhaps having been led beyond his capacity by the rainy New Year's Day, he poured cup after cup for himself, almost ignoring his father. His expression was not his usual one. Shingo had heard how, at the establishment of his mistress, Shuichi had gotten violently drunk, and how he had made the woman cry by insisting that her friend sing to him.

"Kikuko," called Yasuko. "Would you mind bringing us some oranges too?" Kikuko slid open the door. "Come and sit over here. I have a pair of silent drinkers on my hands."

Kikuko glanced at Shuichi. "I don't think Father is drinking all that much."

"I've been thinking a little," muttered Shuichi. "About Father's life."

"About my life?"

"Oh, nothing very definite. But if I had to summarize my speculations, I suppose they would go something like this: has Father been a success or a failure?"

"You think you would be able to judge?" Shingo was silent for a moment. "Well, the food this New Year has a little of the taste it had before the war. In that sense you can say I'm a success."

"The food—did you say?"

"I did. And wouldn't that be about it? If you say you've been giving a little thought to your father's life."

"A little."

"An ordinary, mediocre life that's come as far as it has, and now it runs into good food at New Year's. Lots of people have died, you know."

"True."

"But whether or not a parent is a success *would* seem to have something to do with whether or not his children's marriages are successful. There I haven't done too well."

"That's your feeling, is it?"

"Oh, stop it, you two." Yasuko looked up. "You aren't

getting the year off to a very good start." She lowered her voice. "And don't forget that Fusako is here. Where is she, by the way?"

"Asleep," said Kikuko.

"Satoko?"

"Satoko and the baby too."

"Well, now. All three of them sleeping away?" Yasuko's eyes were round and on her face was something of the innocence that comes with old age.

The gate opened. Kikuko went out. Tanizaki Eiko had come to make her New Year's call.

"Well, now. And in this rain." Shingo was indeed surprised, but that "Well, now" he had borrowed from Yasuko.

"She says she won't come in," said Kikuko.

"Oh?" Shingo went to the door.

Eiko was standing with her coat over her arm. She had on a black velvet dress. Her makeup was heavy despite the fact that she seemed to have shaved away the fuzz. Bowing from the hips, she looked even smaller.

Her greeting was a little stiff.

"It was good of you to come in this downpour. I hadn't expected callers, and I hadn't thought of going out. Come in and warm yourself."

"Thank you."

Eiko had come through the cold of the wind and rain. He had trouble knowing whether she had come to register a protest, or whether she really had something to talk about.

He felt, in any case, that it had been brave of her.

Eiko seemed reluctant to come inside.

"In that case I'll pull myself together and go out with

you. Why don't you wait inside while I get ready? I always go at least to see Mr. Itakura. The old president of the company."

Itakura had been on his mind all morning, and Eiko's arrival had made the decision for him. He hurried to change clothes.

Shuichi had apparently lain back, his feet in the *ko-tatsu*, when Shingo had gone out. He got up again as Shingo started to change.

"Tanizaki is here," said Shingo.

"Yes." Shuichi spoke as if the matter were no concern of his, and did not seem disposed to greet her.

As Shingo went out, Shuichi looked up and followed with his eyes. "Don't stay out after dark."

"I'll be back early."

Teru was at the gate.

A black puppy came running out and, imitating its mother, cut across in front of Shingo toward the gate. It staggered and fell, wetting one side of its body.

"What a shame," said Eiko. She seemed about to kneel down beside it.

"We had five of them. We've given four away, and this is the only one left. It's promised too."

The train on the Yokosuka Line was empty.

Looking at the rain, driven horizontal by the wind, Shingo felt somehow happy that she had braved it.

"There are generally swarms of people from the Hachiman Shrine."

Eiko nodded.

"Yes, it's true—you always do come on New Year's Day."

"Yes." Eiko looked down for a time. "I'd like to keep coming even after I've quit work."

"You won't be able to once you're married. Did you have something on your mind?"

"No."

"You needn't feel shy. I'm a little dull and absent-minded these days."

"Stop pretending." It was an odd remark. "But I think I'll have to ask you to let me quit work."

This announcement had not been wholly unexpected, but Shingo was troubled for an answer.

"I didn't come especially on New Year's Day to tell you." Her manner seemed old beyond her years. "We'll talk about it later."

"Oh?" Shingo no longer felt as happy.

She had been in his office for three years, and now, suddenly, she seemed a different woman. She was not her usual self.

Not that he had paid a great deal of attention to her. She had only been his secretary.

He felt, of course, that he would like to keep her. Yet she was in no sense his captive.

"But I think it's my fault that you want to quit. I had you show me that house, and I made things unpleasant for you; and I imagine it isn't easy to have to see Shui-chi."

"It has been hard." Her answer was unequivocal. "But when I thought about it all afterwards, it seemed the natural thing for a father. And I saw that I had been wrong, too. I was very proud of myself when he took me dancing, and I went to Kinu's house. It was depraved of me."

"That seems a little strong."

"But I did get worse." Her eyes were half closed, in sorrow. "If I quit work, I'll ask Kinu to give him up. To pay you back for all you've done."

Shingo was startled. It was as if something had brushed against a ticklish spot.

"That was his wife at the door?"

"Kikuko?"

"Yes. It was very hard for me. I decided I really had to speak to Kinu."

He felt a certain lightness in her, and a lightening of his own spirits.

It was not impossible, the thought came to him, that by even such light devices the problem might be solved, and with unexpected dispatch.

"I can't really ask you to do that."

"I'm doing it of my own free will, to pay you back for all you've done." That such a grand statement should have come from Eiko's small lips made Shingo once again feel aware of the ticklish spot.

And he thought of telling her not to rush into affairs that were no concern of hers.

But Eiko seemed much affected by her own "decision."

"I can't understand him, when he has such a good wife. I don't like watching him with Kinu, but I couldn't be jealous of his wife, I don't care how close they might seem to be. Or is it that men are dissatisfied with women who don't make other women jealous?"

Shingo smiled wryly.

"He was always saying what a child she is."

"To you?" There was sharpness in the words.

"Yes, and to Kinu. He said you were fond of her because she was a child."

"The fool!" Shingo looked at her.

"But he doesn't any more," said Eiko in some confusion. "He doesn't talk about her anymore."

Shingo was almost trembling with anger.

He sensed that Shuichi had referred to her body.

Had he wanted to find a prostitute in his bride? There was astonishing ignorance in the fact, and Shingo felt in it too a frightening paralysis of the soul.

Did the immodesty with which he spoke of his wife to Kinu and even to Eiko arise from that same paralysis?

He sensed cruelty in Shuichi. And not only in him: in Kinu and Eiko too he sensed cruelty toward Kikuko.

Did Shuichi not feel the cleanness in her?

The pale, delicate, childlike face of Kikuko, baby of her family, floated before him.

It was a little abnormal, Shingo could see, for him to feel a sensual resentment toward his son because of his son's wife; but he could not help himself.

There was an undercurrent running through his life, the abnormality that made Shingo, drawn to Yasuko's sister, marry Yasuko, a year his senior, upon the sister's death; was it exacerbated by Kikuko?

When Shuichi had found another woman so remarkably early in their marriage, Kikuko had seemed at a loss to control her jealousy; and yet it seemed that, in the presence of Shuichi's cruelty and moral paralysis, indeed because of them, she had awakened as a woman.

He remembered that Eiko was less well developed physically than Kikuko.

Shingo fell silent, seeking somehow to control his anger through his sadness.

Eiko too was silent. Taking off her gloves, she smoothed her hair.

4

Shingo was in Atami. In the garden of the inn a cherry tree was in full bloom. It was January.

Winter cherries, he had been told, had been blooming from before the end of the year; but he felt as if he had come upon spring in a wholly different world.

He mistook the red plum blossoms for peaches, and wondered if the white might be apricots.

Attracted to the cherry blossoms as they were reflected by the pond, he went over to stand on the bank. He had not yet been shown to his room.

He crossed the bridge to the opposite bank, there to look at a plum tree shaped like an umbrella and covered with red blossoms.

Several ducks came running out from under the tree. In their yellow bills and the slightly deeper yellow of their feet he again felt spring.

Tomorrow the firm would be entertaining guests, and Shingo had come to make the arrangements. His business was over once he had conferred with the innkeeper.

He sat on the veranda and looked out at the garden.

There were also white azaleas.

Heavy rain clouds were bearing down from Jikkoku Pass, however, and he went inside.

On the desk were a pocket watch and a wristwatch. The wristwatch was two minutes the faster.

It was seldom that the two were exactly together, which fact sometimes bothered him.

"But if they worry you so, why don't you just carry one?" said Yasuko.

She had a point, to be sure. But the habit had formed over the years.

Already before dinner there were heavy rains and strong winds.

The lights failed and he went to bed early.

He awoke to the howling of a dog in the garden, and the sound of wind and rain, like a raging sea.

There were drops of perspiration on his forehead. The room had a heaviness about it, like the beginning of a spring storm beside the sea. The air was tepid, and seemed to press down upon his chest.

Taking a deep breath, he felt a surge of disquiet, as if he were about to spit blood.

"It's not in my chest," he muttered to himself. He was only having an attack of nausea.

An unpleasant tightness in his ears moved through his temples to gather at his forehead. He rubbed his forehead and throat.

The sound like a raging sea was a mountain downpour and above it the sharp rasp of the wind came nearer.

In the depths of the storm there was a roaring.

A train was passing through the Tanna Tunnel, he thought. Such was no doubt the case. A whistle blew as the train emerged.

Shingo was suddenly afraid; he was now wide awake.

The roaring had gone on and on. The tunnel being some five miles long, the train would have taken perhaps seven or eight minutes to pass through. His impression was that he had heard it entering the far mouth, beyond Kannami. But was it possible that, a half mile from the Atami exit, he could have heard it at such a distance?

He had somehow felt the presence of the train in the tunnel as if it were inside his head. He had felt it all the way to the near mouth, and heaved a sigh of relief as it came out.

But he was perplexed. He would make inquiries of the inn people the next morning, he decided, and he would telephone the station.

For a time he was unable to sleep.

"Shingo-o-oh! Shingo-o-oh!" Half asleep and half awake, he heard someone calling him.

The only person who called with that particular lilt was Yasuko's sister.

For Shingo it was a piercingly sweet awakening.

"Shingo-o-oh! Shingo-o-oh! Shingo-o-oh!"

The voice had stolen into the back garden and was calling from under the window.

Shingo was awake. The sound of the brook behind the inn had become a roar. There were children's voices.

He got up and opened the back shutters.

The morning sun was bright. It had the warm brightness of a winter sun that was damp with the rain of spring.

On the path beyond the brook seven or eight children had gathered, on their way to grammar school.

Had he then heard them calling one another?

But Shingo leaned out of the window and searched through the bamboo thickets on the near side of the stream.

Water in the Morning

Told by his son on New Year's Day that his hair was getting white, Shingo had replied that at his age a person had more white hairs every day, indeed that he could see hairs growing white before his eyes. He had remembered Kitamoto.

His schoolmates were now in their sixties. Among them were considerable numbers whose luck, from the middle of the war on into the defeat, had not been good. Since they were already then in their late fifties, the fall was cruel and recovery difficult. And they were of an age to lose sons in the war.

Kitamoto had lost three sons. When his company

turned to war production, he was a technician whose services were no longer needed.

"They say it happened while he was sitting in front of a mirror pulling out white hairs," said an old friend who, visiting Shingo's office, told him of Kitamoto. "He was at home with nothing to do, and at first his family didn't take it too seriously. They thought he was just pulling out white hairs to keep himself busy. It was nothing to be all that worried about. But every day he would squat in front of the mirror. Where he thought he had pulled them all out the day before there would be white hairs again. I imagine there were actually too many for him to get them all. Every day he would spend more time in front of the mirror. They would wonder where he was, and there he would be in front of the mirror pulling out hair. He'd be nervous and jumpy if he was away from the mirror for even a minute, and rush back to it again. Finally he was spending all his time there."

"It's a wonder he didn't lose all his hair." Shingo was on the point of laughter.

"It's no laughing matter. He did. He pulled out every last hair."

This time Shingo laughed openly.

"But it's no lie," said the friend, looking into Shingo's face. "They say that even while he was pulling out white hair his hair would get whiter. He'd pull out one white hair, and two or three hairs next to it would be white. He would look at himself in the mirror with a sort of desperate expression on his face, and he would be getting whiter as he pulled out white hairs. His hair got thinner and thinner."

Shingo restrained his laughter. "And his wife let him go on pulling?"

But the friend went on as if the question needed no answer. "Finally he had almost no hair left, and what was left was white."

"It must have hurt."

"When he was pulling it out? No, it didn't hurt. He didn't want to lose any black hair, and he was careful to pull out the white hairs one by one. But when he had finished, the skin was drawn and shriveled. It hurt when you ran your hand over it, the doctor said. It didn't bleed, but it was raw and red. Finally he was put in a mental hospital. They say it was in the hospital that he pulled out what little was left. But think of the will-power and the concentration. They almost scare you. He didn't want to be old, he wanted to be young again. No one seems to know whether he started pulling it out because he had lost his mind, or he lost his mind because he pulled out too much."

"But I suppose he's better?"

"Yes. And there was a miracle. A fine crop of black hair came out on his naked head."

"You can't mean it!" Shingo was laughing again.

"But it's true," said the friend, unsmiling. "Lunatics have no age. If we were crazy, you and I, we might be a great deal younger." He looked at Shingo's hair. "There's still hope for you. For me it's too late."

The friend had lost most of his hair.

"Shall I pull out one of my own?" muttered Shingo.

"Have a try at it. But I doubt if you have the will-power to pull them all out."

"I doubt it too. And white hair doesn't worry me. I have no mad desire for black hair."

"You've had security. You calmly swam through while everyone else was going under."

"You make it seem so easy. You might as well have said to Kitamoto that he would save himself trouble by dyeing his hair."

"Dyeing is cheating. If we're going to let ourselves think of cheating, then I doubt if we can hope for miracles like Kitamoto's."

"But isn't Kitamoto dead? Even though there was a miracle."

"Did you go to the funeral?"

"I didn't know of it at the time. I didn't hear of it till the war was over and things had settled down a little. I doubt if I would have gone into Tokyo anyway. It was during the air raids."

"You can't hold on to miracles for very long. Kitamoto may have pulled out his white hair and fought against the years, but life goes its own way. You don't live longer just because your hair goes dark again. It might even be the opposite. It might be that he used up all his energy growing that crop of dark hair, and his life was actually shortened. But don't think the struggle means nothing to you and me." He nodded to emphasize this conclusion. Hair was combed across his bald crown like the strips of a blind.

"Everyone I meet these days has white hair," said Shingo. "It wasn't so bad with me during the war, but I've gotten whiter and whiter since."

Shingo did not believe all the details of the story. He suspected embroidering.

That Kitamoto had died was a fact, however. He had learned of it from someone else.

As Shingo turned the story over in his mind, his thoughts took a strange turn. If it was true that Kitamoto was dead, then it must also be true that his white hair had grown out black. If it was true that he had lost his mind, then it must also be true that he had pulled out all his hair. If it was true that he had pulled out his hair, then it must also be true that it had grown white as he sat before the mirror. Was not the whole of the story true? Shingo was surprised at his own conclusion.

"I forgot to ask whether Kitamoto's hair was white or black when he died," he said, laughing. But neither the words nor the laughter were audible. They were for him alone.

Even if the story he had heard was true and without embroidery, there had probably been an element of parody in the manner of its telling. One old man had told of the death of another old man with derision and not without cruelty. The taste left by the encounter was not pleasant.

Among the friends of his student days, Kitamoto and Mizuta had been the ones to die strange deaths. Mizuta had died suddenly at a hot-spring resort. He had gone there with a young girl. Shingo had been importuned late the year before to buy his No masks. It had been because of Kitamoto that he had hired Tanizaki Eiko.

Mizuta having died since the war, Shingo had been able to go to the funeral. He did not hear until later of Kitamoto's death, which occurred during the air raids; and when Tanizaki Eiko came with her introduction, Kitamoto's wife and children were still in Gifu Prefecture, where they had taken refuge from the raids.

Eiko was a schoolfriend of Kitamoto's daughter. But it seemed altogether too unceremonious that he should be asked this favor by the daughter. He had not met her, and Eiko said that she had not seen her since the war. It seemed too precipitous on the part of both girls. If Kitamoto's widow, at the daughter's prompting, had remembered Shingo, then she should have written herself.

Shingo felt no obligation toward the daughter and her letter of introduction.

As for Eiko, who brought it, she seemed slight in body and frivolous in mind.

Yet he hired her, and took her into his own office. She had been working there for three years.

The three years had gone by swiftly, but it seemed odd, now, that she had lasted so long. It was perhaps not surprising that she had, in the course of the three years, gone dancing with Shuichi, but she had even been in the house of Shuichi's woman. And Shingo himself, under her guidance, had gone to see it.

Eiko seemed to feel intimidated by these events. She had come to dislike her work.

Shingo had not spoken to Eiko of Kitamoto. Probably she did not know that he had lost his mind. She and the daughter were probably not such close friends as to frequent each other's houses.

He had thought her frivolous, but now that she had quit work he sensed certain traces of conscience and benevolence in her. And with them a purity, for she was not yet married.

2

"You're up early, Father." Pouring out the water with which she was about to wash her face, Kikuko drew water for him.

Drops of blood fell into it, and spread and thinned.

Remembering how he himself had coughed up a small amount of blood, and thinking how much cleaner was Kikuko's, he was afraid that she too might be spitting up blood; but it was a nosebleed.

She held a cloth to her nose. The blood traced a line from her wrist down to her elbow.

"Look up, look up." He put his arm over her shoulders. She fell slightly forward, as if avoiding him. He pulled her back by the shoulders, and, taking her forehead, made her look up.

"I'm all right, Father. I'm sorry."

"Keep quiet and kneel down. Lie down."

Supported by Shingo, Kikuko leaned against the wall.

"Lie down," he said again.

But she remained in the same position, her eyes closed. On her face, white as if she had fainted, there was an innocent quality, as of a child who has quit resisting. He saw the small scar on her forehead.

"Has it stopped? If it has, go in and lie down."

"Yes. I'm all right." She wiped her nose with the cloth. "The basin is dirty. I'll wash it for you."

"Please don't bother."

Shingo poured out the water in some haste. Faintly, melting away, there were traces of blood at the bottom of the basin.

Shingo did not use it. He washed his face directly from the faucet.

He thought of rousing Yasuko and sending her to help.

But then he decided not to. Kikuko might not want to reveal her discomfort to her mother-in-law.

The blood had fallen as from a bursting pod. To him

it had been as if pain itself were bursting forth.

Kikuko passed while he was combing his hair.

"Kikuko."

"Yes?" She looked over her shoulder at him, but went on to the kitchen. She came back with charcoal in a firepan. He saw it send off sparks. She had lighted charcoal for the *kotatsu* over the kitchen gas.

Shingo was startled at himself. He had quite forgotten that his own daughter, Fusako, had come home. The breakfast room was dark because Fusako and her two children were asleep in the next room. The shutters had not yet been opened.

Rather than his old wife, he could have roused Fusako to help Kikuko. It was odd that Fusako had not come into his mind when he had thought to call Yasuko.

At the *kotatsu*, Kikuko poured tea for him.

"Are you dizzy?"

"Just a little."

"It's still early. Why don't you rest this morning?"

"It's time I was up and around." Kikuko spoke as of a triviality. "The cold wind was good for me when I went to get the paper. And I've always been told that a woman's nosebleed is nothing to worry about. Why are you up so early yourself? It's cold again this morning."

"I wonder. I was awake before the temple bell rang. It rings at six, summer and winter, the whole year round."

Shingo was up earlier than Shuichi, but later in starting for the office. Such was their way in the winter.

He took Shuichi to lunch at a nearby occidental restaurant.

"You know about the scar on Kikuko's forehead?" he asked.

"Yes."

"The mark of the forceps, I imagine. It was a difficult birth. You couldn't exactly call it the remains of suffering at birth, I suppose, but it stands out when she's in pain."

"You mean this morning?"

"Yes."

"It was probably because of the nosebleed. It stands out when her color is bad."

Shingo felt somehow forestalled. When had Kikuko told Shuichi?

"But she didn't sleep last night."

Shuichi frowned. After a moment of silence he said: "You needn't behave so properly with an outsider."

"An outsider? Isn't she your own wife?"

"That's what I'm saying. You needn't behave yourself so properly with your son's wife."

"What do you mean?"

Shuichi did not answer.

3

When Shingo returned to his office, Eiko was seated in the reception room. Another woman was standing beside her.

Eiko too stood up. She offered the usual sort of greetings about the weather and her remissness.

"It's been a long time. Two months."

Eiko seemed to have put on a little weight, and her face was more heavily made up. He remembered how, when he had gone dancing with her, her breasts had seemed just enough to fill his hands.

"This is Mrs. Ikeda. You will remember that I spoke of her." Eiko's eyes were most appealing, as if she might be on the point of tears. So it was with her on solemn occasions.

"How do you do." Shingo could not bring himself to thank the Ikeda woman, as ceremony required, for her ministrations to Shuichi.

"I dragged Mrs. Ikeda here. She said she didn't want to come. She said there was no point in coming."

"Oh? Shall we talk here, or would you rather go out?"

Eiko looked inquiringly at the other woman.

"This will do nicely, as far as I am concerned," she said curtly.

Shingo was confused. Eiko had said, he seemed to remember, that she would introduce him to the woman who was living with Shuichi's woman. He had not pursued the matter.

It seemed to him very odd indeed that two months after she had quit work Eiko should acquit herself of the undertaking.

Had Shuichi and his woman at length agreed on a separation? Shingo waited for Eiko or the Ikeda woman to speak.

"Eiko pestered me into coming. But it won't do any good." Her manner was hostile. "I've been telling Kinu that she ought to leave Shuichi. I thought if I came I might get your help."

"I see."

"Eiko is in your debt, and she sympathizes with his wife."

"A very nice lady," put in Eiko.

"Eiko has said that to Kinu too. But there aren't many

women these days who will withdraw just because a man has a nice wife. Kinu says if she is to give another man back, then let her have her own husband back. He was killed in the war. Just bring him back to me alive she says, and I'll let him do exactly what he wants. He can have as many affairs with other women and as many mistresses as he wants. She asks if I don't agree. Anyone who lost her husband in the war has to agree. Didn't we send them off to war? And what are we to do now that they're dead? He's in no danger of getting killed when he comes to see me, she says. I send him back undamaged."

Shingo smiled wryly.

"I don't care how good a wife she is, she isn't a war widow."

"That's a blunt way to put it."

"Yes. That's what she says when she's in her cups. She and Shuichi are ugly drinkers. She says to tell his wife she's never had to wait for someone to come home from a war. She waits for someone who's sure to come back. All right, he shouts back. He *will* tell her. I'm a war widow, too. Doesn't it always go bad when a war widow falls in love?"

"What do you mean?"

"Shuichi too—he's an ugly drinker. He's been very rough with her. He told her to sing for him. She doesn't like to sing, and there was nothing for me to do but sing in her place. I sang in a very small voice. If I hadn't done something to quiet him down we'd have been the scandal of the neighborhood. I felt so insulted myself that I could hardly go on. But I wonder if it's really because of drink. Mightn't it be because of the war? Don't you suppose he had women that way somewhere? When I saw him out of control, I thought I was seeing my own husband during the war. I went dizzy and I could hardly breathe, and it seemed to me that I was the woman he was having. I cried and I sang some songs that weren't very proper. I said to Kinu that I wanted to think of my husband as the only exception; but I suppose it was that way with him too. Afterwards, when Shuichi made me sing, Kinu would be crying with me."

Shingo's face clouded over. It was a morbid story.

"The best thing would be to put an end to it as soon as possible."

"I agree. After he's gone, she's always saying that this sort of thing means complete ruin. If that's how she feels, then of course she ought to leave him. But I suspect she's afraid that what would come afterwards would really be ruin. A woman. . . ."

"She needn't worry," put in Eiko.

"You're right I suppose. She has her work. You've seen how it is."

"Yes."

"She did this for me." The Ikeda woman gestured toward her own suit. "I suppose she's about the most important after the chief cutter. They think very highly of her. They took in Eiko on the spot because of her."

"You're working in the same shop?" Shingo looked at Eiko in surprise.

"Yes." Eiko nodded, and flushed slightly.

He found it hard to understand her. First she had Shuichi's mistress get her a job in the same shop, and now she brought the Ikeda woman to see him.

"And so I doubt if she costs Shuichi much money," said the latter.

"It's not a matter of money." Shingo was irritated, but he controlled himself.

"There's something I often say to her after he's been bad to her." She sat with bowed head. Her hands were folded on her knees. "He goes home wounded, too, I say. He goes home a wounded soldier." She looked up. "Can't he and his wife live away from you? I often think that if he and his wife were alone together, he would leave Kinu. I've thought about it a great deal."

"Possibly so. I'll give it some thought myself."

He considered her forward, but he had to agree with her.

4

Shingo had had no intention of asking anything of the woman named Ikeda, and he had had nothing to say to her. He had just let her talk on.

To the woman the visit must have seemed pointless. Without going so far as to seem a suppliant, Shingo should have discussed the matter candidly with her. She had done well to say as much as she had. It had been as if she were apologizing for Kinu, and doing yet something more.

Shingo felt that he should be grateful to both Eiko and Ikeda.

The visit had aroused neither doubts nor suspicions.

But, perhaps because his self-respect was on trial, he answered irritably when, going into a business dinner, a geisha whispered something in his ear.

"What? I'm deaf, damn it. I can't hear you."

He clutched at her shoulder. He took his hand away immediately, but the geisha frowned with pain and rubbed at the shoulder.

"Come out here for a minute," she said, reading the irritation on his face. She pressed her shoulder to his and led him to the veranda.

He was back in Kamakura at about eleven. Shuichi was not yet home.

In her room, next to the breakfast room, Fusako raised herself on an elbow and looked up at him. She was nursing her younger child.

"Is Satoko asleep?"

"She just now went to sleep. Mother, she said, which is bigger, a thousand yen or a million yen? Which is bigger? We laughed and laughed. Ask Grandfather when he comes home, I said. She went to sleep while she was waiting for you."

"If she was asking about a thousand yen before the war and a million yen since, it was a good question," laughed Shingo. "May I have a glass of water, please, Kikuko?"

"Water? A glass of water?" Kikuko got up, but she spoke as if it were an odd request.

"From the well. I don't want all those chemicals."

"Yes."

"Satoko wasn't born before the war," said Fusako, still in bed. "I wasn't married yet."

"It would be better if you hadn't married at all, before the war or after," said Yasuko. They heard water being drawn at the well. "The pump doesn't sound cold any more. In the winter when Kikuko goes out early to get water for your tea, that squeaking makes me shiver even when I'm warm in bed."

"I'm thinking of having them live away from us," he said in a low voice.

"Away from us?"

"Don't you think that would be better?"

"Maybe. If Fusako is going to stay on."

"I'll leave, Mother, if it's a question of living away from you." Fusako got out of bed. "I'll move out. Isn't that the thing to do?"

"It has nothing to do with you," Shingo half snarled at her.

"It does have something to do with me. A great deal, in fact. When Aihara said that you made me what I am by not liking me, I almost choked. I've never been so hurt in my life."

"Control yourself, control yourself. Here you are in your thirties."

"I can't control myself because I have no place to control myself in."

Fusako brought together her night kimono over her rich breasts.

Shingo got up wearily. "Let's go to bed, Granny."

Kikuko brought his glass of water. In her other hand she had a large leaf.

"What is it?" he asked, drinking the water down in one breath.

"A loquat leaf. There's a new moon, and there was a white blur by the well. I wondered what it might be. A new loquat leaf, already this big."

"Very school-girlish of you," said Fusako sardonically.

The Voice in the Night

❁

Shingo woke to a sound as of a man's groaning.

He was not sure whether it was a dog or a man. At first it sounded like the moaning of a dog. It would be Teru, in her death agonies. Had she been poisoned?

His heart was racing.

He held his hand to his chest. It was as though he had had a seizure.

But when he was fully awake, he knew that it was not a dog but a man. He was being throttled; his voice was thick. Shingo was in a cold sweat. Someone was being attacked.

"Kiko-o-oh. Kiko-o-oh," the voice seemed to say. "Tell me, tell me." There was pain in it, the words caught in the throat and refused to take shape.

"Kiko-o-oh. Kiko-o-oh."

About to be killed, would he be asking his assailant's reasons or demands?

Shingo heard someone fall against the gate. He hunched his shoulders, preparing to get up.

"Kikuko-o-oh. Kikuko-o-oh."

It was Shuichi calling Kikuko. His speech was muddled, and the second syllable was lost. He was dead drunk.

Exhausted, Shingo sank back on the pillow. His heart was still racing. He rubbed his chest and breathed deeply and regularly.

"Kikuko-o-oh, Kikuko-o-oh."

Shuichi seemed not to be knocking on the gate but falling against it.

Shingo thought he would go out after he had rested a moment.

But then he decided that that might not be the best thing to do. Shuichi seemed to be calling out in heartbroken love and in sorrow. It was the voice of one for whom there is nothing else. The groaning was like a child calling out for its mother in a moment of pain and sorrow, or of mortal fear. And it seemed to come from depths of guilt. Shuichi was calling out to Kikuko, seeking to endear himself to her, with a heart that lay cruelly naked. Perhaps, his drunkenness his excuse, he called out in a voice that begged for affection, thinking he would not be heard. And it was as if he were doing reverence to her.

"Kikuko-o-oh, Kikuko-o-oh."

The sadness came across to Shingo.

Had he ever himself, even once, called out to his wife in a voice filled with such hopeless love? Perhaps, unconsciously, it had in it the hopelessness of a certain moment on a foreign battlefield.

He listened on, wishing that Kikuko would awaken. At the same time he felt a little embarrassed to have his daughter-in-law hear that misery-ridden voice. He thought he would rouse Yasuko if Kikuko did not get up soon; but it would be better for Kikuko to go.

He pushed the hot-water bottle to the foot of the bed. Was it because he still had a hot-water bottle, even now in spring, that his heart raced so?

Kikuko was in charge of the bottle. He would occasionally ask her for one. The water stayed warm longer when she heated it, and the lid was secure.

Perhaps because Yasuko was stubborn, perhaps because she was healthy, she disliked hot-water bottles even at her age. She had warm feet. As late as his fifties, Shingo had still taken warmth from his wife, but now they slept apart.

She never moved to touch his hot-water bottle.

"Kikuko-o-oh, Kikuko-o-oh." Again the voice came from the gate.

Shingo turned on the light by his pillow. It was almost two-thirty.

The last train on the Yokosuka line got to Kamakura before one. Shuichi had evidently held out in one of the taverns by the station.

Shingo thought, from the tone of the voice, that the

end was in sight for Shuichi and the woman in Tokyo.

Kikuko went out through the kitchen.

Much relieved, Shingo turned off the light.

"Forgive him," he muttered, addressing the words to Kikuko.

She seemed to be holding Shuichi up.

"Please. You're hurting me." It was Kikuko. "You're pulling my hair with your left hand."

"Am I?"

The two of them fell down in the kitchen.

"Steady, now. On my knees. Your legs swell when you're drunk."

"My legs swell? You're a liar."

Kikuko seemed to be taking off his socks, his legs on her knees.

She had forgiven him. Perhaps he need not have worried. Perhaps, as his wife, she took pleasure in sometimes being able to forgive. And perhaps she had listened well to the voice.

His legs on her knees, she pulled off the socks of a husband drunk and back from visiting another woman. Shingo felt the gentleness in her.

When she had put Shuichi to bed, she went out to lock the back gate and the kitchen door.

Shuichi's snoring was so loud that even Shingo could hear it.

Here was Shuichi, put to bed by his wife and promptly asleep; and what would be the position of the woman Kinu who, until just now, had been made his companion in ugly drunkenness? Had Shingo not heard that he drank and resorted to violence and made her weep?

And Kikuko: she had sometimes been pale and drawn because of Kinu, but the flesh at her hips had grown richer.

2

The snoring soon stopped, but Shingo could not get back to sleep.

He wondered if Yasuko's snoring had been handed on to their son.

Probably not. Probably he snored tonight because he had had so much to drink.

Yasuko did not seem to snore these days. She seemed to sleep even better in cold weather.

Shingo disliked mornings after he had slept badly because his memory was worse than usual, and he was overtaken by fits of sentimentality.

It might have been sentimentality that had made him hear Shuichi's voice as he had. Possibly it had been a voice thick from drink, nothing more. Had Shuichi hidden his discomfiture behind his drunkenness?

It also seemed to Shingo that the love and the sadness he had sensed in that fuddled voice had only been what he hoped for in his son.

Because of that voice, Shingo himself had forgiven Shuichi. And he thought that Kikuko had forgiven him. The selfishness of blood ties bore itself in on Shingo.

He thought himself good to his daughter-in-law, and yet he seemed in some respects to side with his son.

It was an ugly picture. Shuichi had drunk too much at the house of the woman in Tokyo, and come home to fall against the gate.

If Shingo himself had gone to open the gate, he probably would have glared at Shuichi, and Shuichi would have sobered up. It was better that Kikuko had gone. Shuichi had thus been able to come in hanging on her shoulder.

Kikuko the injured party was Kikuko the absolver.

How many times would Kikuko, now in her early twenties, have to forgive Shuichi before she had lived with him to the ages of Shingo and Yasuko? Would there be no limit to her forgiving?

A marriage was like a dangerous marsh, sucking in endlessly the misdeeds of the partners. Kinu's love for Shuichi, Shingo's love for Kikuko—would they disappear without trace in the swamp that was Shuichi's and Kikuko's marriage?

It seemed to Shingo quite proper that in postwar domestic law the basic unit had been changed from parent and child to husband and wife.

"In other words, the husband-wife marsh," he muttered to himself. "They'll have to have their own house."

It was because of his age that he had this way of muttering what came into his mind.

The expression "husband-wife marsh" meant only that a husband and wife alone, putting up with each other's misdeeds, deepened the marsh with the years.

That was probably because the wife awoke to herself in confrontation with the husband's misdeeds.

Shingo rubbed at an itching eyebrow.

Spring was near.

He did not dislike awakening in the night as he had during the winter.

He had awakened from a dream before Shuichi's voice had awakened him. At the time he remembered it well, but when he was awakened the second time he had almost forgotten it.

Perhaps it was the pounding of his heart that had erased it.

He remembered only the fact that a girl fourteen or fifteen years old had an abortion, and the words: "And she has become a holy child forever."

He had been reading a novel. Those were the concluding words.

He had read the novel as words, and seen the plot as a movie or play. He had not appeared in it himself. He had been completely the onlooker.

A girl who had an abortion at fourteen or fifteen and was at the same time a holy child was something of an oddity; but there had been a long story. Shingo's dream had read a masterpiece about pure love between a boy and a girl. His feelings were still with him when he woke at the end of the reading.

Had it been that the girl did not know she was pregnant and did not think of it as an abortion, and went on longing for the boy from whom she had been separated? But such a twist in the dream would be unnatural and unclean.

A forgotten dream could not be put together again. And his feelings upon reading the novel were a dream.

The girl must have had a name, and he must have seen her face, but only her size, or more properly her smallness, remained vaguely in his mind. She seemed to have been in Japanese dress.

He asked himself whether it had been a vision of

Yasuko's beautiful sister, but decided that it could not have been.

The source of the dream was no more than an article in last night's paper.

"Girl Has Twins. Misguided Awakening of Spring in Aomori." Under the large headline was this article: "According to a survey by the Aomori Prefectural Public Health Service of legal abortions under the Eugenics Law, five girls fifteen years old, three girls fourteen, and one girl thirteen have undergone abortions. There have been four hundred cases of abortion among girls of high-school age, sixteen to eighteen, and of these twenty per cent have been high-school students. There has been one middle-school pregnancy in Hirosaki and one in Aomori, and there have been four in South Tsugaru District and one in North Tsugaru District. Though the girls have gone to specialists, a lack of sexual knowledge has produced the horrifying results of death in .2 per cent of the cases and serious illness in 2.5 per cent. The thought that others, in secret, go to their deaths at the hands of unlicensed doctors makes one tremble for 'young mothers.'"

Four actual cases were listed. A second-year middle-school student, fourteen years old, in North Tsugaru District, had, in February of the year before, suddenly felt the coming on of birth pangs, and borne twins. Mother and children were healthy, and the girl was back in school, now a third-year student. Her parents had not known of her pregnancy.

A high-school student in Aomori, having promised herself to a classmate, became pregnant the summer before. The parents of the two, on the grounds that they were still in school, decided upon an abortion. But the boy said: "We weren't playing. We're going to get married soon."

The article had been a shock to Shingo; and so he had gone to bed and dreamed of an abortion.

But his dream had seen nothing ugly in the boy and girl. It had told a story of pure love, and made the girl "a holy child." He had not so viewed the matter before going to sleep.

The shock had become something beautiful. Why should there have been such a transformation?

Perhaps, in the dream, he had rescued the girl, and himself, too.

In any case, benevolence had emerged from the dream.

Shingo reflected upon himself, wondering whether for him benevolence woke in dreams.

And he became somewhat sentimental. Had a flicker of youth given him a dream of pure love in old age?

The sentimentality had remained after the dream, and perhaps made him greet Shuichi's voice, like a loud moaning, with benevolence, made him feel in it love and sadness.

3

Still in bed, Shingo heard Kikuko arousing Shuichi.

He woke too early these days. Yasuko, a late sleeper, had reprimanded him. "Old people aren't popular when they make fools of themselves and get up too early."

He too thought it improper to be up before Kikuko,

and so he would go quietly to the front door for the paper and read it in bed.

Shuichi seemed to have gone to wash.

There was a sound of vomiting. He had evidently gagged while brushing his teeth.

Kikuko ran to the kitchen.

Shingo got up. On the veranda he met Kikuko coming back from the kitchen.

"Father!"

She stopped, almost running into him, and flushed. Something spilled from the cup in her hand. It seemed to be a cold sake, a remedy for Shuichi's hangover.

Shingo thought her very beautiful, a flush on the somewhat pale face, without cosmetics, shyness in the still sleepy eyes, the beautiful teeth showing between plain, unpainted lips upon which floated a smile of embarrassment.

Was there still this childlike quality in her? Shingo thought of his dream.

But it was not so very strange that girls no older than those in the article should marry and bear children. In ancient times that had been the ordinary thing.

And when he was no older than the boys, Shingo himself had been strongly drawn to Yasuko's sister.

Seeing that he had come into the breakfast room, Kikuko opened the shutters in some haste.

Spring sunlight flooded in.

Kikuko seemed startled by the brightness. Shingo was watching her from behind. She brought both hands to her head and pulled at her hair, still tangled from sleep.

The great gingko in the shrine precincts was not yet sending out new shoots. Yet somehow, in the morning light and the morning nostrils, there was something akin to a scent of buds.

Quickly putting herself in order, Kikuko brought him *gyokuro*.

"Here you are, Father. I'm being very slow this morning."

Always when he got up in the morning, Shingo had *gyokuro* in very hot water. The hotter the water the more difficult the steeping, and Kikuko did it best.

Shingo wondered whether *gyokuro* might not be even better if it came from an unmarried girl.

"You're very busy," he said cheerfully. "Sake for the drunkard, *gyokuro* for the dotard."

"You knew about it?"

"He woke me up. At first I thought it was Teru."

"You did?" Kikuko sat with bowed head, as if unable to move.

"I was awake before you were, Kikuko," said Fusako, in the next room. "It wasn't at all pleasant. I knew it was Shuichi, because Teru is a quieter sort."

Still in her nightgrown, her younger child at her breast, Fusako came into the breakfast room. Her features were bad, but her breasts were white and remarkably full.

"You're a mess," said Shingo. "Put something on."

"Aihara was a mess, and so naturally I'm a mess too. There's nothing else for you to be when you're married to a man who's a mess." Fusako shifted Kuniko from her right breast to her left. "If you didn't want it that way, then it would have been a very good idea for you to look into things before you married me off."

"Men and women are different."

"They are the same. Look at Shuichi."

She started for the washstand.

Kikuko reached for Kuniko. Fusako handed her over so roughly that she began to cry.

Unconcerned, Fusako walked off.

Yasuko, back from washing her face, took the child. "What do you suppose her father means to do? It was New Year's Eve when Fusako came back. More than two months ago. He says that Fusako is a mess, but I think that Father here is even messier in the matter that is most important. You said on New Year's Eve that it was good to have a clean break, and since then you've done exactly nothing. And there's not been a word from Aihara." She was looking down at the baby as she spoke. "The Tanizaki girl you had in your office—Shuichi says she's half a widow. I suppose Fusako is half a divorcee."

"What does 'half a widow' mean?"

"She wasn't married, but the man she was in love with was killed in the war."

"But Tanizaki would have been a mere child."

"She was sixteen or seventeen by the old count. Old enough to have a man you can't forget."

Shingo thought the expression "a man you can't forget" an odd one to come from Yasuko.

Shuichi left without breakfast. He was late, and probably not feeling well.

Shingo killed time until the morning mail came. Among the letters Kikuko brought was one addressed to her.

He handed it to her.

She had apparently brought them in without looking at them. She rarely got letters. Nor did it seem that she expected them.

She read the letter in the breakfast room.

"It's from a friend. She had an abortion and hasn't been well since. She's in the University Hospital in Hongo."

"Oh?" He took off his glasses and looked into her face. "Did she fall into the clutches of some unlicensed old midwife? Very dangerous."

The newspaper article last night and Kikuko's letter —Shingo was struck by the coincidence. And he had dreamed of an abortion.

He was tempted to tell Kikuko of the dream.

But, as he gazed at her, unable to speak, he felt in himself a flicker of something youthful, and was startled as another thought flashed across his mind, that Kikuko was pregnant and was thinking of an abortion.

4

"See how the plums are blooming," said Kikuko wonderingly as the train passed through the North Kamakura valley.

In North Kamakura there were large numbers of plums very near the train window. Shingo saw them every day but paid no particular attention to them.

The white blossoms were past their prime. In the warm sunlight, they were beginning to look dirty.

"But our plums are in bloom too," said Shingo. There were only two or three of them, however, and perhaps this was the first real display that Kikuko had seen.

It was rare for her to get letters, and it was rare for her to go out, save to shop in Kamakura.

On her way to pay a sick call on her friend in the University Hospital, she had left with Shingo.

The house of Shuichi's woman was near the University. That fact troubled Shingo.

He wanted, along the way, to ask whether Kikuko was pregnant.

The question was not such a difficult one, and yet it seemed quite possible that he would let the opportunity pass.

How many years had it been since he had stopped asking Yasuko about her physiological processes? Since the change of life, Yasuko herself had said nothing. Had it become a question not of vigor but of decay?

Shingo had forgotten a matter of which Yasuko had stopped speaking.

As he thought to ask Kikuko the question, Yasuko came into his mind.

Perhaps if Yasuko had known that Kikuko was going to an obstetric ward, she would have suggested an examination.

Yasuko sometimes spoke to Kikuko of children. To Shingo it seemed that Kikuko found the subject forbidding.

Kikuko had without doubt said something to Shuichi. Long ago Shingo had listened with admiration to a friend's theory that for a woman the man to whom she made the revelation was everything. If she had another man, she kept the secret of her condition to herself.

A daughter did not make it to her own father.

Shingo seemed to avoid talking to Kikuko of Shuichi's woman, and she to him.

If she was pregnant, it might be because of a ripening brought on by Shuichi's woman. An unpleasant thought, but a part of being human; and it seemed to him that there was cruelty hidden in speaking to Kikuko of children.

"Did Mother tell you that Grandfather Amamiya came around yesterday?"

"No."

"He came to say that he was being taken into the Tokyo house. And he brought two big sacks of cookies and asked us to be good to Teru."

"Are the cookies for Teru?"

"Mother thinks so. Or maybe one is for us. Grandfather Amamiya was very happy. He said that young Mr. Amamiya's business was doing well, and that he had built on to the house."

"That's how it is. A good businessman sells his house right away and starts all over again, and before you know it he is building on to a new house. With people like me, ten years go by like a day. Even this train ride gets to seem like too much trouble. The other day we had dinner together, all of us old men. It's remarkable how we go on year after year, doing the same old things. We get tired and bored, and ask when they'll come for us."

It did not seem that Kikuko quite understood the last remark.

"Someone said that when we go before the judge we should tell him that spare parts commit no sins. That's what we are, life's spare parts. And while we're alive, shouldn't life at least be kind to us?"

"But. . . ."

"It's true. I doubt whether anyone in any age can say he has really lived life for everything in it. Think of the man who checks your shoes at the restaurant. All he does day after day is put away shoes and take out shoes. One of us old men had a theory all his own—that things are actually easier for that kind of spare part. But the waitress didn't agree. The old man who takes care of shoes has a hard life, she said. He has to work in a hole with shoe shelves all around him, and there he sits hugging a charcoal fire and shining shoes. It's cold in the winter there in the doorway and hot in the summer. You've noticed how our own granny likes to talk about old people's homes?"

"Mother? But with Mother it's not that serious. It's like young people who keep saying they wish they were dead."

"That's true, I suppose. She assumes she's going to outlive me. But what young people are you talking about?"

"Young people. . . ." Kikuko hesitated. "In my friend's letter."

"The letter this morning?"

"Yes. She's not married."

"Well!"

He fell silent. Kikuko could not go on.

It was as the train left Totsuka. Hodogaya, the next stop, was some distance away.

"Kikuko. I've been thinking. Wouldn't you and Shuichi like to live away from us?"

Kikuko looked at him, waiting for him to say more. Then, a pleading note in her voice: "Why, Father? Because Fusako has come back?"

"It has nothing to do with Fusako. I know it's hard for you, having a half-divorcee with us; but even if she divorces Aihara, she probably won't be with us long. No, it has nothing to do with her. It has to do with the two of you. Don't you think it would be better?"

"No. You are good to me, and I would rather be with you. I don't think you can imagine how lonely I'd be away from you."

"You're being very kind."

"Oh, no. I'm taking advantage of you. I'm the baby, the spoiled child of the family. I was always my father's favorite and I like being with you."

"I can understand why your father favored you, and it's good having you with us. I wouldn't be happy to see you go. But Shuichi is the way he is, and I haven't once talked the problem over with you. A useless sort of parent to be living with. If the two of you were by yourselves, mightn't you come up with your own solution?"

"No. You don't say anything, but I know that you're worrying about me and sympathizing with me. That's how I manage to go on." There were tears in the large eyes. "I think I'd be afraid if you made us live away. I don't think I could stand to wait at home alone. I'd be too lonely, and frightened."

"I see—waiting for him by yourself. But this isn't the sort of thing to talk about on a train. Think it over."

She did seem to be frightened. Her shoulders were trembling.

He saw her to Hongo in a taxi.

Perhaps because she had been pampered by her father, or perhaps because she was upset, she did not seem to think the service unnatural.

It was most unlikely that Shuichi's woman would be out walking, and yet he was concerned. He waited until Kikuko was safely inside the hospital.

The Bell in Spring

❀

In Kamakura in the season of cherry blossoms, the seven-hundredth anniversary of the Buddhist capital was being celebrated. The temple bell rang all through the day.

There were times when Shingo could not hear it. Kikuko heard it, apparently, even when she was working or talking; but Shingo had to listen carefully.

"There," Kikuko would inform him. "There. It rang again."

"Oh?" said Shingo, cocking his head to one side. "And how is it with Granny?"

Yasuko was no comfort. "Of course I can hear it. It's practically deafening."

She was reading at her own pace through the five days' accumulation of newspapers before her.

"There it goes, there it goes," said Shingo. Once he had caught the sound, it was easy to follow succeeding strokes.

"You seem very pleased." Yasuko took off her glasses and looked at him. "The priests must get tired, ringing away at it day after day."

"No, they have the pilgrims ring, at ten yen a stroke," explained Kikuko. "It's not the priests."

"A clever idea," said Shingo.

"They call it the bell for the dead, or something of the sort. The angle is to have a hundred thousand people or a million people or something of the sort ring the bell."

"The angle?" Her choice of words struck Shingo as amusing.

"It has a dark sound to it." said Kikuko. "I don't really like it."

"You think it's dark?"

Shingo himself had been thinking how pleasantly quiet and relaxed it was, sitting in the breakfast room on an April Sunday, looking at the cherry blossoms and listening to the bell.

"What is this the seven-hundredth anniversary of, anyway?" asked Yasuko. "Some say it has to do with the Great Buddha, and some say it's Nichiren."

Shingo could not answer.

"Do you know, Kikuko?"

"No."

"Very odd. And here we all are living in Kamakura."

"Isn't there anything in your newspapers, Mother?"

"There might be." Yasuko passed them on to Kikuko. They were neatly folded and stacked. Yasuko kept one for herself. "I believe I did see something. But I was so struck by the piece about the old couple who left home that I forgot everything else. You saw it, I suppose?" she asked Shingo.

"Yes."

"A great benefactor of Japanese boat racing. The vice-chairman of the Japanese Rowing Association." She began to read the article, and then went on in her own words. "He was the president of a company that makes boats and yachts. He was sixty-nine, and she was sixty-eight."

"And what was there about it that struck you so?"

"He left behind notes to their daughter and son-in-law and grandchildren. Here it is in the paper." Yasuko began reading again. " 'Miserable old creatures, living our leftover lives, forgotten by the world? No, we have decided that we do not want to live so long. We quite understand the feelings of Viscount Takagi.* People should go away while they are still loved. We shall go now, still in the embrace of family affection, blessed with numbers of comrades and colleagues and school-mates.' That's to the daughter and son-in-law. And this is the one to the grandchildren: 'The day of Japanese independence is approaching, but the way ahead is dark. If young students who know the horrors of war really want peace, then they must persist to the end in the non-violent methods of Gandhi. We have lived too long and

---

* *Father-in-law of the present Emperor's youngest brother. His death, in 1948, is commonly believed to have been at his own hand.*

no longer have the strength to lead and to pursue the way we believe right. Were we to live idly on into "The Spiteful Years," * then we would have made meaning-less the years we have lived thus far. We want to leave behind memories of a good grandfather and grand-mother. We do not know where we are going. We but go quietly off.' "

Yasuko fell silent.

Shingo turned aside, to look at the cherries in the garden.

Yasuko was still looking at the newspaper. "They left their house in Tokyo and disappeared after they had visited his sister in Osaka. The sister is in her eighties."

"Did the wife leave a note?"

"What?" Yasuko looked up in surprise.

"Didn't the wife leave a note?"

"The wife? The old woman?"

"Of course. If they went off together, it would have been natural for the wife to leave a note too. Suppose you and I were to commit suicide. You'd have something you wanted to say, and write it down."

"That wouldn't be necessary," said Yasuko briskly. "It's when young people commit suicide that they both leave notes. They want to talk about the tragedy of being kept apart. What would I have to say? With a husband and wife it's enough for the husband to leave a note."

"You really think so?"

"It would be different if I were to die by myself."

"I suppose you'd have mountains of pains and re-grets."

"They wouldn't matter. Not at my age."

Shingo laughed. "Comfortable remarks from an old

* *A reference to a story (1947) by Niwa Fumio.*

woman who doesn't plan to die and isn't about to die. And Kikuko?"

"Me?" It was a low, hesitant voice.

"Supposing you were to commit suicide with Shuichi. Would you want to leave a note?"

He knew immediately that it had not been the thing to say.

"I don't know. I wonder how it would be." She looked at Shingo. The forefinger of her right hand was in her obi, as if to loosen it. "I have a feeling I'd want to say something to you, Father." Her eyes had a youthful moistness, and then there were tears in them.

Yasuko had no intimations of death, thought Shingo, but Kikuko was not without them.

Kikuko leaned forward. He thought she was about to collapse in tears, and then she got up.

Yasuko looked after her. "Odd. She has nothing to cry about. Hysteria, that's what it is. Plain hysteria."

Shingo unbuttoned his shirt and put his hand to his chest.

"Is your heart pounding?"

"No. The nipple itches. It's hard and itches."

"Like a teen-age girl."

Shingo rubbed his left nipple with his forefinger.

When a couple committed suicide together the husband left a note and the wife did not. Did the wife have the husband substitute for her, or act for the two in concert? The question had puzzled and interested Shingo as Yasuko read from the newspaper.

Living together for long years, had the two become one? Had the old wife lost her identity, was she without a testament to leave behind?

Was it that the woman, with no compulsion to die,

went in attendance upon her husband, had her part in the husband's testament, without bitterness, regrets, hesitation? It all seemed very odd to Shingo.

But his own old wife had in fact said that if they were to commit suicide she would not need to leave a note. It would be enough for him to.

A woman who went uncomplainingly to death with a man—there were times when the opposite was the case, but usually the woman followed the man. Somehow it startled Shingo that such a woman, grown old, should be here beside him.

Kikuko and Shuichi had not been together long, and already they were having their troubles.

It might be that he had been cruel to Kikuko, that he had injured her when he asked whether she would want to leave a note.

He knew that she stood on a dangerous brink.

"You're too good to her. That's why she cries over such silly things." said Yasuko. "You pamper her, and you've done not one single thing about the most important problem. It's the same with Fusako."

Shingo was looking at the cherry tree, heavy with blossoms.

Under the great cherry was a rich growth of *yatsude*.*

Disliking *yatsude*, Shingo had meant to cut it away before the cherry bloomed; but there had been heavy snowfalls in March, and now the blossoms had come.

Though he had cut it down three years ago, it had come back all the more luxuriantly. He had thought then that he should dig up the roots, and he had been right.

Yasuko's observations made him dislike the heavy

* FATSIA JAPONICA.

green of the leaves all the more. Without the *yatsude* the cherry would stand alone, spreading until its branches fell in the four directions. It had spread well even with the *yatsude* crowding it.

And it was so laden with blossoms that one wondered how a tree could bear so many.

The blossoms floated up grandly in the light of the afternoon sky. Neither the shape of the tree nor its color was particularly strong, but one felt that it quite filled the sky. The blossoms were at their best. It was hard to think that they would fall.

But two or three petals were constantly falling, and the ground was carpeted with them.

"When you read that a young person has been killed or committed suicide, you just say to yourself it's happened again," mused Yasuko. "But with old people it really hits you. 'People should go away while they are still loved.'" She had evidently read the article over two and three times. "The other day there was a story about a sixty-one-year-old man who brought his grandson down from Tochigi to put him in St. Luke's Hospital. The boy was seventeen and had had infantile paralysis. The grandfather carried the boy around on his back to show him Tokyo. But the boy absolutely refused to go to the hospital, and so finally the grandfather strangled him with a towel. It was in the paper the other day."

"Oh? I didn't notice." Shingo's answer was indifferent, but he remembered how deeply he had been impressed by the article about young girls and their abortions, how he had even dreamed of it.

The difference between him and the old woman who was his wife was very considerable.

2

"Kikuko," called Fusako. "This sewing machine is always breaking the thread. Is something wrong with it? Come and have a look. It's a Singer and ought to be a good machine. I wonder if I've lost my touch. I wonder if maybe I'm hysterical."

"It might be going to pieces. I've had it since I was in school." Kikuko came into the room. "But it listens when I speak to it. Let me have a try."

"Oh? I get so nervous with Satoko hanging onto me. I'm always sewing her hand. Of course I don't sew her hand, but she puts it up here like this, and while I'm watching the seam everything gets blurry and she and the cloth run together."

"You're tired."

"Just as I said. Hysterical. You're tired yourself. The only ones in this house who aren't tired are Grandfather and Grandmother. Here Grandfather is in his sixties and he complains about an itching nipple. Ridiculous."

On her way back from the sick call in Tokyo, Kikuko had bought material for the two children.

Fusako was at work on dresses, and well disposed toward Kikuko.

Displeasure was plain on Satoko's face, however, as Kikuko changed places with Fusako.

"Aunt Kikuko bought the material, and now you're going to have her sew it?"

"Don't listen to her, Kikuko. She's exactly like Aihara." Apologies did not come easily from Fusako.

Kikuko put her hand on Satoko's shoulder. "Get

Grandfather to take you down to the Buddha. There will be a procession with little princes and all, and there will be dancing."

At Fusako's urging, Shingo went out with Fusako and Satoko.

As they walked down the main street of the Hase district, Shingo's eye was caught by a dwarf camellia before a tobacco shop. Buying a package of Hikari cigarettes, he offered a word of praise. The blossoms, of which there were five or six, were double, with crinkly petals.

No, replied the tobacconist. Double blossoms were not right for dwarf trees. One should stay with the single-petalled wild camellia. He led them to the garden behind. Dwarf trees in pots were lined up by a vegetable patch some four or five yards square. The wild camellia was an old tree with a powerful trunk.

"I've pinched off the buds," the man said. "It wouldn't do to wear the tree out."

"It does have buds?"

"Plenty of them. But I leave very few. The one out in front must have had twenty or thirty."

The man talked of the techniques of dwarfing, and of people in Kamakura with a fondness for dwarf trees. Shingo had frequently seen them in shop windows.

"Thank you very much," he said, leaving the shop. "I envy you."

"I don't have any really good ones, but the wild camellia does have its points. You get yourself a tree, and then you're responsible for seeing that it doesn't die or lose its shape. It's good medicine for laziness."

Shingo lit one of the cigarettes he had just bought. "It

has the Buddha on it," he said, handing the package to Fusako. "Especially made for Kamakura."

"Let me see." Satoko stretched for the cigarettes.

"You remember last fall when you ran away from home and went off to Shinano?"

"I did not run away from home."

"Were there any dwarf trees in the old house?"

"I didn't see any."

"Probably not. It must be forty years ago. The old man was addicted to dwarf trees. Yasuko's father. But you know how Yasuko is, and he preferred her sister. It was her sister he had help him with the trees. She was such a beauty that you'd never have dreamed she was Yasuko's sister. I can see her now, dressed in a red kimono, bangs on her forehead, going down of a morning when snow was piled on the shelves to brush it away from the branches. I can see it right here in front of me, all fresh and clean. Shinano is cold, and her breath was white."

The white breath was scented with the softness of the young girl.

Sunk in memories, Shingo was taking advantage of the fact that Fusako, of a different generation, was not interested.

"I imagine that camellia has been at it for more than forty years." It seemed to be of a venerable age. How many years would it take for a dwarfed trunk to become like flexed biceps?

The maple that had glowed red on the altar after Yasuko's sister died—would it, in someone's hands, still be alive?

3

When the three came to the temple precincts, the "procession of little princes" was weaving its way up the flagstone walk before the Great Buddha. The little boys had walked a considerable distance, it seemed. Some of them were exhausted.

Fusako lifted Satoko to see over the wall of people. Satoko gazed at the boys in their flowery kimonos.

Having heard that there was a stone in the precincts bearing a poem by Yosano Akiko,* they went behind the statue to look for it. It seemed to be in Akiko's own hand, enlarged, and carved on the stone.

"I see it has Sakyamuni," said Shingo.

He was astounded that Fusako did not know this most famous of poems.

Akiko had written:

A summer grove, Kamakura; a Buddha he may be,
But a handsome man he also is, Lord Sakyamuni.

"But the Great Buddha isn't a Sakyamuni. He's actually an Amitabha. Seeing that she had made a mistake, she rewrote the poem, but by that time the Sakyamuni version was too well known, and to change it to the Great Buddha or something of the sort would spoil the rhythm—and bring in Buddha twice. But it *is* a mistake. A mistake carved on stone, right here in front of us."

Ceremonial tea was being served in a curtained-off space near the stone. Kikuko had given Fusako tickets.

The tea in the open sunlight had its own special color.

* 1878–1942.

Shingo wondered whether Satoko too would drink it. Satoko clutched at the edge of the bowl with one hand. It was a most ordinary bowl, but Shingo reached to help her.

"It's bitter."

"Bitter?"

Even before she had tasted the tea, Satoko's face announced that it was bitter.

The little dancing girls came inside the curtain. Perhaps half sat down on stools by the door. The others crowded in front of them, one against another. They were all heavily made up and had on long-sleeved festive kimonos.

Behind them, two or three young cherries were in full bloom. Defeated by the powerful colors of the girls' kimonos, they seemed pale and wan. The sun was shining on the green of the tall trees beyond.

"Water, Mother, water," said Satoko, glaring at the dancers.

"There is no water. You can have some when we get home."

Suddenly Shingo too wanted water.

One day in March, from the Yokosuka train, Shingo had seen a girl about Satoko's age drinking at a fountain. She laughed in surprise when, as she turned it on, the water shot high in the air. The laughing face was very pretty. Her mother adjusted the fountain for her. Watching her drink as if it were the world's most delicious water, Shingo thought to himself that this year too spring had come. The scene returned to him now.

He wondered what it was about the cluster of little girls dressed for dancing that had made both him and

Satoko want water. Satoko was grumbling again. "Buy me a kimono, Mother, buy me a kimono."

Fusako got up.

Among the girls was a most appealing one a year or two older than Satoko. Her eyebrows were painted on in thick, short, sloping lines, and at the edges of her eyes, round as bells, there was rouge.

Satoko stared at the girl as Fusako led her off, and as they started out through the curtain, lunged in her direction.

"A kimono," she persisted. "A kimono."

"Grandfather said he'll buy you one for Three-five-seven Day," * said Fusako insinuatingly. "She hasn't once worn a kimono. Only diapers from an old cotton kimono, an outcast of a kimono."

They went into a tea stall, and Shingo asked for water. Satoko gulped down two glasses.

They had left the precincts of the Great Buddha and were walking toward home when a girl in a dancing kimono hurried past on her mother's hand, apparently also on the way home. This would not do, thought Shingo, taking Satoko by the shoulder; but he was too late.

"A kimono," said Satoko, reaching for the girl's sleeve.

"Don't!" Pulling away, the girl tripped over her long sleeve and fell.

Shingo gasped and brought his hands to his face.

The child was being run over. Shingo heard only his own gasp, but it seemed that numbers of other people had cried out.

* *November 15. Children those ages are presented at shrines.*

The automobile screeched to a stop. Three or four ran forward from among the horrified outlookers.

The girl jumped up. Clinging to her mother's skirt, she began screaming as if set afire.

"Good, good," someone said. "The brakes worked. An expensive car."

"If it had been a broken-down wreck you wouldn't be alive."

Satoko was terrified. Her eyes were rolled back into her head as if she were having a convulsion.

Was the girl hurt, had she torn her kimono, asked Fusako, apologizing profusely to the girl's mother. The mother was looking absently into space.

When the girl had finished screaming, her thick powder had run; but her eyes were shining, as if washed clean.

Shingo had little to say the rest of the way home.

They heard the baby wailing.

Singing a lullaby, Kikuko came out to greet them.

"I'm sorry," she said to Fusako. "I have her crying. I'm a failure."

Perhaps led on by her sister, perhaps surrendering now that she was safe at home, Satoko too was wailing.

Ignoring Satoko, Fusako pulled her kimono open and took the baby from Kikuko.

"Just look, will you. I'm all in a cold sweat here in the hollow between."

Shingo glanced up at a framed inscription that purported to be a Ryokan: * "In the heavens, a high wind." He had bought it when Ryokans were still cheap, but it was a forgery all the same. A friend having pointed this fact out, he could see that it must be true.

* *Poet, 1757–1831.*

"We had a look at the Akiko stone," he said to Kikuko. "It's in Akiko's own hand, and it says 'Sakyamuni.'"

"It does, does it?"

4

After dinner Shingo went out alone to look through the new and used kimono shops.

But he found nothing that seemed appropriate for Satoko.

The matter weighed even more heavily on his mind.

He felt a dark foreboding.

Did even so young a girl covet another's bright kimono?

Was it only that Satoko's envy and greed were somewhat stronger than the usual? Or were they quite extraordinarily powerful? In either case, the outburst had struck Shingo as lunatic.

What would be happening now if the girl in the dancing clothes had been run over and killed? The pattern of the girl's kimono came up vividly before him. There was seldom anything so festive in the shop windows.

But the thought of returning empty-handed made the street seem dark.

Had Yasuko given Satoko only old cotton kimonos to be made into diapers? Or was Fusako lying? There had been poison in the remark. Had Yasuko not given the girl a swaddling kimono, or a kimono for her first visit to a shrine? Had Fusako perhaps asked for western clothes?

"I forget," he muttered to himself.

He had forgotten whether or not Yasuko had con-

sulted with him in the matter; but if they, he and Yasuko, had paid more attention to Fusako, they might
have been given a pretty grandchild even by so ill-
favored a daughter. Feelings of inescapable guilt dragged
at him.

"Because I know how it was before birth, because I
know how it was before birth, I have no parent to love.
Because I have no parent, neither have I child to be
loved by."

A passage from a No play came to Shingo, but that
alone scarcely brought the enlightenment of the dark-
cloaked sage.

"The former Buddha has gone, the later not yet come.
I am born in a dream, what shall I think real? I have
chanced to receive this human flesh, so difficult of re-
ceiving."

Had Satoko, about to pounce upon the dancing girl,
inherited her violence and malice from Fusako? Or did
she have them from Aihara? If from Fusako, then did
Fusako have them from Yasuko or from Shingo?

If Shingo had married Yasuko's sister, then probably
he would have had neither a daughter like Fusako nor a
granddaughter like Satoko.

This was hardly a proper occasion to stir in him so in-
tense a yearning for a person long dead that he wanted
to rush into her arms.

He was sixty-three, and the girl who had died in her
twenties had been older than he.

When he got home, Fusako was in bed, the baby in her
arms. The door between her room and the breakfast
room was open.

"She's asleep," said Yasuko. "Her heart was pounding

and pounding, and Fusako gave her sleeping medicine. She went right off to sleep."

Shingo nodded. "Suppose you pull the door shut."

"Yes." Kikuko got up.

Satoko was tight against Fusako's back. But her eyes seemed to be open. She had a way of staring at a person, silently and rigidly.

Shingo said nothing about having gone out to buy her a kimono.

It appeared that Fusako had not told her mother of the crisis that had arisen from Satoko's desire for a kimono.

He went into his room. Kikuko brought charcoal.

"Have a seat," he said to her.

"In just a second." She went out, and came back with a pitcher on a tray. One did not need a tray for a pitcher; but there seemed to be flowers beside it.

"What are they?" He took a flower in his hand. "*Kikyo,** maybe?"

"Black lilies, I'm told."

"Black lilies?"

"Yes. A friend I take tea lessons with gave them to me a little while ago." She opened the closet door behind Shingo and took out a little vase.

"Black lilies, are they?"

"She said that on the anniversary of Rikyu's death this year the head of the Enshu School arranged a tea ceremony in the museum tea cottage. There was an old narrow-necked bronze vase in the alcove with black lilies and white hyacinths in it. A very interesting combination, she said."

* *Sometimes called bell flowers.*

"Oh?"

Shingo gazed at the black lilies. There were two of them, with two flowers on each stem.

"It must have snowed eleven or thirteen times this spring."

"We did have a lot of snow."

"She said that there were four or five inches of snow on the anniversary of Rikyu's death. It was very early in the spring, and black lilies seemed even more unusual. They're mountain flowers, you know."

"The color is a little like a black camellia."

"Yes." Kikuko poured water into the vase. "She said that Rikyu's testament was on display, and the dagger he committed suicide with."

"Oh? Your friend gives tea lessons?"

"Yes. She's a war widow. She worked hard, and now the returns are coming in."

"What school?"

"Kankyuan. The Mushanokoji family."

This meant nothing to Shingo, who knew little about tea.

Kikuko waited, ready to put the flowers in the vase, but Shingo still had one in his hand.

"It seems to droop a little. I don't suppose it's wilting?"

"No. I had them in water."

"Do *kikyo* droop too?"

"I beg your pardon?"

"It seems a little smaller than *kikyo*."

"I believe so."

"At first it looks black, but it isn't. It's like dark purple, but not that either—touched with crimson. I'll have to have a good look at it tomorrow in daylight."

"In the sun it's a transparent purple touched with red."

The flowers, fully opened, would be scarcely an inch across. There were six petals. The tips of the pistils parted in three directions, and there were four or five stamens. The leaves spread in the four directions at stages about an inch apart. They were small for lily leaves, not two inches long.

Finally Shingo sniffed at the flower.

"The smell of a dirty woman." It was a badly chosen remark.

He had not meant to suggest wantonness, but Kikuko looked down and flushed slightly around the eyes.

"The smell is a disappointment," he corrected himself. "Here. Try it."

"I think I'll not investigate as thoroughly as you, Father." She started to put the flowers into the vase. "Four is too many for a tea ceremony. But shall I leave them as they are?"

"Yes, do."

Kikuko set the vase in the alcove.

"The masks are in that closet, the one you took the vase from. Would you mind getting them out?"

He had thought of the No masks when that passage from a No play had come to him.

He took up the *jido*. "This one is a sprite. A symbol of eternal youth. Did I tell you about it when I bought it?"

"No."

"Tanizaki, the girl who was in the office. When I bought it I had her put it on. She was charming. A great surprise."

Kikuko put the mask to her face. "Do you tie it behind?"

No doubt, deep behind the eyes of the mask, Kikuko's eyes were fixed on him.

"It has no expression unless you move it."

The day he had brought it home, Shingo had been on the point of kissing the scarlet lips. He had felt a flash like heaven's own wayward love.

"It may be lost in the undergrowth, but while it still has the flower of the heart. . . ."

Those too seemed to be words from a No play.

Shingo could not look at Kikuko as she moved the glowing young mask this way and that.

She had a small face, and the tip of her chin was almost hidden behind the mask. Tears were flowing from the scarcely visible chin down over her throat. They flowed on, drawing two lines, then three.

"Kikuko," said Shingo. "Kikuko. You thought if you were to leave Shuichi you might give tea lessons, and that was why you went to see your friend?"

The *jido* Kikuko nodded.

"I think I'd like to stay on with you here and give lessons." The words were distinct even from behind the mask.

A piercing wail came from Satoko.

Teru barked noisily in the garden.

Shingo felt something ominous in it all. Kikuko seemed to be listening for a sign at the gate that Shuichi, who evidently went to visit the woman even on Sunday, had come home.

The Kite's House

In summer and in winter, the bell in the temple rang at six; and in summer and winter, Shingo told himself, when he heard it, that he was awake too soon.

This did not necessarily mean that he got out of bed.

Six o'clock was of course not in summer what it was in winter. Because the bell rang at the same time, he could tell himself that it was six; but in summer the sun was already up.

He had a large pocket watch at his pillow. He had to turn on the light and put on his glasses, however, and so he seldom looked at it. Without his glasses, he had trouble distinguishing the hour hand from the minute hand.

He had no worries about oversleeping. The trouble was the reverse, that he woke too early.

Six of a winter morning was very early, but, unable to stay in bed, Shingo would go for the paper.

Since the maid had left them, Kikuko had been getting up to do the morning work.

"You're early, Father," she would say.

"I'll sleep a little longer," Shingo would reply, embarrassed.

"Yes, do. I don't even have hot water yet."

With Kikuko up, Shingo would feel that he had company.

At what age had it been that he had begun to feel lonely, waking before the winter sun was up?

With spring, the waking became warmer.

Mid-May had passed, and after the bell he heard the cry of a kite.

"So it's here again," he muttered to himself, listening from bed.

The kite seemed to be strolling grandly over the roof, and then it flew off toward the sea.

Shingo got up.

He scanned the sky as he brushed his teeth, but the kite was not to be seen.

But it was as if a fresh young voice had departed and left the sky over the roof serene.

"Kikuko. You heard our kite, I suppose?" he called to the kitchen.

"No, I didn't. Careless of me." Kikuko was transferring rice, hot and steaming, from the pot to the serving cask.

"It makes its home with us. Wouldn't you say so?"

"Yes, I suppose so."

"We heard a lot from it last year, too. What month was it, I wonder? About now? My memory isn't what it ought to be."

With Shingo looking at her, Kikuko untied the ribbon around her hair.

It would seem that she sometimes slept with her hair tied up.

Leaving the cask uncovered, she hurried to make Shingo's tea.

"If our kite is here, then our buntings ought to be here too."

"Yes. And crows."

"Crows?" Shingo laughed. If it was "our" kite, then it should also be "our" crows. "We think of it as a house for human beings, but all sorts of birds live here too."

"And the fleas and mosquitoes will be coming out."

"That's a nice thought. But fleas and mosquitoes don't live here. They don't live over from one year to the next."

"I imagine the fleas do. We have them in the winter."

"I've no idea how long fleas live, but I doubt if this year's fleas are last year's."

Kikuko looked at him and laughed. "That snake will be coming out one of these days."

"The *aodaisho* * that scared you so?"

"Yes."

"He's the master of the place."

* *A large, harmless snake.*

Back from shopping, one day last summer, Kikuko had seen the snake at the kitchen door, and come in trembling with fright.

Teru ran up at Kikuko's scream and raised a mad barking. Teru would lower her head as if to bite at the snake, jump back four or five feet, and come in for the attack again. The process was repeated over and over.

The snake raised its head and put out a red tongue, then turned and slithered off past the kitchen doorsill.

From Kikuko's description, it stretched more than twice the width of the door, or more than two yards; and it was thicker than her wrist.

Kikuko was greatly agitated, but Yasuko was calm. "It's the master of the place," she said. "It was here I don't know how many years before you came."

"What would have happened if Teru had bitten it?"

"Teru would have lost. She would have gotten all tangled up in it. She knew it well enough, and that's why she only barked."

Kikuko was still trembling. For a time she avoided the kitchen door, and went in and out through the front door.

It bothered her to think that there was such a monster under the floor.

But it probably lived on the mountain behind and rarely came down.

The land behind the house did not belong to Shingo. He did not know whose it was.

The mountain pressed down in a steep slope upon Shingo's house, and for animals there seemed to be no boundary marking off his garden, into which leaves and flowers from the mountain fell liberally.

"It's back again," he muttered to himself. And then, cheerfully: "Kikuko, the kite seems to be back."

"Yes. This time I hear it." Kikuko glanced at the ceiling.

The crying of the kite went on for a time.

"It flew off to the sea a few minutes ago?"

"So it seemed."

"It went off for something to eat and then came back."

Now that Kikuko had said so, that seemed a most likely possibility. "Suppose we put fish out where it will see them."

"Teru would eat them."

"Some high place."

It had been the same last year and the year before: Shingo felt a surge of affection when, on waking, he heard the call of the kite.

He was not alone, it would seem. The expression "our kite" was current throughout the house.

Yet he did not know for certain whether it was one kite or two. It seemed to him that he had, one year or another, seen two kites dancing on the roof.

And was it the same kite whose voice they heard year after year? Had a new generation taken the place of the old? Had the parent kite perhaps died, and was its young now calling out in its place? The thought came to Shingo this morning for the first time.

It seemed to him an interesting thought, that the old kite had died last year, and that, without knowing it, half asleep and half awake, they should be listening to a new kite this year, and thinking it their own.

And it seemed strange that, with all the mountains in

Kamakura, the kite should have chosen to live on the mountain behind Shingo's house.

"I have met with what is difficult of meeting, I have heard what is difficult of hearing." * Perhaps it was so with the kite.

If the kite was living with them, it let them have the pleasure of its voice.

2

Because Shingo and Kikuko were the early risers, they could say what they had to say to each other early in the morning. Shingo talked alone with Shuichi only when the two of them happened to be on the same train.

"We're almost there," he would say to himself as they crossed the railway bridge into Tokyo and the Ikegami grove came in sight. It was his habit to look out the window of the morning train at the grove.

But, for all the years he had taken the same train, he had but recently discovered two pine trees in the grove.

The pine trees stood out above the grove. They leaned toward each other, as if about to embrace. The branches came so near that it was as if they might embrace at any moment.

Since they so stood out, the only tall trees in the grove, they should have caught his eye immediately. Now that he had noticed them, it was always the two pines he saw first.

This morning they were blurred by wind and rain.

* *A common saying in pietist Buddhism.*

"Shuichi," he said. "What's wrong with Kikuko?"

"Nothing in particular." Shuichi was reading a weekly magazine.

He had bought two in Kamakura station and had handed one to his father. Shingo's lay unread.

"What's wrong with her?" Shingo repeated quietly.

"She complains of headaches."

"Oh? The old woman says she was in Tokyo yesterday and went to bed when she got back last night. She's not her usual self. Something happened in Tokyo, the old woman thinks. She didn't have dinner last night, and when you got home and went to your room, it must have been about nine, we heard her crying. She tried to smother it, but we could hear."

"She'll be all right in a few days. I don't think it's anything to worry about."

"Oh? She wouldn't cry if it were only a headache. And wasn't she crying again early this morning?"

"Yes."

"Fusako says that when she went in with breakfast, Kikuko refused to look at her. Fusako was very unhappy about it. I thought I might ask you to tell me what's wrong."

"All the eyes in the family seem to be on Kikuko." Shuichi cocked an eye up at his father. "She gets sick occasionally, like everyone else."

"And what is the ailment?" he asked irritably.

"An abortion." Shuichi flung out the words.

Shingo was aghast. He looked at the seat ahead of them. It was occupied by two American soldiers. He had started the conversation on the assumption that they would not understand.

He lowered his voice. "She went to a doctor?"

"Yes."

"Yesterday?" It was a hollow mutter.

Shuichi had laid down his magazine. "Yes."

"And came back the same day?"

"Yes."

"You had her do it."

"She wanted it done, and wouldn't listen to anything I said."

"Kikuko wanted to? You're lying."

"It's the truth."

"Why? What could make her feel that way?"

Shuichi was silent.

"Don't you think it's your fault?"

"I suppose so. But she said she didn't want it now and that was that."

"You could have stopped her if you'd tried."

"Not this time, I think."

"What do you mean, this time?"

"You know what I mean. She won't have a baby with me as I am."

"While you have the other woman?"

"I'd say so."

"You'd say so!" Shingo's chest was tight with anger. "It was half a suicide. Don't you think so? It wasn't so much that she was getting back at you as that she was half killing herself." Shuichi fell back before the assault. "You've destroyed her spirit and the damage can't be undone."

"I'd say her spirit is still pretty strong."

"But isn't she a woman? Your wife? If you'd done one thing to comfort her she'd have been happy to have the baby. Quite aside from the other woman."

"Oh, but it isn't quite aside."

"Kikuko knows how much Yasuko wants grandchildren. So much that she feels guilty about taking so long. She doesn't have the baby she wants to have, and that's because you've murdered her spiritually."

"It's a little different, actually. She has her own squeamishness."

"Squeamishness?"

"Resents being put in that situation."

"Oh?" It was a matter between husband and wife. He wondered whether Shuichi had in fact made Kikuko feel so debased and insulted. "I don't believe it. She may have talked and acted as if she felt that way, but I doubt if she really did. For a husband to make so much of his wife's squeamishness is a sign that he's short on affection. Does a husband take a fit of pouting so seriously?" Shingo had somewhat lost his momentum. "I wonder what Yasuko will say when she hears she's lost a grandchild."

"I'd think she'd feel relieved. She knows now that Kikuko can have children."

"What's that? You guarantee that she will have children later?"

"I'm prepared to guarantee it."

"Anyone who can say that has no fear of heaven and no human affection."

"A difficult way to put it. Isn't it a simple enough matter?"

"It's not simple at all. Think about it a minute. Think about the way she was crying."

"It's not that I don't want children myself. But with things between us as they are now, I doubt if it would be a very superior child."

"I don't know about things with you, but there is nothing wrong about things with Kikuko. It's only you that things are wrong with. She's not that way. You do nothing to help her get rid of her jealousy. That's why she lost the child. And maybe more than the child, too." Shuichi was looking at him in surprise. "Suppose you have a try at getting blind drunk with that woman and coming into the house with your dirty shoes on and putting them on Kikuko's knee and having her take them off for you."

3

Shingo went to the bank that morning on company business, and had lunch with a friend who worked there. They talked until about two-thirty. After telephoning the office from the restaurant, he started for home.

Kikuko was sitting on the veranda with Kuniko on her lap.

She got up hastily, surprised at his early return.

"No, please." He came out to the veranda. "Shouldn't you be in bed?"

"I was about to change her diaper."

"Fusako?"

"She's gone to the post office with Satoko."

"What business does she have at the post office? Leaving the baby behind."

"Just a minute," said Kikuko to the baby. "I'll get out Grandfather's kimono first."

"No, please. Get her changed first."

Kikuko looked up smiling. Her small teeth showed between her lips.

"He says I'm to get you changed first." She was in *déshabille*, her bright silk kimono tied with a narrow obi. "Has it stopped raining in Tokyo?"

"Raining? It was raining when I got on the train, but clear when I got off. I didn't notice where it stopped."

"It was raining here until just a few minutes ago. Fusako went out when it stopped."

"It's still wet up the hill."

Laid face up on the veranda, the baby raised her bare feet and took her toes in her hands. The feet moved more freely than the hands. "Yes, have a look up the mountain," said Kikuko, wiping the baby's rear.

Two American military planes flew low overhead. Startled by the noise, the baby looked up at the mountain. They did not see the planes, but great shadows passed over the slope. Probably the baby saw them too.

Shingo was touched by the gleam of surprise in the innocent eyes.

"She doesn't know about air raids. There are all sorts of babies who don't know about war." He looked down at the baby. The gleam had already faded. "I wish I had a picture of her eyes just now. With the shadow of the airplanes in it. And the next picture. . . ."

Of a dead baby, shot from an airplane, he was about to say; but he held himself back, remembering that Kikuko had the day before had an abortion.

In fact, there were numberless babies like Kuniko as he had seen her in the two pictures.

Kuniko in her arms and a rolled-up diaper in one hand, Kikuko went off to the bath.

Shingo had come home early out of concern for Kikuko. He went into the breakfast room.

"What brings you back so soon?" said Yasuko, joining him.

"Where were you?"

"I was washing my hair. It stopped raining and the sun came blazing out, and my head got to feeling all itchy. An old person's head seems to itch for no reason at all."

"Mine doesn't."

"Probably because it's such a good head," she laughed. "I knew you were back, but I thought if I came in with my hair all which-way I'd get a scolding."

"The old woman's hair all undone—why not cut it off and make a tea whisk out of it?"

"Not at all a bad idea. Men have their whisks too. It used to be, you know, that both men and women cut their hair short and pulled it back like a tea whisk. You see it in the Kabuki."

"I don't mean hair tied up. I mean hair cut off."

"I wouldn't mind. We both have too much hair."

"Kikuko is up and around?" he asked in a low voice.

"She's been having a try at it. She doesn't look at all well."

"She shouldn't be taking care of the baby."

"Take care of her for a minute, please, Fusako said, and dumped her by Kikuko's bed. The baby was sound asleep."

"Why didn't you take her?"

"I was washing my hair when she started crying." Yasuko went for his kimono. "I wondered if something might be wrong with you, too, you got home so early."

Shingo called to Kikuko, who seemed to be going from the bath to her room.

"Yes?"

"Bring Kuniko in here."

"We'll be there in a minute."

Her hand in Kikuko's, Kuniko was having a walk. Kikuko had put on a more formal obi.

Kuniko clutched at Yasuko's shoulder. Yasuko, who was brushing Shingo's trousers, took the baby on her knee.

Kikuko went off with Shingo's suit.

Having put it away in the next room, she slowly closed the doors of the wardrobe.

She seemed taken aback by her face in the wardrobe mirror, and she wavered between going to her room and returning to the breakfast room.

"Wouldn't you be better off in bed?" said Shingo.

"Yes." A spasm passed across Kikuko's shoulders. She went off to her room without looking back.

"Doesn't she seem strange to you?" Yasuko frowned.

Shingo did not answer.

"And it's not at all clear what's the matter. She gets up and walks around, and then starts breaking down again. I'm very worried."

"So am I."

"You have to do something about Shuichi and that affair of his."

Shingo nodded.

"Suppose you have a good talk with Kikuko. I'll take the baby out to Fusako and while I'm about it do some shopping for dinner. That Fusako—she's another one."

Yasuko got up, the baby in her arms.

"What business does she have at the post office?"

Yasuko looked back. "I wondered myself. Do you suppose she's written to Aihara? They've been separated for six months. It's almost six months since she came back. It was New Year's Eve."

"If it was just a letter she could have put it in the mailbox down the street."

"I imagine she thinks it will be quicker and safer if she sends it from the post office. Maybe the thought of Aihara comes into her head and she can't sit still a minute."

Shingo smiled wryly. He sensed optimism in Yasuko.

It would seem that optimism put down deep roots in a woman who had been given charge of a household on into old age.

He took up the heap of newspapers, four or five days' worth of them, that Yasuko had been reading. Though he was not really interested, his eye fell on a remarkable headline: "Lotus in Bloom, Two Thousand Years Old."

The spring before, in the course of a Yayoi excavation in the Kemigawa district of Chiba, three lotus seeds had been found in a dugout canoe. They were judged to be two thousand years old. A certain "doctor of lotuses" succeeded in making them sprout, and in April of this year the shoots were planted in three places, the Chiba Agricultural Experimental Station, the pond of a Chiba park, and the house of a sake brewer in Hatake-machi, Chiba. The brewer apparently had been among the sponsors of the excavation. He had put his shoot in a water cauldron and set it out in the garden, and his was the first to bloom. The lotus doctor rushed to the spot upon hearing the news. "It's in bloom, it's in bloom," he said, stroking the handsome flower. It would go from the "vase shape" to the "cup shape" to the "bowl shape," the newspaper reported, and finally, at the "tray shape," shed its petals. There were twenty-four petals, it was further reported.

Below the article was a picture of the bespectacled, apparently graying doctor, the stem of the opening lotus in his hand. Glancing back over the article, Shingo saw that he was sixty-nine.

Shingo looked for a time at the photograph of the lotus, then took the paper into Kikuko's room.

It was her room and Shuichi's. On the desk, which was part of her dowry, lay Shuichi's felt hat. There was stationery beside it—perhaps she thought of writing to someone. A piece of embroidery hung over the drawer.

He seemed to catch the scent of perfume.

"How are you? You shouldn't be jumping out of bed all the time." He sat down by the desk.

Opening her eyes, she gazed at him. She seemed embarrassed that he should have ordered her to stay in bed. Her cheeks were faintly flushed. Her forehead was a wan white, however, and her eyebrows stood out cleanly.

"Did you see in the paper that a lotus two thousand years old has come into bloom?"

"Yes."

"Oh, you did," he muttered. "If you had only told us, you wouldn't have had to overdo it. You shouldn't have come back the same day."

Kikuko looked up in surprise.

"It was last month, wasn't it, that we talked about a baby? I suppose you already knew."

Kikuko shook her head. "No. If I had known, I would have been too embarrassed to say anything."

"Oh? Shuichi said it was squeamishness." Seeing tears

in her eyes, he dropped the subject. "You won't have to go to the doctor again?"

"I'll look in on him tomorrow."

When he came back from work the next day, Yasuko was waiting impatiently.

"Kikuko's gone back to her family. They say she's in bed. There was a call from the Sagaras, it must have been at about two. Fusako took it. They said that Kikuko had come by and wasn't feeling well, and had gone to bed, and they wondered if they might let her stay and rest for two or three days."

"Oh?"

"I told Fusako to say we'd send Shuichi around tomorrow. It was Kikuko's mother, Fusako said. Do you suppose Kikuko went to Tokyo especially for that?"

"No."

"What can be the matter with her?"

Shingo had taken off his coat and, lifting his chin, was slowly untying his tie.

"She had an abortion."

"What!" Yasuko was stunned. "Without telling us? Kikuko could do that? People these days are too much for me."

"You're very unobservant, Mother," said Fusako, coming into the breakfast room with Kuniko in her arms. "I knew all about it."

"And how did you know?" The question came of its own accord.

"That I can hardly tell you. But there's cleaning up afterwards, you know."

Shingo could think of nothing more to say.

A Garden in the Capital

"Father is a very interesting man, isn't he, Mother?" said Fusako, noisily loading the dinner dishes onto a tray. "He's more reserved with his daughter than with the girl who came in from outside."

"Please, Fusako."

"But it's true. If the spinach was overdone, why didn't he come out and say so? It wasn't as if I'd cooked it to a pulp. You could still see the shape of spinach. Maybe he should have it done in a hot spring."

"A hot spring?"

"They cook eggs and dumplings in hot springs, don't they? I remember you once gave me something called radium eggs, from somewhere or other, with the whites hard and the yolks soft. And didn't you say they could cook a fine egg at the Squash House in Kyoto?"

"Squash House?"

"Oh, the Gourd House. Every beggar knows that much. I'm just saying you can squash your ideas about good and bad cooking for all the difference they make to me."

Yasuko laughed.

But Fusako went on unsmiling. "If he takes it to a raduim spring and watches the time and the temperature very, very closely, he'll be as healthy as Popeye, even without Kikuko to look after him. Myself, I've had enough of all this moping." Pushing herself up from her knees, she went off with the heavy tray. "Dinner doesn't seem to taste the same without a handsome son and a beautiful daughter-in-law."

Shingo looked up. His eyes met Yasuko's. "She does talk."

"Yes. She's been holding back both the talk and the tears because of Kikuko."

"You can't keep children from crying," muttered Shingo.

His mouth was slightly open, as if he meant to say more, but Fusako, staggering off toward the kitchen, spoke first. "It's not the children. It's me. Of course children cry."

They heard her flinging dishes into the sink.

Yasuko half stood up. They heard sniffling in the kitchen.

Rolling her eyes up at Yasuko, Satoko ran off after her mother.

A most unpleasing expression, thought Shingo.

Yasuko put Kuniko on Shingo's knee. "Watch her for a minute," she said, following them to the kitchen.

The baby was soft in his arms. He pulled her close to him. He took her feet in his hand. The hollow of the ankles and the swelling of the calves were also in his hand.

"Does it tickle?" But Kuniko evidently did not think so.

It seemed to Shingo that when Fusako, still a babe in arms, had lain naked, having a change of clothes, and he had tickled her armpits, she had wrinkled her nose and waved her arms at him, but he could not really remember.

Shingo had seldom spoken of what a homely baby she was. To speak of the matter would have been to bring back the image of Yasuko's beautiful sister.

His hope that Fusako would change faces several times before she grew up had not been realized, and the hope itself had faded with the years.

His granddaughter Satoko seemed somewhat better favored than her mother, and there was hope for the baby.

Was he searching for the image of Yasuko's sister even in his grandchildren? The thought made Shingo dislike himself.

And even while disliking himself, he was lost in fantasy: would not the child Kikuko had done away with, his lost grandchild, have been Yasuko's sister, reborn, was she not a beauty refused life in this world? He was even more dissatisfied with himself.

As he loosened his grip on her feet, Kuniko climbed

from his knee and started off toward the kitchen. Her arms were bent in front of her, and her legs were unsteady.

"You'll fall," said Shingo. But the baby had already fallen.

She fell forward and rolled to her side, and for a time did not cry.

The four of them came back into the breakfast room, Satoko clinging to Fusako's sleeve, Yasuko with Kuniko in her arms.

"Father is very absent-minded these days, Mother," said Fusako, wiping the table. "When he was changing clothes this evening, he was quite a sight. He was starting to put on an obi, and he had his kimono and *juban* * with the right side pulled over the left. Can you imagine it? I don't suppose he's ever done that before. He must be getting senile."

"I did it once before. I had the right side over the left, and Kikuko said that in Okinawa it didn't matter whether you had the left side or the right side over."

"In Okinawa? I wonder if that's true."

Fusako was scowling again. "Kikuko knows how to please you. That was very clever of her. In Okinawa, was it?"

Shingo controlled his irritation. "The word *juban* comes from Portuguese. I don't know whether they wear the left or the right side on top in Portugal."

"Another piece of information from Kikuko?"

Yasuko sought to intercede. "Father is always putting on summer kimonos inside out."

* *A singlet worn under a kimono.*

"There is a difference between accidentally putting a kimono on inside out and standing there like a fool bringing the right side over the left."

"Let Kuniko have a try at putting on a kimono. You can't be sure which side will come out in front."

"It's early for second childhood, Father," said Fusako, unflagging. "Isn't it a little too much, Mother? So his daughter-in-law does go home for a day or two, that's no excuse for losing track of which side of his kimono goes in front. Hasn't it been six months now since his own daughter came home to Mother?"

It was true: six months had passed since that rainy New Year's Eve. There had been no word from her husband, Aihara, nor had Shingo seen Aihara.

"Six months," nodded Yasuko. "Not that there's any relation between that and Kikuko."

"No relation? I think both have some relation to Father."

"You *are* his children. It would be nice if he could find an answer."

Fusako looked down in silence.

"All right, Fusako, now is your chance. Come out with everything. Say what you have to say. You'll feel better. Kikuko is away."

"I was wrong, and I'm not going to complain. But I should think you could eat it even if it didn't come from Kikuko's hands." Fusako was weeping again. "Isn't it the truth? You sit there grimly forcing it down. I'm not happy myself."

"Fusako. You must have all sorts of things to say. When you went to the post office the other day—I imagine it was to mail a letter to Aihara?"

A tremor seemed to pass over Fusako, but she shook her head.

"I decided it had to be Aihara, because I couldn't think of anyone else you'd have any reason to write to." Yasuko's voice was not often so sharp. "Did you send money?"

So Yasuko had been giving Fusako money.

"Where is Aihara?" Shingo looked at Fusako, waiting for an answer. "He doesn't seem to be at home. I've been sending someone around from the office once a month or so to have a look at the place. No, not that so much, really, as to give a little money to his mother. If you were there you might be the one to take care of her."

Yasuko sat open-mouthed. "You send someone from the office?"

"Don't worry. He's someone you can depend on. Someone who doesn't give away secrets or ask questions. If Aihara were there I'd go and talk your problem over, but there's no point in talking to a lame old woman."

"What is Aihara doing?"

"Peddling drugs or something of the sort, it would seem. I imagine he was being used to peddle the stuff, and he moved from drink to drugs."

Yasuko gazed at him in fright. It seemed possible that she was less frightened by the matter of Aihara than by her own husband, who had kept his secret so long.

Shingo went on. "But now it seems that the old woman isn't there either. Someone else is in the place. In other words, Fusako no longer has a house."

"And what about Fusako's things?"

"My chests and trunks have been empty for a long time, Mother."

"I see." Yasuko sighed. "You're an easy target for him and come home with everything you own tied up in one kerchief."

Shingo wondered whether Fusako might know where Aihara was, and whether she might be in communication with him.

And as he looked out at the garden, moving into dusk, he wondered who it was that had been unable to keep Aihara from falling, Fusako or Shingo or Aihara himself. Or perhaps no one at all.

2

Shingo got to the office at about ten to find a note from Tanizaki Eiko.

She wanted to talk to him about the young mistress, and would come again later.

The young mistress could only be Kikuko.

Shingo questioned Iwamura Natsuko, who had replaced Eiko as his secretary.

"What time was Tanizaki here?"

"I had just come in and was dusting the desks. I suppose it would have been a little after eight."

"Did she wait?"

"Yes, for a while."

Shingo disliked the dull, heavy way in which Natsuko said "Yes." Perhaps it had to do with her native dialect.

"Did she see Shuichi?"

"I believe she went away without seeing him."

"Oh?" Shingo was talking to himself. "If it was a little after eight, then. . . ."

Eiko had probably come on her way to work. She would probably come again at noon.

After rereading the note, tiny at the edge of a large sheet of paper, he looked out of the window.

He looked out at the clear sky of the most May-like of May days.

He had seen it from the train. All the passengers looking out had their windows open.

The birds skimming low over the shining stream that marked the limits of Tokyo shone silver themselves. It seemed more than accidental that a red-banded bus should be crossing the bridge to the north.

"In the heavens, a high wind." For no particular reason, he repeated the motto on his counterfeit Ryokan.

"Well!" The Ikegami grove came into view, and he leaned forward as if he meant to jump out. "Maybe the pines aren't in the Ikegami grove at all."

This morning the two pines that stood out above the grove seemed nearer.

Had it been that, in the rains and the spring mists, the perspective had been blurred?

He gazed on, trying to make sure.

He gazed at them every morning, and he thought he would like to go and inspect the site itself.

But though he saw the grove every morning, he had only recently discovered the two pines. He had looked at it absently over the years, knowing that it was the grove of the Ikegami Hommonji Temple.

Today, in the clear May sky, he had discovered that the pine trees did not seem to be in the Ikegami grove at all.

And so he had twice discovered the two pines that

leaned toward each other as if about to embrace.

When, last night after dinner, he had told of seeking out Aihara's house and giving modest help to his old mother, the agitated Fusako had fallen silent.

He had felt sorry for her. He thought that he had discovered something in her, but what he had discovered was by no means as clear as the discovery in the Ike-gami grove.

Some days earlier, looking out at this same grove, he had questioned Shuichi, and drawn from him the news of Kikuko's abortion.

The pines were no longer just pines. They were entangled with the abortion. Perhaps he would always be reminded of it when he passed them to and from work.

This morning, of course, it had been so again.

On the morning of Shuichi's admission, the pines had melted back into the grove, dim in the wind and rain. This morning, standing apart, associated in his mind with Kikuko's abortion, they somehow looked dirty. Perhaps the weather was too good.

"Even when natural weather is good, human weather is bad," he muttered to himself, somewhat inanely. Turning away from the clear sky framed in the office window, he set about the day's work.

Shortly after noon there was a telephone call from Eiko. Busy with summer clothes, she would not be able to come by today.

"You're so good at it that you're kept busy?"

"Yes." Eiko fell silent.

"You're at the shop?"

"Yes. But Kinu isn't here." The name of Shuichi's woman came out smoothly. "I waited for her to leave."

"Oh?"

"Hello? I'll stop by tomorrow morning."

"Tomorrow morning? At eight again?"

"No. I'll wait for you."

"It's all that pressing?"

"Yes. Well, it is and it isn't. To me it seems pressing. I want to talk to you as soon as I can. I'm rather worked up about it."

"Worked up? About Shuichi?"

"I'll tell you when I see you."

He did not attach much importance to her being "worked up," but he was uneasy that she should so want to talk as to come two days in a row.

The uneasiness increased. At about three he called Kikuko's family house.

The Sagawa maid answered. Music came over the telephone as he waited for Kikuko.

He had not talked to Shuichi of Kikuko since she had gone home to her family. Shuichi seemed anxious to avoid the subject.

And Shingo had avoided going to inquire after Kikuko, because to do so would only have been to give the matter unnecessary emphasis.

Shingo thought that, being what she was, Kikuko would have spoken to her family neither of Kinu nor of the abortion. But he could not be sure.

Kikuko's voice came up from the symphony over the telephone. "Father?" There was affection in it. "I've kept you waiting."

"Hello." A surge of relief swept over him. "And how are you?"

"Oh, I'm fine again. I'm pampering myself."

"Not at all." He found it hard to go on.

"Father," said Kikuko happily. "I want to see you. May I come now?"

"Now? Is it all right?"

"Yes. The quicker I see you the easier it will be for me to go home again."

"I'll be waiting here for you." The music went on. "Hello, hello," Shingo did not want to let her hang up. "That's very good music."

"I forgot to turn it down, didn't I? It's ballet music. *Les Sylphides*, by Chopin. I'll steal it from them and bring it home with me."

"You're coming right away?"

"Yes. But let me think a minute. I don't really want to go to the office."

She suggested that they meet at the Shinjuku Garden.

Shingo laughed, somewhat disconcerted at this proposed rendezvous.

Kikuko seemed to think that she had hit upon a remarkably good idea. "The green will bring you to life."

"The Shinjuku Garden? I've been there exactly once. For some reason or other I went to a dog show there."

"Come and let me show you myself instead." And after her laughter, *Les Sylphides* played on.

3

He went in through the main gate of the Shinjuku Garden.

A notice beside the gate announced that perambulators were available for thirty yen per hour, and straw mats for twenty yen per day and up.

There was an American couple ahead of him. The

husband had a little girl in his arms, and the wife was leading a German pointer. There were other people too, all young couples. Only the Americans were walking at an easy pace.

Shingo fell in after them.

To the left of the path, what at first seemed to be a stand of deciduous pines proved to be deodars. When he had come to the dog show, a benefit given by an organization for the prevention of cruelty to animals, he had seen a remarkable stand of deodars; but he could not remember where.

To the right were signs identifying trees and shrubs as Oriental arborvitae and *utsukushimatsu* * and the like.

He walked on at his leisure, thinking he would be ahead of Kikuko; but he found her on a bench under a gingko, by the pond to which the path shortly led.

Turning toward him and half rising to her feet, Kikuko bowed.

"You're early. It's still fifteen minutes to half-past four." He looked at his watch.

"I was so pleased when you called that I ran right out of the house." She spoke rapidly. "I can't tell you how pleased I was."

"So you've been waiting? Shouldn't you have on something heavier?"

"I've had this sweater since I was in school." A note of shyness came into her voice. "I don't have any clothes at home anymore. I couldn't very well borrow a kimono from my sister."

Kikuko was the youngest of eight children, and all her

* A pine, to judge from the name. Not identified in botanical dictionaries.

sisters were married. It was probably to a sister-in-law that she had reference.

The dark green sweater had short sleeves. It seemed to Shingo that he was seeing her bare arms for the first time this year.

She apologized in a somewhat more formal manner for having gone home to her family.

"Can you come back to Kamakura yet?" he asked softly, not knowing what sort of reply was called for.

"Yes." She nodded simply and quickly. "I've been wanting to come back." The beautiful shoulders moved as she gazed at Shingo. His eye had not caught the exact motion, but a gentle scent came from her to surprise him.

"Did Shuichi go to see you?"

"Yes. But if you hadn't called. . . ."

It would have been difficult for her to go back?

The remark unfinished, Kikuko stepped out of the shade.

The green of the giant trees, so rich as to be almost heavy, seemed to fall upon the slender neck of the retreating figure.

The lake was Japanese, after a fashion. On the little island, his foot on a stone lantern, a foreign soldier was joking with a prostitute. There were other couples on the benches around the lake.

Shingo followed Kikuko out through the trees to the right of the lake. "Enormous," he said, surprised at the vastness of the expanse before them.

"It *has* brought you to life, Father," she said, openly pleased with herself. "I told you it would."

Shingo stopped before a loquat beside the path. He

did not immediately go out upon the broad lawn.

"A splendid loquat. It has nothing to get in its way, and it spreads out just as it wants to, all the way to the bottom."

Shingo was deeply moved by the form the tree had taken in free and natural growth.

"Beautiful. Yes—when I came to the dog show there was a row of deodars growing just as they wanted to, spreading as far as they could spread, all the way down to the bottom. I felt like growing with them. I wonder where it was."

"Over in the direction of Shinjuku."

"Yes. I came in from Shinjuku."

"You said on the telephone that you came to look at dogs?"

"There weren't so many of them, but it was a benefit given by the Society for the Prevention of Cruelty to Animals. There were more foreigners than Japanese. Diplomats and people from the Occupation, I imagine. It was summer. The Indian girls were the most beautiful, all done up in red and blue silk gauzes. There were Indian and American stalls. We didn't have many such affairs in those days."

It had been two or three years before, but Shingo could not remember exactly when.

As he spoke, he moved away from the loquat tree.

"Let's get rid of the *yatsude* at the foot of the cherry. Remind me when you get home."

"I will."

"We've never cut back the cherry. I like it as it is."

"It has all those tiny branches loaded with flowers. We listened to the temple bell when it was in full bloom. Remember? Last month during the festival."

"Such a small thing—it's good of you to remember."

"I'll never forget. And there was the kite."

She came close to him. They walked from the shadow of a great *keyaki* * out over the broad lawn.

The vast green expanse set Shingo free.

"You can stretch out. It's like getting out of Japan—I wouldn't have dreamed that there was a place like this right in the middle of Tokyo." He gazed at the distant expanse of green toward Shinjuku.

"They paid a great deal of attention to the vista. It looks even farther off than it is."

"What's a vista?" Kikuko had used the Italian word.

"A line of vision, you might say. See how all the paths and the borders are in gentle curves."

Kikuko had come on a school outing, and her teacher had told them all about the garden. The wide lawn, with trees scattered over it, was in the English fashion, it seemed.

There were few people other than young couples, lying down, sitting up, strolling casually about. There were also children, and schoolgirls in groups of five and six. Shingo was surprised, and somehow thought it inappropriate, that the park should be an Eden for assignations.

Did the scene tell one that the youth of the land had been liberated, just as the imperial garden had been?

No one paid the slightest attention to the two of them as they made their way over the lawn, weaving in and out among the couples. Shingo stayed as far from them as he could.

And what would Kikuko be thinking? He was an old man who had brought his young daughter-in-law to the

* ZELKOVA SERRATA, *related to the elms.*

garden, but there was something about the situation that did not rest well with him.

He had not given much thought to the matter when Kikuko had suggested over the telephone that they meet in the Shinjuku Garden, but now that they had come it all seemed very odd.

Shingo was drawn to one particularly high tree out on the lawn.

As he approached, looking up at it, the dignity and the mass of the towering green came grandly down to him, to wash away his and Kikuko's gloom. She had been right to think that the garden would bring him to life.

The tree was what is called in Japan a "lily tree." Coming nearer, he saw that it was in fact three trees. The sign explained that, since the flowers resemble both the lily and the tulip, it is also known as a tulip tree. A fast grower, it came originally from North America. These specimens were about fifty years old.

"Fifty years old? They're younger than I am." Shingo looked up in surprise.

The broad-leafed branches spread out as if to enfold and hide the two of them.

Shingo sat down on a bench, but he felt restless.

Kikuko looked at him, puzzled, as he stood up again.

"Let's go have a look at the flowers over there," he said.

There was a bed of white flowers, fresh in the distance beyond the lawn, about as high as the dipping branches of the tulip tree.

"They had a victory reception here for the generals in the Russo-Japanese War. I was in my teens, still out in the country."

There were trees in grand rows on either side of the flower bed. Shingo chose a bench set among them.

Kikuko stood before him. "I'll come home tomorrow morning. Tell Mother, and see that she doesn't scold me." She sat down beside him.

"Do you have anything you want to say to me first?"

"Say to you? All sorts of things, but. . . ."

4

Shingo waited hopefully the following morning, but Kikuko had not yet come back when he left for the office.

"She said I was to see that you didn't scold her."

"Scold her?" Yasuko's face was bright and happy. "We ought to apologize."

He had said only that he had telephoned Kikuko.

"You have a remarkably strong influence on her." Yasuko saw him to the door. "But that's all right."

Eiko came shortly after he arrived at the office.

"You're prettier," he said affably. "And you brought flowers."

"I can't get away once I'm at the shop, and so I walked around killing time. The florist's was beautiful."

But the expression on her face was solemn as she approached his desk. "Get rid of her," she wrote with her finger on the desk.

"What?" He was startled. "Would you mind leaving us alone for a minute?" he said to Natsuko.

Waiting for Natsuko to go, Eiko found a vase and put three roses in it. She was wearing a slip-on dress that gave her the look of one who worked for a *modiste*. She had put on a little weight, he thought.

"I'm sorry about yesterday." Her manner was strangely tense. "I—coming two days in a row, and all that."

"Have a seat."

"Thank you." She sat with bowed head.

"I'm making you late for work."

"It doesn't matter." Looking up at him, she drew in her breath sharply, as if she were about to weep. "Is it all right to talk to you? I'm boiling over, and I may be a little hysterical."

"Oh?"

"It's about the young mistress." She choked over the words. "I believe she had an abortion."

Shingo did not answer.

How could she have known? Shuichi would hardly have spoken to her of it. But Eiko worked with Shuichi's woman. He braced himself for unpleasantness.

"It's all right for her to have an abortion." Eiko hesitated again.

"Who told you?"

"Shuichi got the hospital money from Kinu."

Shingo felt a tightening in his chest.

"I thought it was outrageous. Really too insulting, too unfeeling. I felt so sorry for the young mistress that I wanted to cry. He gives Kinu money, and so I suppose you can think of it as his money, but it wasn't the right thing to do. He comes from a different class than the rest of us, and he could put together that amount of money any way he pleased. Does being on a different level make it all right for him to do things like that?" She fought to keep her slender shoulders from trembling. "And then there was Kinu, letting him have the money. I couldn't understand her. I was boiling over. I wanted to talk to you even if it meant that I couldn't work with her any more. I know I'm telling you more than I ought to, of course."

"Thank you."

"You were good to me here. I only met the young mistress once, but I liked her." Tears glistened in her eyes. "Have them separate."

"Yes."

She meant Shuichi and Kinu, of course—and yet the remark could also be interpreted as referring to Shuichi and Kikuko.

Into such depths Shuichi had been pushed.

Shingo was astonished at his son's spiritual paralysis and decay, but it seemed to him that he was caught in the same filthy slough. Dark terror swept over him.

Having had her say, Eiko prepared to leave.

"Don't rush off." He sought to detain her, but without enthusiasm.

"I'll come again. Today I'd weep for you and make a fool of myself."

He felt benevolence and a sense of responsibility in her.

He had thought it remarkably indelicate of her to go to work in the same shop as Kinu; but how much worse were Shuichi and Shingo himself.

He gazed absently at the crimson roses Eiko had brought.

Shuichi had said that squeamishness had kept Kikuko from bearing a child "with things as they are now." Was she not being trampled on for her squeamishness?

Unknowing, Kikuko would now be back in Kamakura. He closed his eyes.

The Scar

❁

On Sunday morning, Shingo sawed down the *yatsude* at the foot of the cherry.

He knew that to be quite rid of it he would have to dig up the roots; but he told himself that he could cut the shoots as they came up.

He had sawed it down before, and the effect had been to make it spread. Once again, however, digging up the roots seemed too much trouble. Perhaps he did not have the strength.

Though they put up little resistance to the saw, there

were large numbers of stalks. His forehead was bathed
in sweat.

"Shall I help you?" Shuichi had come up behind him.

"No, I can manage," he answered somewhat curtly.

Shuichi pulled up short.

"Kikuko called me. She said that you were cutting
down the *yatsude*, and I should go help."

"Oh? But there's only a little more."

Sitting down on the *yatsude* he had cut away, Shingo
looked toward the house. Kikuko, in a bright red obi,
was leaning against a glass door at the veranda.

Shuichi took up the saw on Shingo's knee. "You're
cutting it all, I suppose."

"Yes." He watched the youthful motions as the remaining four or five stalks were cut down.

"Shall I cut these too?" Shuichi turned toward
Shingo.

"Just a minute." Shingo got up. "I'll have a look."

There were two or three young cherry trees; or possibly they were not independent trees but branches. They
seemed to come up from the roots of the parent tree.

At the thick base of the trunk, as if grafted on, there
were little branches with leaves.

Shingo backed off some paces. "I think it would look
better if you cut the ones coming from the ground."

"Oh?" But Shuichi was in no hurry to set about cutting them down. He did not seem to think Shingo's idea
a very good one.

Kikuko too came down into the garden.

Shuichi pointed the saw at the young trees. "Father is
in process of deliberating whether to cut them or not."
He laughed lightly.

"Yes, do cut them." Kikuko's solution came readily.

"I don't know whether they're branches or not," said Shingo to Kikuko.

"Branches don't come from the ground."

"What *do* you call a branch coming from the roots?" Shingo laughed with the others.

In silence, Shuichi cut the shoots.

"I want to leave all the branches and let it grow and spread as it wants to. The *yatsude* was in the way. Leave the little branches there at the base."

"Tiny little branches, like chopsticks or toothpicks." Kikuko looked at Shingo. "They were very sweet when they were in bloom."

"Oh? They had blossoms, did they? I didn't notice."

"Oh, yes. One little cluster, and two and three. And I believe the ones like toothpicks had single blossoms."

"Oh?"

"But I wonder if they'll really grow. By the time they're like the bottom branches of the loquat and the wild cherry in the Shinjuku Garden, I'll be an old woman."

"Oh, no. Cherries are quick growers." He looked into Kikuko's eyes.

He had told neither his wife nor Shuichi of the visit to the Shinjuku Garden.

And had Kikuko revealed the secret to her husband immediately upon her return to Kamakura? Since it was not really a secret, she had probably spoken of it as a matter of no moment at all.

"I understand you met Kikuko at the Shinjuku Garden," Shuichi might have said; but if it was hard for him to broach the subject, then possibly Shingo should speak first. Both were silent, and there was a certain strain between them. Perhaps, having heard of the visit from Kikuko, Shuichi was feigning ignorance.

But there was no sign of embarrassment on Kikuko's face.

Shingo gazed at the tiny branches at the base of the tree. He painted in his mind a picture of them, now feeble, mere sprouts in an improbable place, growing and spreading like the under-branches in the Shinjuku Garden.

They would make a splendid sight, dipping to the ground and heavy with flowers; but he could not remember having seen such a cherry tree. He could not remember having seen a great cherry tree with branches sweeping from its base.

"What shall I do with the *yatsude?*" asked Shuichi.

"Throw it away in a corner somewhere."

Gathering the *yatsude* under his arm, Shuichi dragged it off. Kikuko followed with several branches he had left behind.

"Don't bother," he said. "You still have to take care of yourself."

Kikuko nodded and stood where she had dropped the branches.

Shingo went into the house.

"What was Kikuko doing in the garden?" asked Yasuko, taking off her glasses. She was trimming an old mosquito net to use for the baby's naps. "The two of them out in the garden together on a Sunday. Very unusual—they seem to be getting along better since she went home."

"She's lonely," muttered Shingo.

"Not necessarily." Yasuko spoke with emphasis. "She has a nice laugh, and it's been a long time since I last heard her laughing so. She's a little thinner, and when I see her laughing. . . ."

Shingo did not answer.

"He comes back early from the office, and he's at home on Sunday. Storms make trees take deeper root, they say."

Shingo still did not answer.

Shuichi and Kikuko came in together.

"Father, Satoko tore off your much-prized branches." Shuichi held the little branches between his fingers. "She was having a great time dragging away *yatsude*, and then she ripped off your branches."

"Oh? The sort of branches a child would be likely to rip off."

Kikuko was half hidden behind Shuichi.

2

When Kikuko came back from Tokyo, she brought Shingo an electric razor of Japanese make. Yasuko received an obi binder, and Fusako dresses for the two children.

"Did she bring Shuichi anything?" Shingo asked Yasuko.

"A collapsible umbrella. And she seems to have brought an American comb with a mirror on the case. I've always been told that you don't give people combs, because that means breaking off relations or something of the sort. I imagine Kikuko doesn't know."

"I don't suppose they'd say so in America."

"She brought a comb for herself, too. A little smaller, and a different color. Fusako admired it, and got it. It probably meant a lot to Kikuko to come back with a comb like Shuichi's; and Fusako reached in and grabbed it. Just a silly little comb."

Yasuko seemed to find her daughter hard to excuse. "The children's dresses are good silk, real party dresses. It's true that Fusako herself didn't get anything, but the children's dresses were really presents for her. Kikuko must have felt guilty about Fusako when she gave away the comb. I don't see how any of us can expect presents from her."

Shingo agreed, but had causes for gloom unknown to Yasuko.

Kikuko had no doubt borrowed money from her family. Since Shuichi had gone to Kinu for the medical expenses, it did not seem that either he or Kikuko had money for presents. Under the impression that the medical expenses had been paid by Shuichi, Kikuko had probably importuned her parents.

Shingo was sorry that for some time now he been giving Kikuko nothing resembling an allowance. He had, to be sure, had good intentions; but as Shuichi and Kikuko had drifted apart and he had drawn closer to Kikuko, it had become more difficult for him to give her money as if in secret. But perhaps, in his failure to put himself in her place, he had resembled Fusako as she took possession of the comb.

And since it was because of Shuichi's philandering that she was short of money, Kikuko could hardly come crying to her father-in-law for an allowance. Yet if Shingo had shown more sympathy, she would not have had to submit to the indignity of having the money for her abortion come from her husband's mistress.

"I would have felt better if she hadn't brought anything," said Yasuko meditatively. "How much do you suppose it all came to? A great deal, I'd imagine."

"I wonder." He made a mental reckoning. "I have no idea how much an electric razor costs. I've never noticed."

"Nor have I." Yasuko emphasized this admission with a nod. "If you think of it as a lottery, you got the top prize. That's the way Kikuko would want things to be. It makes noise and moves."

"The blades don't move."

"They must. How else would they cut?"

"No. I've stared and stared, and they don't move."

"Oh?" Yasuko was smiling broadly. "The top prize, absolutely, if only from the way it makes you look like a child with a new toy. You buzz and grind away every morning, absolutely delighted, and you feel your pretty, smooth skin all through breakfast. It embarrasses Kikuko a little. Not that she's not pleased, too, of course."

"I'll let you use it." He smiled, but Yasuko shook her head emphatically.

Shingo and Shuichi had come home together on the night of Kikuko's return; and the electric razor had been the object of much breakfast-room attention.

The electric razor, it might have been said, did the honors in place of the awkward greetings that would otherwise have been exchanged between Kikuko, absent without leave, and the family of Shuichi, by whom she had been driven to an abortion.

Fusako too smiled happily, getting the children into their new dresses and praising the good taste of the embroidery at the necklines. Having mastered the instruction booklet, Shingo gave the razor a trial.

The inquiring eyes of the whole family were upon him.

He moved his chin over the razor, the instruction booklet in his other hand. "It says here that it does well too with the downy hair at the nape of a lady's neck." His eyes met Kikuko's.

The hairline at her forehead was very beautiful. It seemed to him that he had not really seen it before. It drew a delicately graceful curve.

The division between the fine skin and the even, rich hair was sharp and clean.

For some reason the cheeks of the otherwise wan face were slightly flushed. Her eyes were shining happily.

"Father has a nice new toy," said Yasuko.

"It's not a toy," said Shingo. "It's a finely tooled product of modern civilization. A precision instrument. It has a number, and it's initialed by technicians for the trial and the adjustment and the final inspection."

In fine spirits, Shingo tried shaving with and against the grain.

"You won't cut yourself or give yourself a rash, I'm told," said Kikuko, "and you don't need soap and water."

"An old man is always getting his razor caught in wrinkles. It will do nicely for you too." He offered the razor to Yasuko.

But Yasuko pulled back as if in fright. "If you think I have whiskers, you're quite mistaken," she said.

He looked at the blades, and put on his glasses and looked again. "They don't move. I wonder how it cuts. The motor revolves, but the blades don't move."

"Let me see." Shuichi reached for the razor, but passed it on immediately to Yasuko.

"It's true. The blades don't seem to move. Maybe it's like a vacuum cleaner. You know how a vacuum cleaner sucks in dirt."

"Can you tell where the whiskers go?" asked Shingo. Kikuko looked down and smiled.

"Suppose we give a vacuum cleaner in return for the electric razor. Or a washing machine—that would do too. It would be a help to Kikuko."

Shingo agreed with his old wife.

"We don't have a single finely tooled product of modern civilization in this house. Every year you say you'll buy a refrigerator, and it's time for one again this year. And toasters. There are toasters that turn off automatically and send the bread flying when it's done."

"An old wife's views on domestic electrification?"

"You are very fond of Kikuko, and a lot of good it does her."

Shingo unplugged the electric razor. There were two brushes in the case. One was like a small toothbrush, the other like a small bottle brush. He gave them a try. Cleaning the hole behind the blades with the bottle brush, he looked down and saw that very short white hairs were falling on his knee. He could see only white hairs.

He slapped them from his knee.

3

Shingo at once bought a vacuum cleaner.

It struck him as amusing that, before breakfast, his electric razor and Kikuko's vacuum cleaner should be buzzing along together.

Perhaps he was hearing the sound of renewal in the house.

Satoko trailed after Kikuko, fascinated with the cleaner.

It may have been because of the electric razor that Shingo had a dream of chin-whiskers.

He was not a participant but a spectator. In a dream, however, the division between the two is not clear. It took place in America, where Shingo had never been. Shingo suspected that he had dreamed of America because the combs Kikuko had brought back were American.

In his dream, there were states in which the English were most numerous, and states in which the Spanish prevailed. Accordingly, each state had its own characteristic whiskers. He could not clearly remember, after he awoke, how the color and shape of the beards had differed, but in his dream he had clearly recognized differences in color, which is to say in racial origins, from state to state. In one state, the name of which he could not remember, there appeared a man who had gathered in his one person the special characteristics of all the states and origins. It was not that all the various whiskers were mixed in together on his chin. It was rather that the French variety would be set off from an Indian beard, each in its proper place. Varied tufts of whiskers, each for a different state and racial origin, hung in sprays from his chin.

The American government designated the beard a national monument; and so he could not of his own free will cut or dress it.

That was the whole of the dream. Looking at the

wondrous assortment of colors in the beard, Shingo half felt that it was his own. Somehow he felt the man's pride and confusion as his own.

The dream had had scarcely any plot. He had just seen a bearded man.

The beard was of course a long one. Perhaps it was because he shaved his own face clean every morning that he had dreamed of that unfettered beard. He liked the idea of its becoming a national monument.

A naïve, uncomplicated dream, and he looked forward to telling it in the morning. He woke to the sound of rain, however, and, shortly going back to sleep, woke again, this time from an unpleasant dream.

His hands were against drooping, vaguely pointed breasts. They remained soft, refusing to rise. The woman was refusing to respond. All very stupid.

Even though he was touching her breasts, he did not know who the woman was. It was not so much that he did not know as that he did not seek to find out. She had no face and no body; just two breasts floating in space. Asking for the first time who she was, he saw that she had become the younger sister of a friend of Shuichi's; but the recognition brought neither excitement nor feelings of guilt. The impression that it was the sister was a fleeting one. She remained a dim figure. Her breasts were those of a woman who had not had children, but Shingo did not think she was a virgin. He was startled to find traces of her purity on his finger. He felt disconcerted, but not especially guilty.

"We can say that she was an athlete," he muttered.

Startled at the remark, he awoke.

"All very stupid"—he recognized Mori Ogai's * dying

* *Writer, 1862–1922.*

words. It seemed he had once read them in a newspaper.

But it had probably been an evasion on his part, waking from an unpleasant dream, to think first of Mori
Ogai's dying words and then to tie them to the dream.

The Shingo of the dream had felt neither delight nor
affection, nor even wantonness. All very stupid indeed.
And a dreary way to wake up.

He had not sought to assault the girl. Perhaps he had
been about to. Had he assaulted her, trembling with love
or terror, the dream would have had more life after he
waked.

He thought of wanton dreams he had had in recent
years. They had generally been of women he would have
to call coarse and vulgar. So it had been tonight. Was it
that even in a dream he feared adultery?

He remembered the friend's sister as having full
breasts. Before Shuichi married there had been some
not-very-serious talk of arranging a marriage with her,
and the two had kept company.

A bolt flashed across his mind.

Had not the girl in the dream been an incarnation of
Kikuko, a substitute for her? Had not moral considera-
tions after all had their way even in his dream, had he
not borrowed the figure of the girl as a substitute for
Kikuko? And, to coat over the unpleasantness, to ob-
scure the guilt, had he not made her a less attractive girl
than she was?

And might it not be that, if his desires were given free
rein, if he could remake his life as he wished, he would
want to love the virgin Kikuko, before she was married
to Shuichi?

Suppressed and twisted, the subconscious wish had taken an unlovable form in his dream. Even in the dream, had he sought to hide it, to deceive himself?

That he had transferred it to the girl who had been talked of for Shuichi, that he had given her an elusive, uncertain form—was it not because he feared in the extreme having the woman be Kikuko?

And the fact that, upon awakening, he had difficulty remembering it, that his companion in the dream, and the plot as well, was blurred, and the fact that there had been no pleasure in the hand against the breast— might these be because, at the moment of awakening, a certain cunning went adroitly to work at erasing the dream?

"A dream. And the national monument was a dream too. Don't put faith in what dreams decide for you." He wiped his face with the palm of his hand.

The dream had had a chilling effect, but when he woke Shingo was bathed in a disagreeable sweat.

The rain which after the dream of whiskers had been only enough to tell him that it was rain was now driven by a wind, and beating against the house. The dampness seemed to come up through the floor mats. It had the sound of a rain, however, that would have its brief rampage and go.

He remembered an ink wash by Watanabe Kazan * that he had seen at a friend's house a few days before.

It had been of a single crow at the tip of a leafless tree, and had born the legend: "A stubborn crow in the dawn: the rains of June. Kazan."

Shingo thought he understood Kazan's feelings, and

* *Scholar and painter, 1793–1841.*

the intent of the picture. The crow, high in a naked tree, bearing up under strong wind and rain, was awaiting the dawn. The storm was shown in faint ink. He did not remember the tree very well, but he thought it had been broken off, leaving only a thick trunk. He remembered the crow vividly. Perhaps from sleep, perhaps from the wind—most likely both—its feathers were somewhat ruffled. It had a heavy bill. The upper bill, blackly stained where the ink had run, was thicker and heavier than the lower. The eyes were sleepy, as if it had not yet fully awakened. Yet they were strong, and somehow angry. It was a large figure for the size of the picture.

Shingo knew of Kazan only that he had been impoverished and that he had committed suicide, but he could see that this "Crow in the Stormy Dawn" gave expression to Kazan's feelings at a certain point in his life.

No doubt the friend had put the painting up to match the season.

Shingo ventured an opinion: "A very strong-minded bird. Not at all likeable."

"Oh? I used to look at it during the war. Damned crow, I used to think. Damned crow it is. But it has a quietness about it. If Kazan had to kill himself for no better reasons than he had, then you and I probably ought to kill ourselves time after time. It's a question of the age you live in."

"We waited for the dawn, too."

The crow would be hanging in the friend's parlor this rainy night, thought Shingo.

He wondered where his own kite and crow would be.

4

Unable to sleep after waking from the second dream, Shingo lay waiting for the dawn. He did not wait with the stubborn resistance of the Kazan crow, however.

Whether the woman in the dream had been Kikuko or the friend's sister, he thought it altogether too dreary that no flicker of lust had come over him.

The dream had been uglier than any waking adultery. The ugliness of old age, might it be?

Women had left his life during the war, and had been absent since. He was not very old, but that was how it was with him. What had been killed by the war had not come to life again. It seemed too that his way of thinking was as the war had left it, pushed into a narrow kind of common sense.

He wanted to inquire among his friends whether many old men his age felt as he did. But perhaps he would but be laughed at and called weak and feckless.

What was wrong with loving Kikuko in a dream? What was there to fear, to be ashamed of, in a dream? And indeed what would be wrong with secretly loving her in his waking hours? He tried this new way of thinking.

But a *haiku* by Buson came into his mind: "I try to forget this senile love; a chilly autumn shower." The gloom only grew denser.

Shuichi's marital relations had ripened since he had taken a mistress. Since Kikuko had had her abortion, they had softened, warmed. On the night of that wild storm, Kikuko had been much more coquettish toward

Shuichi than usual: on the night he had come home drunk, she had forgiven him more gently than usual.

Was she sad, or silly?

And was she aware of these facts herself? Perhaps, not alive to them, she was but giving herself in all innocence to the wonders of creation, riding the wave of life.

She had protested by not having the baby and by going back to her family, and so given expression to an unbearable loneliness; and then, returning a few days later, she had drawn closer to Shuichi, as if apologizing for some misdeed, or treating a wound.

Shingo could, if he chose, think that this too was "all very stupid." But probably it was to the good.

He was even able to think that he might as well wait for the Kinu affair to settle itself.

Shuichi was his son; but were they so ideal a couple, were they so fated for each other, that Kikuko must put up with such treatment? Once he began doubting, the doubts were endless.

Not wanting to arouse Yasuko, he could not turn on the light to look at his watch; but dawn seemed to be breaking, and it would soon be time for the temple bell.

He remembered the bell at the Shinjuku Garden.

It had signaled closing time, but he had said to Kikuko: "It sounds like a church bell."

He had felt as if he were making his way through some wooded park on his way to a Western church, and as if the cluster of people at the gate were also going to church.

He got up without having had enough sleep.

He left early with Shuichi. He did not want to have to face Kikuko.

Suddenly he asked: "Did you kill anyone during the war?"

"I wonder. If anyone got in the way of a bullet from my machine gun, he probably died. But you might say I wasn't shooting the machine gun."

Shuichi looked away in displeasure.

The rain stopped during the day and began again in the evening. Tokyo was wrapped in a heavy fog.

When he left the restaurant after a business dinner, he found himself in the predicament of having to see the geisha home in the last automobile.

Two elderly geisha and Shingo were side by side, and three young ones sat on their knees.

"Please." Shingo put his hand to the front of the girl's obi.

"If you'll excuse me, then." Reassured, she settled in his lap. She was four or five years younger than Kikuko.

He meant to write her name down in his memorandum book once he was on the train. It was only a passing thought, however, which he seemed likely to forget.

In the Rain

❁

Kikuko was the first to read the newspaper that morning.

Rain had apparently blown into the mailbox. She dried the paper over the gas as she was cooking breakfast.

Sometimes, when he was awake early, Shingo went for the newspaper and took it back to bed with him; but now going for it seemed to have become Kikuko's work.

Usually he saw the newspaper only after Shuichi had left for the office.

"Father, Father," Kikuko called softly through the door.

"What is it?"

"If you're awake, would you come out for a minute?"

"Is something wrong?"

Alarmed by the tone of her voice, he got up immediately.

She was standing on the veranda with the newspaper in her hand.

"What's happened?"

"Mr. Aihara is in the paper."

"Has Aihara been taken in by the police?"

"No." Retreating a step, she handed him the paper. "It's still wet."

He reached for it, reluctantly. It sagged limply from his hand. Kikuko held it up for him.

"I can't see. What happened to Aihara?"

"It was suicide with a woman."

"Is he dead?"

"He will probably be saved, it says."

"Wait a minute." He started off, leaving the newspaper with Kikuko. "I suppose Fusako is here?"

"Yes."

It was scarcely likely that Fusako, who had gone to bed here with her two children late the night before, had committed suicide with Aihara, or that she would be in the paper.

Looking at the wind-driven rain outside the toilet window, Shingo sought to calm himself. The drops fell in rapid succession from the long leaves of pampas grass at the foot of the mountain.

"It's a real downpour. Not the usual thing for June."

In the breakfast room, he took up the newspaper, but before he could begin reading his glasses slipped down

over his nose. Snorting in annoyance, he took them off
and rubbed impatiently at the bridge of his nose. It was
damply unpleasant.

His glasses slipped down again as he was reading the
short article.

The incident had occurred at Rendaiji Spa on the Izu
Peninsula. The woman was dead. She was twenty-five or
-six and had the look of a maid or waitress, but had not
been identified. The man seemed to be a drug addict. The
probability was that he would be saved. Because of his
addiction and because there was no suicide note, there
was a suspicion that he had himself been playing a game
and had lured the woman on.

Shingo clutched at his glasses, which had slipped to
the tip of his nose, as if to give them a cuffing. He did not
know whether he was angry that Aihara had tried suicide
or angry that his glasses slipped.

Rubbing at his face, he went off to the washstand.

The newspaper said that Aihara had given the inn a
Yokohama address. Fusako was not mentioned.

The article was thus unrelated to Shingo's family.

Perhaps the registration was false, and Aihara was in
fact a vagrant. And perhaps Fusako was no longer his
wife.

He washed his face before he brushed his teeth.

Was it only sentimentality that left him troubled and
confused at the thought that Fusako might still be Aihara's wife?

"Is this what they call letting time take care of
things?" he muttered to himself.

Had time finally brought the solution he had so put off
seeking?

But might it not be that Shingo had had no recourse other than to hope for desperate action on Aihara's part?

He did not know whether Fusako had pushed Aihara to destruction, or whether Aihara had led her into misery. There were no doubt those whose nature it was to push their partners into misery and destruction, and those whose it was to be led into misery and destruction.

"Kikuko," he said, going back into the breakfast room and sipping at hot tea. "You knew, didn't you, that Aihara mailed us a divorce notice five or six days ago?"

"Yes. You were furious."

"That I was. And Fusako said there was a limit to the insults a person could take. But maybe he was getting ready for suicide. He wasn't pretending, he meant to kill himself. I imagine he just took the woman along for company."

Kikuko wrinkled her beautiful eyebrows and did not answer. She had on a striped silk kimono.

"Would you get Shuichi up, please?"

The retreating figure seemed taller than usual, perhaps because of the broad vertical stripes.

"So Aihara did it?" Shuichi took up the newspaper. "Has Fusako sent in the notice?"

"Not yet."

"Not yet?" Shuichi looked up. "Why not? Send it in this morning. We won't want to be sending in a divorce notice from a corpse."

"But what about the children? Aihara said nothing about them, and they're too young to decide for themselves which family they want to be in."

The divorce notice, with Fusako's seal on it, had been

going to and from the office in Shingo's briefcase.

He had occasionally sent money to Aihara's mother. He had thought to have the same messenger take the divorce notice to the ward office, but he had delayed from day to day.

"They're here, and you can't do a damned thing about it. I imagine the police will be coming."

"What for?"

"Looking for someone to hand Aihara over to."

"I don't think so. I think that must have been exactly why he sent the notice."

Banging the door open, Fusako came in, still in her night kimono.

She ripped the newspaper to pieces and flung it away after only glancing at it. Though she had put more than enough strength into the ripping, it did not rebound when she threw it. Falling to the floor on her knees, she pushed violently at the fragments.

"Close the door, please, Fusako," said Shingo.

He could see the sleeping children through the open door.

Her hands trembling, Fusako tore the newspaper into smaller pieces.

Shuichi and Kikuko were silent.

"Fusako. Do you feel like going for Aihara?"

"No!" Raising herself on an elbow, she turned and glared at Shingo, her eyes rolled upwards. "How do you feel about your daughter, Father? You coward. Seeing your own daughter into this, and not upset, not the least little bit. Swallow your pride and go for him yourself. You be the one to do it. Who was it that married me to a man like that?"

Kikuko went off to the kitchen.

Shingo had only said what floated into his mind; but he continued to think that if Fusako went for Aihara in this extremity, the two might come together again, they might make a new start. Human beings were capable of such things.

2

There was nothing more in the newspaper to tell them whether Aihara was dead or alive.

Since the ward office had accepted the divorce notice, it would seem that he was not registered as dead.

Or if he was dead, had his identity not been established? It hardly seemed likely. There was his lame mother. Even if she had not seen the newspaper, someone among their acquaintances and relatives would surely have noticed. Shingo concluded that Aihara had been saved.

But, having taken in Aihara's two children, was it enough for him just to conclude? For Shuichi the answer was clear, but Shingo himself still had doubts.

The two children were now Shingo's responsibility. Shuichi apparently did not consider the fact that they might one day be his.

Quite aside from the worry of rearing and educating the children, it would seem that what chance Fusako and the children had had for happiness had been cut in half; and was that fact too a part of Shingo's responsibility?

As he sent off the divorce notice, Shingo thought of the woman with Aihara.

A woman had died, that much was certain. What were the life and death of a woman?

"Come back and haunt us," he muttered to himself. Startled, he added: "And what a stupid life you had."

If Aihara and Fusako had gone on living together as an ordinary husband and wife, the woman need not have died; and so it was not impossible to call Shingo himself a murderer by remote control. Should there not then come into his mind pious thoughts about the dead woman?

But there was no way of conjuring up her image. Suddenly he saw Kikuko's baby. He could not of course see the face of a baby disposed of so early in pregnancy. Still he pictured the varieties of beauty in children.

The baby had not been born; and was he not then twice a distant murderer?

Unpleasantly wet days went on, when even his glasses seemed damp and clammy. He felt a heaviness in his right chest.

The sun blazed forth during lulls in the June rains.

"The house that had sunflowers last summer," said Shingo as he stepped into his trousers. "This year it has some white flower, I don't know the name of it. Something like a Western chrysanthemum. Four or five houses in a row have the same flower. They must have arranged it. Last year they all had sunflowers."

Kikuko stood in front of him, holding his coat.

"I imagine it's because the sunflowers were blown over in the storm."

"Probably so. Haven't you grown a little, Kikuko?"

"I've been getting taller since I came here, but lately I've begun to shoot up. Shuichi was very surprised."

"When?"

Flushing scarlet, Kikuko stepped behind him to help him into his coat.

"I thought you were taller, and it wasn't just the kimono. It's a good idea to keep growing for years after you're married."

"I've been too small. A late bloomer."

"Not at all. I think it's splendid." Shingo did feel something splendidly fresh in this new blossoming. Had Kikuko so grown that Shuichi noticed the difference when he held her in his arms?

It also seemed to Shingo, as he left the house, that the lost life of the child was growing in Kikuko herself.

Squatting at the edge of the street, Satoko was watching some little girls of the neighborhood play house.

Shingo too stopped to watch. He looked admiringly at the neatly clipped mounds of grass on the abalone shells and *yatsude* leaves they were using as dishes.

Dahlia and marguerite petals, also cut into fine bits, had been added for color.

They had spread a straw mat, over which marguerites cast a heavy shadow.

"Marguerites. That's what they are," said Shingo, remembering.

Marguerites had been planted before the several houses that had last year had sunflowers.

It seemed that Satoko was too young to be admitted to the company.

"Grandfather." She followed after him.

He led her by the hand to the corner of the main street. There was summer in the figure running back toward home.

Natsuko, her white arms bare, was polishing the office windows.

"Did you see the newspaper this morning?" he asked lightly.

"Yes." The word was, as usual, dull and heavy.

"The newspaper. Which paper was it, I wonder?"

"Which newspaper?"

"I don't remember which newspaper it was, but some sociologists at Harvard University and Boston University sent out a questionnaire to a thousand secretaries, asking what it was that gave them the greatest pleasure. Every last one of them said that it was being praised when there was someone around to hear it. Every last one of them. Are girls the same in the East and in the West? How is it with you?"

"But wouldn't it be embarrassing?"

"Embarrassing things and pleasant things often go together. Isn't it that way when a man makes a pass at you?"

Natsuko looked down and did not answer. Not the sort of girl one often comes upon these days, thought Shingo.

"I imagine that's how it was with Tanizaki. I should have praised her more often when there were people around."

"Miss Tanizaki was here," said Natsuko awkwardly. "At about eight-thirty."

"And?"

"She said she'd come again at noon."

Shingo sensed the approach of unhappiness.

He did not go out for lunch.

Eiko stood in the door. She was breathing heavily and seemed on the edge of tears.

"No flowers today?" Shingo hid his uneasiness.

She approached him solemnly, as if reprimanding him for his own want of solemnity.

"You want me to get rid of her again?" But Natsuko had gone to lunch and he was alone.

He was offered the startling news that Shuichi's woman was pregnant.

"I told her she must *not* have the baby." Eiko's thin lips were trembling. "I got hold of her yesterday on the way home from work, and told her so."

"I see."

"But isn't that right? It's too awful."

Shingo had no answer. He was frowning.

Eiko was thinking of Kikuko.

Kikuko, Shuichi's wife, and Kinu, his mistress, had become pregnant the one after the other. The sequence was of course not impossible, but it had not occurred to Shingo that his own son could be the agent. And Kikuko had had an abortion.

3

"Would you see whether Shuichi is here, please. If he is, ask him to come in for a minute."

"Yes, sir." Eiko took out a small mirror. "I'd be ashamed to have him see me this way," she added, somewhat hesitantly. "And then Kinu will find out that I've been bringing stories."

"I see."

"Not that I'd mind having to leave the shop."

"Don't do that."

Shingo inquired by telephone. He did not, at this moment, want to have to face Shuichi in front of other employees. Shuichi was out.

Inviting Eiko to a foreign restaurant nearby, Shingo left the office.

Eiko, who was small, walked close to him and looked up into his face. "Do you remember?" she asked nonchalantly. "You took me dancing just once when I was in your office."

"Yes. You had a white ribbon in your hair."

"No." She shook her head. "I had the white ribbon the day after the typhoon. I remember because I was very upset. It was the day you first asked about Kinu."

"Was that it?"

It had been that day, he remembered. Eiko had told him that Kinu's husky voice was erotic.

"Last September. I really asked too much of you." Shingo had come without a hat. The sun was hot on his bare head.

"I was no help at all."

"Because we didn't give you anything to work with. A family to be ashamed of."

"I admire you. Even more since I left the office." Her voice was strained and unnatural. After a moment she went on: "When I told her she must not have the child, she hit back at me as if I were a child myself that needed a spanking. I knew nothing about it, she said, and I couldn't understand. I'd do better to mind my own business. And finally she said she had it there inside her."

"Oh?"

"Who had asked me to give her stupid advice? If it had to do with being separated from Shuichi, there was nothing she could do but be separated when he left her. But the child was hers and no one else's. No one could do anything about it. If I could I should ask a baby inside my own self whether it was wrong to have it. I'm young and she was making fun of me. She said I wasn't to make fun of *her*. She may intend to go on and have it. I remembered afterwards that she and her husband had no children. He was killed in the war."

Walking beside her, Shingo nodded.

"Maybe she just said it because I irritated her. Maybe she doesn't mean to have it."

"How far along is it?"

"Four months. I didn't notice, but some of the others in the shop did. They say the owner heard and told her not to have it. She's very talented, and I imagine it would be a loss to the shop." She raised a hand to her face. "I didn't know what to do to. I thought if I told you you might speak to Shuichi."

"Yes."

"I think you should see her as soon as possible."

Shingo had been thinking the same thing. "The lady who came to the office with you that day—are they still living together?"

"Mrs. Ikeda."

"Yes. Which is older?"

"I believe Kinu is two or three years younger."

Eiko saw him back as far as his building. Her smile seemed on the edge of tears.

"Thank you."

"Thank *you*. Are you going back to the shop?"

"Yes. Kinu generally leaves early these days. The shop is open till six-thirty."

"You don't mean I'm to go there!"

It had been as if Eiko were urging him to see Kinu even today; but the thought was more than he could tolerate. And it would not be easy to face Kikuko when he got back to Kamakura.

Evidently, from her squeamishness, her irritation at being pregnant while Shuichi had another woman, Kikuko had refused to bear her child. Doubtless she had not even dreamed that the other woman was pregnant.

Kikuko had come back from a few days with her family after Shingo had heard of the abortion, and had since seemed closer to Shuichi. Home early every day, he was considerate as he had not been before. What did it all mean?

The more favorable interpretation was that Shuichi, deeply troubled by Kinu and her resolution to have the baby, was pulling away from her, apologizing to Kikuko.

But a scent of ugly decay and want of principle filled Shingo's nostrils.

Wherever it came from, the embryonic life itself seemed evil.

"And if it's born it will be my grandchild," Shingo muttered.

The Cluster of Mosquitoes

❀

Shingo walked up the main Hongo street on the side that skirted the Tokyo University campus.

He had left the cab on the side lined by shops, and would of course turn from that side into Kinu's lane. He had purposely crossed the car tracks to the other side.

He was most reluctant to visit the house of his son's mistress. He would be meeting her for the first time, and she was already pregnant. Would he be able to ask her not to have the child?

"So there is to be another murder," he said to himself.

"Can't it be accomplished without adding to the crimes of an old man? But all solutions are cruel, I suppose."

The solution in this case should have been up to the son. It was not the father's place to interfere. Shingo was going off to see Kinu without telling Shuichi; and he was thus no doubt providing evidence that he had lost faith in his son.

When, he asked himself, startled, had this gap come between them? Might it be that this visit to Kinu was less out of a wish to find a solution for Shuichi than out of pity and anger at what had been done to Kikuko?

The strong evening sunlight touched only the tips of the branches. The sidewalk was in shade. On the university lawns, men students in shirt sleeves were talking to girl students. It was a scene that told of a break in the early summer rains.

Shingo touched a hand to his cheek. The effects of the sake had left him.

Knowing when Kinu would be finishing work, he had invited a friend from another company to a Western restaurant. He had not seen the friend in rather a long time and had forgotten what a drinker he was. They had had a short drink downstairs before going up to dinner, and after dinner they had again sat for a time in the bar.

"You're not going already?" the friend had asked in surprise. Thinking that, at this first meeting in such a long time, they would want to have a talk, said the friend, he had called for reservations in the Tsukiji geisha district.

Shingo had replied he would come after paying an unavoidable visit of perhaps an hour or so. The friend had written the Tsukiji address and telephone number on a calling card. Shingo had had no intention of going.

He walked along the wall of the University, looking across the street for the mouth of the lane. He was relying on vague memories, but they did not prove wrong.

Inside the dark doorway, which faced north, there was a shabby chest for footwear. On it was a potted occidental plant of some description from which hung a woman's umbrella.

A woman in an apron came from the kitchen.

Her face went tense as she started to take off the apron. She had on a navy-blue skirt, and her feet were bare.

"Mrs. Ikeda, I believe. You once honored us at the office with a visit."

"Yes. It was rude of me, but Eiko dragged me along."

Her apron wadded in one hand, she looked at him inquiringly. There were freckles even around her eyes, all the more conspicuous because she did not seem to be wearing powder. She had a delicate, well-shaped nose, and one saw a certain elegance in the narrow eyes and the fair skin.

No doubt the new blouse had been made by Kinu.

"I was hoping to see Miss Kinu."

He spoke as if requesting a favor.

"She should be home soon. Would you like to wait?"

A smell of grilling fish came from the kitchen.

Shingo thought it might be better to come later, when Kinu had had her dinner. On the urging of the Ikeda woman, however, he went inside.

Fashion magazines were piled in the alcove of the medium-sized parlor, among them considerable numbers of what seemed to be foreign magazines. Beside them were two French dolls, their frills quite out of harmony with the shabby old walls. From the sewing machine hung a length of silk. The bright, flowery pattern made the dirty floor matting look all the dirtier.

To the left of the machine was a little desk on which were numerous primary-school textbooks and a photograph of a small boy.

Between the machine and the desk was a dressing table, and in front of the closet to the rear a full-length mirror, the most conspicuous piece of furniture in the room. Perhaps Kinu used it to try on clothes she had made, perhaps she gave fittings to customers for whom she did extra work. There was a large ironing board beside it.

The Ikeda woman brought orange juice from the kitchen.

"It's my son," she said immediately. Shingo was looking at the picture.

"Is he in school?"

"I don't have him here. I left him with my husband's family. The books—I don't have regular work like Kinu, and so I do tutoring. There are six or seven houses I go to."

"I see. I thought there were too many for one child."

"They're all ages and grades. The schools these days are a great deal different from before the war, and I'm afraid I don't really do very well. But when I'm teaching I feel as if he were with me."

Shingo nodded. There was nothing he could say to the war widow.

The other, Kinu, was working.

"How did you find the place? Did Shuichi tell you?"

"No. I came once before, but I couldn't make myself come inside. It must have been last autumn."

"Really?" She looked up at him, and looked down again. "Shuichi hasn't been coming around lately," she said abruptly, after a time.

Shingo thought it might be better to tell her why he had come. "I understand that Kinu is going to have a child," he said.

The woman shrugged her shoulders very slightly and turned to the photograph of her son.

"Does she mean to go ahead and have it?"

She continued to look at the photograph. "I think you'd better ask her."

"I agree. But won't it be a great misfortune for both mother and child?"

"I think you can call Kinu unfortunate whether she has the child or not."

"But I'd imagine that you yourself might have been advising her to break with Shuichi."

"That's what I think she should do. But Kinu is much stronger than I, and it hasn't amounted to advice. We're two very different people, but somehow we get along well. She's been a great help to me since we started living together. We met at the war widows' club, you know. Both of us have left our husbands' families and not gone back to our own—we're free agents, you might say. We want our minds to be free too, and so we've put our husbands' pictures away. I do have the boy's out, of course. Kinu reads all sorts of American magazines, and then she can get the gist of French too with a dictionary, she says. After all, it's about sewing and there aren't many words. She wants to have a shop of her own some day. We both say that when the chance comes we'll remarry. And so I don't understand why she had to be all tangled up with Shuichi."

The front door opened. She got up somewhat hastily and went out to the hall.

"Mr. Ogata's father is here," Shingo heard her say.

"Do I have to see him?" replied a husky voice.

2

Kinu went to the kitchen and seemed to be having a glass of water.

"You come in too," she said, looking back toward Mrs. Ikeda as she came into the room.

She had on a very bright suit. Perhaps because she was so large, it was not apparent to Shingo that she was pregnant. He found it hard to believe that the hoarse voice could have come from the small, puckered mouth.

The mirrors were in the parlor, and it seemed that she had retouched her face from a compact.

Shingo's first impression was not unfavorable. The face, round yet hollow, did not suggest the strength of will which the Ikeda woman had described. There was a gentle roundness about the hands too.

"My name is Ogata."

Kinu did not answer.

"You've kept us waiting," said Mrs. Ikeda, seating herself before the mirror stand. Still Kinu said nothing.

Perhaps because surprise and hostility did not show themselves well on the essentially cheerful face, she seemed about to weep. Shingo remembered that in this house Shuichi had gotten drunk and had made her weep by insisting that the Ikeda woman sing for him.

Kinu had hurried home through muggy streets. Her face was flushed, and her rich breasts rose and fell.

"It must seem strange that I should be calling on you," said Shingo, unable to approach his subject with complete directness, "but I imagine that you will have guessed what brings me."

Kinu still did not answer.

"Shuichi, of course."

"If it's about Shuichi, then I have nothing to say." Suddenly she pounced. "Are you asking that I apologize?"

"No. I think the apologies should come from me."

"We've separated, and I will be no more trouble to you." She looked at Mrs. Ikeda. "Shouldn't that take care of things?"

Shingo had difficulty replying, but at length he found words: "There is still the question of the child, you know."

"I don't know what you're talking about." Kinu blanched, but all her strength seemed to go into the words. As her voice fell it was even huskier.

"You must forgive me for asking, but I believe you are to have a child?"

"Do I have to answer that sort of question? If a woman wants to have a child, are outsiders to step in and prevent it? Do you think a man would understand that sort of thing?" She spoke rapidly and there were tears in her voice.

"Outsiders, you say—but I *am* Shuichi's father. I imagine your child will have a father too?"

"It will not. A war widow has decided to have a bastard, that's all. I have nothing to ask of you except that you leave me alone to have it. Just ignore it, as an act of charity, if you will. The child is inside me, and it is mine."

"That is true. And when you get married you will have other children. I see no need at this point in having unnatural children."

"And what is unnatural about it?"

"I didn't mean that."

"There is no guarantee that I will marry again, or that I will have children. Are you willing to play God and give us an oracle? I had no children last time."

"Relations between the child and its father are the main point. The child will suffer and so will you."

"A great many children were left behind by men who died in the war, and a great many mothers were left to suffer. Think of it as if he had gone off into the islands and left behind a half-breed. Women bring up children that men have forgotten long ago."

"The matter has to do with Shuichi's child."

"I can't see that it makes any difference as long as I don't mean to bother you. I won't come crying to you, I swear I won't. And Shuichi and I have separated."

"The child will live for a long time. The bond with its father will last after you think you've cut it."

"The child is not Shuichi's."

"You must know that Shuichi's wife did not have *her* child."

"She can have as many as she wants, and if she has none the regrets are hers. Do you think a pampered wife can understand how I feel?"

"And you do not know how Kikuko feels."

In spite of himself, Shingo spoke the name.

"Did Shuichi send you around?" She set upon him like an inquisitor. "He told me I was not to have the child, and beat me and stamped on me and kicked me and dragged me downstairs to try to get me to a doctor. It was a fine show, and I think we have acquitted ourselves of our duty to his wife."

Shingo smiled bitterly.

"It really was quite a display, wasn't it?" she said to the Ikeda woman, who nodded.

"Kinu is already collecting scraps that she thinks might do as diapers."

"I went to the doctor afterwards because I thought the kicking might have injured the child. I told Shuichi it was not his. It most definitely is not yours, I said. And with that we separated. He hasn't been here since."

"Another man's, then?"

"Take it so, and that will be that."

Kinu looked up. She had been weeping for some time, and there were new tears on her face.

Even now, at the end of his resources, Shingo thought the woman beautiful. On close examination her features were not perfect; but the first impression was of beauty all the same.

Despite the apparent softness, she was not a woman to let Shingo come near.

3

His head bowed, Shingo left Kinu's house.

Kinu had accepted the check he had offered her.

"If you're leaving Shuichi it might be better to take it." Mrs. Ikeda had been very direct, and Kinu had nodded.

"So you're buying me off. That's the sort of thing I've come to. Shall I give you a receipt?"

As he got into a cab, Shingo wondered whether it might not be better to effect a reconciliation between Shuichi and the woman. An abortion might still be possible. Or should the separation be considered final?

Kinu had been antagonized by Shuichi and now by Shingo's visit. Her longing for a child seemed unshakable.

It would be dangerous to push Shuichi toward the woman again; and yet as matters stood the child would be born.

Kinu had said that it belonged to another man. Not even Shuichi could be sure. If Kinu made the assertion out of pride and Shuichi was prepared to believe her, then the world might be described as in order. There need be no further complications. Yet the child would be a fact. Shingo would die, and he would have a grandson on whom he had never laid eyes.

"And so?" he muttered.

In some haste, they had submitted the divorce notice after Aihara's attempt at suicide. In effect, Shingo had taken in his daughter and two grandchildren. If Shuichi and his woman were to part, another child would remain, out in the world somewhere. Were they not but a clouding-over of the moment, these two solutions that were no solutions?

He had contributed to no one's happiness.

On a different level, he did not like to think of the ineptness with which he had faced Kinu.

He had intended to take a train home from Tokyo Central Station, but, coming upon the friend's card, he took a cab instead to the Tsukiji geisha district.

He hoped to ask advice of the friend. The latter was getting drunk with two geisha, however, and there was no opportunity.

Shingo thought of a young geisha who had once sat on his lap. It had been after a party, and they had been in an automobile. He called her again tonight. When she arrived the friend made a number of not very interesting remarks: that Shingo was not to be underestimated, that he had a good eye, and the like. It was rather an achievement for Shingo, who could not remember the girl's face, to have remembered her name. She proved to be winsome and elegant.

Shingo went into a small room with her, but did nothing out of the ordinary.

Soon he found her face pressed gently against his chest. He thought she was being coquettish, but she seemed in fact to have gone to sleep.

He looked inquiringly down at her. She was too near for him to see her face.

He smiled. There was warm comfort in having a young girl peacefully asleep in one's arms. She was still in her teens, four or five years younger than Kikuko.

Perhaps there was in his feelings a touch of pity at the plight of the prostitute. In any case, he felt himself bathed in a soft repose, the repose of sleeping with a young girl.

Happiness, he thought, might be just such a matter of the fleeting instant.

He considered vaguely the fact that in sex too there

were riches and poverty, good luck and bad. Slipping away, he caught the last train home.

Yasuko and Kikuko were waiting up in the breakfast room. It was past one.

"Shuichi?" asked Shingo, avoiding Kikuko's eyes.

"He's already in bed."

"Oh? And Fusako?"

"She's in bed too." Kikuko was putting away his suit for him. "The good weather managed to hold out, but it seems to have clouded over again."

"Oh? I hadn't noticed."

As she stood up, she lost her hold on the suit. She straightened the trousers again.

Shingo noticed that her hair was shorter. She seemed to have been to the beauty parlor.

With Yasuko breathing heavily beside him, he slept fitfully. Soon he had a dream.

He was a young army officer in uniform. He had a sword at his hip, and three pistols. The sword seemed to be the family heirloom that Shuichi had taken off to the war.

Shingo was walking a mountain path. He had a woodcutter with him.

"The roads are dangerous at night. I seldom go out," said the woodcutter. "You would do well to walk on the right."

Shingo felt uneasy as he moved to the right. He turned on a flashlight. Diamonds glittered around the edge, making it brighter than most flashlights. A dark form loomed up in the darkness—two or three cedars, one against another. But he looked more carefully and saw instead a great cluster of mosquitoes in the shape of a tree trunk. What to do, he wondered. Cut his way through. He took out his sword and hacked away at the mosquitoes.

Looking back, he saw that the woodcutter was in headlong flight. Here and there flames were shooting from Shingo's uniform. The strange thing was that there were two Shingos. Another Shingo was watching the Shingo along whose uniform the flames were creeping. The flames licked the sleeves and the shoulder seam and the hem of the tunic, and disappeared again. It was less that they blazed up than that they came and went like wisps from a charcoal fire, giving forth tiny noises.

Shingo was finally at home. It seemed to be his childhood home, in Shinshu. Yasuko's beautiful sister was there. Though exhausted, Shingo felt no itching from the mosquitoes.

The woodcutter who had fled in such haste also made his way to Shingo's old home. He fell unconscious as he stepped through the door.

From his body they took a great bucketful of mosquitoes.

Shingo did not know by what process this was accomplished, but he could see the piling up of mosquitoes in the bucket as he awakened.

"A mosquito in the net?" He listened carefully, but his head was heavy.

It was raining.

The Snake's Egg

❁

As autumn came on and the full weariness of summer overtook him, Shingo would sometimes go to sleep on his way home from work.

During rush hours there were trains on the Yokosuka Line every fifteen minutes. The second-class car was not crowded.

In his mind, as he dozed off lightly, was a row of acacia trees in bloom. Not long before, he had passed under the trees that now came to him, and he had marveled, as he looked up, that even in Tokyo rows of acacias came into bloom. It had been on the street leading from the foot of Kudan Hill toward the Palace moat. It had been a damp, drizzly day in mid-August. A single acacia in the row had scattered its flowers on the sidewalk. Why should that be, he had asked, looking back from the cab. The picture was still in his mind. The flowers had been delicate ones, pale yellow tinged with green. Even had there not been the single tree shedding its flowers, the fact of the row of flowering trees would no doubt have left its impression. He had been on his way from a hospital, where he had visited a friend dying of liver cancer.

Although they had been college classmates, the man was not one whom Shingo saw regularly. He was in an advanced state of emaciation and had with him only a nurse.

Shingo did not know whether or not his wife was still living.

"Do you ever see Miyamoto?" asked the friend. "Even if you don't have a chance to see him, would you mind telephoning and asking about it?"

"About what?"

"You remember. What we talked about at the class reunion. At New Year's."

Shingo remembered. It had been about potassium cyanide. The friend apparently knew that he had cancer.

At a gathering of men in their sixties, talk of senile disabilities and mortal ailments tended to loom large in the conversation. Knowing that Miyamoto's factory made use of potassium cyanide, someone had said that, should he perhaps fall victim to an inoperable cancer, he would hope to be given a dose of the poison. To prolong the hideous ailment would only bring meaningless suffering. And, when a person knew he was doomed to die, he would at least wish to choose his own time.

Shingo had trouble finding an answer. "But we were in our cups, after all," he said.

"I won't use it. I won't use it. I just want to have the freedom of choice we were talking about. I think I'll be able to stand the pain if only I know I have a way of being rid of it. You understand, don't you? It's all I have —call it my last liberty, my only way of resisting. But I promise you that I won't use it."

A certain fire came into the man's eyes as he spoke. The nurse, who was knitting a white woolen sweater, said nothing.

Unable to make the request of Miyamoto, Shingo had dropped the matter; but he did not like to think that a man who would soon die might still be depending on him.

At a certain remove from the hospital, the acacia trees, Shingo found, somehow brought relief. And now, as he dozed off on the train, the same row of trees appeared before him. The sick man had not left his mind.

He went to sleep, and when he opened his eyes the train had stopped.

It was not in a station.

The roar as a Tokyo-bound train passed had been more startling with Shingo's train stopped. Probably it had awakened him.

Shingo's train would move forward a little and stop, move forward a little and stop.

A group of children were running down a narrow road toward the train.

Several passengers were leaning out the windows and looking ahead.

Outside the left window was the concrete wall of a factory, a dirty, stagnant ditch between it and the train. The stench flooded in through the window.

To the right was the road along which the children were running. A dog stood motionless by the road, its nose in the green grass.

At the point where the road met the tracks there were two or three little huts, the cracks nailed over with old boards. From a window that was no more than a square hole a girl who seemed to be feeble-minded was beckoning to the train. Her motions were weak and languid.

"The train that left just before us seems to have had an accident in Tsurumi Station," said the conductor. "It is stopped there. We must apologize for keeping you waiting."

The foreigner opposite Shingo shook the Japanese boy sleeping beside him and asked in English what the conductor had said.

Holding the large arm of the foreigner in his hands, the boy had been sleeping with his head on the other's shoulder. In the same position after opening his eyes, he looked up coquettishly. His eyes were somewhat inflamed, and ringed with dark circles. His hair was dyed red, but had grown out black at the roots, to make it a dirty brown. Only the tips were that strange reddish color. Shingo suspected that the boy was a male prostitute who specialized in foreigners.

The boy turned the hand on the foreigner's knee palm up, and pressed it gently with his own, for all the world like a satisfied woman.

The foreigner's arms, below the short sleeves, made one think of a shaggy red bear. Though the boy was not particularly small, he looked like a child beside the giant foreigner. The latter's arms were heavy, his neck thick. Perhaps because he found it too much trouble to turn his head, he appeared quite unaware of the boy clinging to him. He had a fierce countenance, and his florid robustness made the muddy quality of the boy's weary face stand out more.

The ages of foreigners are not easy to guess. The large bald head, the wrinkles at the throat, and the blotches on the bare arms, however, made Shingo suspect that the man's age was not too far from his own. That such a man should come to a foreign country and appropriate a boy for himself—Shingo suddenly felt as if he were faced with a monster. The boy had on a maroon shirt, open at the throat to reveal a bony chest.

He would soon be dead, thought Shingo, averting his eyes.

The foul ditch was lined with green weeds. Still the train did not move.

2

Shingo found mosquito nets heavy and oppressive. He was no longer using one.

Yasuko complained of the deprivation every night and would make a great ceremony of swatting mosquitoes.

"Kikuko and Shuichi still have one."

"Suppose you go sleep with them, then," said Shingo, gazing up at the ceiling now liberated from the net.

"I couldn't very well do that. But I do think I'll move in with Fusako tomorrow night."

"Do. Sleep with one of your grandchildren in your arms."

"Why do you suppose, with the baby there, Satoko has to go on clinging to her mother? Don't you think there's something abnormal about her? She gets the strangest look in her eyes."

Shingo did not answer.

"I wonder if not having a father does that to a child."

"It might help if you were to make yourself more approachable."

"And you might do the same thing. I prefer the baby myself."

"Not a word from Aihara to let us know whether he's dead or alive."

"You sent in the divorce notice. And so it makes no difference."

"And that is that?"

"I know what you mean. But even if he were alive we would have no way of knowing where he might be. We'll have to resign ourselves to it—the marriage failed. But is that the way it should be? You produce two children and then separate? It doesn't give you a great deal of confidence in marriage."

"If a marriage has to break up, the echoes might be a little pleasanter. Fusako hasn't been all that good herself. He was a failure in life, and I don't imagine she gave him much sympathy. He must have suffered."

"There are things a woman can't do when a man is desperate. He won't let her come near. If Fusako and the children had just let themselves be thrown away, then I suppose there would have been nothing left for them but suicide. A man can always find another woman to commit suicide with him. And Shuichi," Yasuko went on after a pause. "He's all right now, but who can tell when he'll be up to something again. It wasn't good for Kikuko."

"You mean the baby?"

Shingo's word referred to two different matters: the fact that Kikuko had refused to have her child, and the fact that Kinu was determined to have hers. Yasuko did not know of the latter.

Kinu had said that the child was not Shuichi's and that she would take no interference from him. Shingo could not be sure of the truth, but he felt all the same that the woman was lying.

"Maybe I should go sleep with Shuichi and Kikuko after all. You can't tell what sort of discussions they might be having."

"And what do you mean by that?"

Yasuko, who had been lying on her back, turned toward him. She seemed about to take his hand, but he did not extend it to her.

She touched the edge of his pillow gently. Then, as if whispering a secret: "It's just possible that she's pregnant again."

"What!"

"I think it's a little too early, but Fusako has suspicions."

Nothing remained in Yasuko's manner from the days when she had announced her own pregnancy.

"Fusako said so?"

"It's a little early," said Yasuko again. "But they say

another often follows along after that sort of thing."

"Did Kikuko or Shuichi speak to Fusako?"

"No. Fusako's own investigations."

"Investigations" was a strange word. It seemed that Fusako, who had left her own husband, was particularly inquisitive in matters having to do with her brother's wife.

"You should say something to her yourself," Yasuko went on. "Persuade her to have it this time."

Shingo felt a tightening at the throat. The news that Kikuko might be pregnant again made the fact of Kinu's pregnancy weigh on him the more oppressively.

It was not so very unusual, perhaps, that two women should simultaneously be pregnant by the same man. But if the man was one's son, then it brought with it a strange fear. It had a hellish aspect, as of retribution, or a curse.

One might look upon these various events as evidence of the healthiest physiological processes; but such magnanimity was at the moment rather beyond Shingo.

This would be Kikuko's second pregnancy. Kinu had been pregnant at the time of the abortion. Before the latter had had her child, the former was pregnant again. Kikuko did not know of Kinu's condition. Kinu would already be attracting attention, and feeling the motions of the child within her.

"If she knows we know, then she won't be able to do quite as she pleases this time."

"I suppose not," said Shingo weakly. "You ought to have a talk with her."

Shingo could not sleep.

He found sinister thoughts coming to him. He asked himself irritably if violence of some description might not prevent Kinu from having her child.

She had said that the child was not Shuichi's; if he were to investigate her activities might he not come upon something to ease his mind?

There was a loud humming of insects in the garden outside. It was past two. The humming was not the clear and distinct sound of bell crickets or pine crickets. It was blurry and ill-defined, rather. It made Shingo think of sleep in dark, dank earth.

He had been much given to dreams lately, and toward dawn he had another long dream.

He did not know by what road he had come. When he awakened he could still see the two white eggs in the dream. He was on a sandy moor, there was sand as far as he could see. Two eggs lay side by side, one of them large, an ostrich's egg, and the other small, a snake's. The shell of the latter was cracked and an engaging little snake was waving its head back and forth. To Shingo it did seem engaging.

There could be no doubt that he had been thinking about Kikuko and Kinu. He did not know which child was the ostrich's, which the snake's.

It occurred to him to wonder whether snakes were oviparous or viviparous.

3

The next day was Sunday. Feeling quite drained of energy, Shingo stayed in bed until nine.

Now, in the morning, both the ostrich egg and the little snake's head seemed vaguely sinister.

He brushed his teeth gloomily and went into the breakfast room.

Kikuko was tying up the accumulated newspapers, no doubt preparing to sell them to a junk dealer.

It was among her duties, for Yasuko's convenience, to arrange the morning and evening newspapers in order.

She went to get tea for him.

"Did you see the news about the lotuses?" She put two newspapers on the table before him. "Two articles. I kept them out for you."

"It does seem to me that I read something of the sort."

He took the papers up all the same.

Lotus seeds some two thousand years old had been dug from a Yayoi tumulus. The "lotus doctor," a botanist who specialized in lotuses, had succeeded in making them sprout. News that they had bloomed had been in the papers earlier, and Shingo had taken it to Kikuko's room. She had been resting, having recently had her abortion.

Items about lotuses had appeared twice since. One described how the lotus doctor had divided the roots and transferred a part of them to Sanshiro's Lake, on the grounds of Tokyo University, from which he had graduated. The other had to do with America. A scientist at Tohoku University had found lotus seeds, apparently fossilized, in a marl stratum in Manchuria and sent them to America. The rock-like outer shell had been removed at the National Botanical Gardens, and the seeds wrapped in permeated cotton wadding and put under glass. They had sent out delicate shoots the year before.

This year, set out in a lake, they had produced two buds, which had opened into pink flowers. The national park service announced that the seeds were from a thousand to fifty thousand years old.

"I thought so when I read it the first time," laughed Shingo. "A thousand to fifty thousand years old—a broadish sort of calculation." He came upon a Japanese scholar's opinion: that, to judge from the nature of the marl stratum, the seeds would be some tens of thousand of years old. Carbon radiation tests run on the shells in America, however, had shown them to be a thousand years old.

The two articles were reports from Washington correspondents.

"Are you finished?" asked Kikuko, picking up the newspapers. No doubt she meant to ask whether she had permission to sell them when next the junk dealer came by.

Shingo nodded. "A thousand years or fifty thousand, a lotus seed lives a long time. Almost an eternity, when you compare it with a human life." He looked at Kikuko. "It would be good to lie in the ground a thousand years or two without dying."

"Lie in the ground!" Kikuko half muttered the words.

"Not in a grave. And not dying. Just resting. If it were possible just to rest in the ground—you would wake up after fifty thousand years and find all your own problems settled and the problems of the world, and you would be in paradise."

"Kikuko, will you see to Father's breakfast, please?" called Fusako from the kitchen, where she seemed to be feeding the children.

Kikuko came back with the breakfast.

"You're all by yourself. The rest of us have eaten."

"Oh? What about Shuichi?"

"He's gone out to the fishing pond."

"And Yasuko?"

"Out in the garden."

"I think I'll do without eggs this morning," he said, handing back the saucer that contained eggs. He disliked the memory it brought of the snake's egg.

Fusako came in with a dried and roasted flounder. She put it down in silence and went back to the children.

Looking Kikuko in the eye as he took the bowl of rice she handed him, Shingo said in a low voice: "Are you going to have a baby?"

"No." She answered readily, and seemed only afterwards to be taken by surprise. "No. Nothing of the sort." She shook her head.

"So it wasn't true."

"No."

She looked at him curiously, and flushed.

"I hope you'll treat it better next time. I argued with Shuichi over the last one. I asked if he could guarantee that you would have another, and he said he could. As if it were all very simple. I told him he ought to be a little more God-fearing. I asked him whether anyone could guarantee that he would be alive the next day. The baby would be yours and Shuichi's, of course, but it would be our grandchild too. A child you would have would be too good to lose."

"I'm sorry," said Kikuko, looking down.

He was sure that she was telling the truth.

And why then had Fusako thought her pregnant? Fusako's investigations had evidently outdone themselves.

She could scarcely be aware of a situation of which Kikuko herself was ignorant.

Shingo looked around, afraid that Fusako might have overheard the conversation. She seemed to be out in front with her children, however.

"Has Shuichi been to the pond before?"

"No. I think he must have heard about it from a friend."

To Shingo the unusual event seemed evidence that Shuichi had in fact left Kinu. He had on occasion used his Sundays to visit her.

"Would you like to go have a look at it yourself?"

"Yes."

Shingo stepped into the garden. Yasuko was looking up at the cherry tree.

"What's the trouble?"

"Nothing. But it's lost most of its leaves. I wonder if something might be eating it. The summer crickets are still singing, and here it has lost most of its leaves."

Even as they talked, yellowish leaves came down, one after another. In the still air, they fell straight to the ground.

"I hear Shuichi's gone fishing. I'm going to take Kikuko for a look."

"Fishing?" Yasuko looked around.

"I asked her about it, and she said it wasn't true. Fusako's investigations have misled her."

"You asked her about it?" There was something a little slow-witted about Yasuko. "What a shame."

"Why does Fusako have to be so energetic with those investigations of hers?"

"Why?"

"I'm the one who's asking."

Back in the house, Kikuko had put on a white sweater and was waiting for him. She had touched her cheeks with rouge, and seemed unusually bright and lively.

4

One day, without warning, there were red flowers outside the train window, equinox lilies all along the railway filling, so near that they seemed to quiver as the train passed.

Shingo gazed too at the lilies on the cherry-lined Totsuka embankment. Just coming into bloom, they were a fresh, clear red.

It was the sort of morning when flowers made one feel the quiet of the autumn meadows.

The pampas grass was beginning to send out plumes.

Taking off his shoe, Shingo raised his right foot to his knee and rubbed at the instep.

"Is there something the matter with it?" asked Shuichi.

"It seems so heavy. Sometimes climbing the stairs in the station my feet seem so heavy. This hasn't been a good year. The life is going out of me."

"Kikuko has been worried. She says you seem tired."

"I'd like to rest in the ground for fifty thousand years —that's the sort of thing I've said to her."

Shuichi looked at him curiously.

"There was something in the paper about old lotuses. Remember? Some ancient lotus seeds that sent out shoots and finally bloomed."

"Oh?" Shuichi lit a cigarette. "You asked her whether she was going to have a baby. She was very upset."

"Well, is she?"

"It's too soon, I think."

"And what about Kinu's? That's more important."

Though cornered, Shuichi took the offensive. "I understand you went to see her. To give her consolation money. There was no need for that."

"When did you hear about it?"

"Oh, I heard indirectly. We've separated, you know."

"Is the child yours?"

"Kinu says it isn't."

"The matter has to do with your own conscience." Shingo's voice was trembling. "What about that?"

"I don't think it's the sort of thing your conscience tells you much about."

"What do you mean by that?"

"Suppose I *am* suffering. Will that do anything to shake her? There is something demented about the woman and that determination of hers to have the baby."

"She's suffering more than you are. So is Kikuko."

"Now that we've separated, I can see that she's been going her own way all along."

"And that's enough for you? You really don't want to know whether or not it's your child? Or does your conscience tell you?"

Shuichi did not answer. His large eyes, almost too good-looking for a man, were blinking.

On Shingo's desk was a black-bordered postcard. The cancer patient had died somewhat more swiftly than the natural course of the illness would have led one to expect.

Had someone brought him poison? Perhaps Shingo had not been the only one of whom the request had been made. Or perhaps the man had found another way to commit suicide.

There was also a letter from Tanizaki Eiko. She had moved to another shop. Kinu had left the earlier shop shortly afterwards, the letter continued, and was in seclusion in Numazu. She meant to open a small business of her own, she had told Eiko. Tokyo would present too many complications.

Although Eiko had not touched upon the matter, it seemed likely that Kinu had retired to Numazu to have the baby.

Was it as Shuichi had said, that she went her own way quite without regard for others, for Shuichi or for Shingo himself?

He sat for a time looking absently into the clear sunlight.

What would the Ikeda woman, now left alone, be doing?

Shingo thought he would like to see either her or Eiko and make inquiries about Kinu.

In the afternoon he went to pay his condolences to the cancer victim's family. He learned for the first time that the wife had died seven years before. The man had apparently lived with his oldest son, and there were five children in the house. It did not seem to Shingo that either the son or the grandchildren resembled the dead man.

Shingo suspected suicide, but could not of course make inquiries. Giant chrysanthemums were conspicuous among the flowers by the coffin.

Going over the mail with his secretary, he had an unexpected telephone call from Kikuko. He feared that something untoward had happened.

"Where are you? In Tokyo?"

"Yes. Visiting my family." There was bright laughter in her voice. "Mother said she had something to talk over with me, and here I am, and it turns out to be nothing at all. She was just lonely and wanted to see my face."

"Oh?" Softness flooded into his chest, and the pleasingly girlish voice over the telephone was not the whole explanation.

"Will you be going home soon?" asked Kikuko.

"Yes. And is everyone well there?"

"Very well. I thought I'd like to go back with you."

"Take your time, now that you're here. I'll tell Shuichi."

"I'm ready to go."

"Suppose you come to the office, then."

"That will be all right? I thought I might wait at the station."

"No, come here. Shall I connect you with Shuichi? The three of us might have dinner together."

"The operator tells me he isn't at his desk."

"Oh?"

"I can start out right away."

Shingo felt warm to the eyelids, and the city beyond the window seemed lighter and clearer.

Fish in Autumn

❁

It was an October morning. Shingo, tying his necktie, felt his hands go wrong.

"Wait a minute." He paused, and a troubled expression came over his face. "How does it go?"

He untied it and tried again, but was no more successful the second time.

Pulling the two ends up to his face, he gazed at them inquiringly.

"What seems to be the trouble?"

Behind him and a little to one side, Kikuko was holding his coat. She came around in front of him.

"I can't tie my tie. Very strange."

Slowly and awkwardly, he wound an end around a finger and tried to pull it through the loop, but the result was a strange lump. The word "strange" was most appropriate for describing the performance, but fear and despair were written on Shingo's face.

It was an expression that seemed to startle Kikuko. "Father!" she cried.

"What shall I do?"

Shingo stood as if without strength for trying to remember.

Unable to watch in silence, Kikuko came up to him, the coat over her arm.

"How do you do it?"

In some consternation, she took up the tie. Her hands were dim to Shingo's old eyes.

"That's what I've forgotten."

"But you tie it yourself every day."

"So I do."

Why should he suddenly this morning have forgotten a process he had repeated every morning through the forty years of his office career? His hands should have moved automatically. He should have been able to tie his tie without even thinking.

It seemed to Shingo that he faced a collapse, a loss of self.

"I've been watching you every morning," said Kikuko solemnly as she twisted the tie and then straightened it out to begin again.

Quite giving himself up to her, he was like a small, spoiled child that is feeling somehow neglected.

The scent of her hair came to him.

"I can't do it." Kikuko flushed.

"Haven't you ever tied Shuichi's?"

"No."

"Just untied it when he's come home drunk?"

She drew back a little and, her shoulders taut, gazed at the tie.

"Mother might know," she said, at length releasing her breath. "Mother," she called, "would you come here, please? Father says he can't tie his tie."

"And why in the world should that be?" Yasuko's face suggested that she had never before been witness to such nonsense. "Why can't he tie it for himself?"

"He says he's forgotten how."

"Something went wrong, and I forgot everything. Very strange."

"Very strange indeed."

Kikuko moved aside and Yasuko took her place.

"I don't seem to remember it all that well myself." She gave his chin a gentle shove upward as she took the tie in her hands. Shingo closed his eyes.

Yasuko did somehow seem to be producing a knot.

Perhaps because of the pressure at the base of his skull, he felt a little giddy, and a golden mist of snow flowed past his closed eyelids. A mist of snow from an avalanche, gold in the evening light. He thought he could hear the roar.

Startled, he opened his eyes. Might he be having a hemorrhage?

Kikuko was holding her breath, and her eyes were on Yasuko's hands.

It was an avalanche he had seen in the mountain home of his boyhood.

"Will this do?"

Yasuko was putting the last touches on the knot.

"Yes."

His fingers brushed against hers as he reached to feel it.

He remembered that when he had left college and first discarded his choke-collared student's uniform for an ordinary business suit, it had been Yasuko's beautiful sister who had tied his tie for him.

Shingo turned to the mirror on the wardrobe, avoiding the eyes of Kikuko and Yasuko.

"This should do nicely. Well, old age has finally caught up with me. It's not a very comfortable feeling when you find all of a sudden that you can't tie your own tie."

To judge from the facility with which she had tied it for him, Yasuko would appear to have performed the function in the early days of their marriage, but he could not remember when it might have been.

Or perhaps, when she had gone to help after the death of her sister, she had tied her handsome brother-in-law's tie.

Slipping into sandals, a worried Kikuko saw him to the gate.

"What are your plans for this evening?"

"Nothing scheduled. I'll be home early."

"Make it very early."

Gazing at Mount Fuji in the autumn blue as the train passed Ofuna, Shingo again felt his tie. He found that left and right were reversed. Facing him, Yasuko had made the left end the longer.

He untied it and retied it with no effort.

That he should earlier have forgotten the process seemed scarcely credible.

2

It was not uncommon now for Shingo and Shuichi to take the same train home.

Normally there were trains on the Yokosuka Line every half-hour, but during rush hours the number was increased to one every fifteen minutes. Sometimes rush-hour trains were emptier than normal ones.

At Tokyo Station a young girl occupied one of the seats opposite them.

"Would you save this for me, please?" she said to Shuichi, putting a red suede handbag on the seat.

"Both seats?"

She murmured an answer that was not entirely clear. As she turned and went out, however, there was no suggestion of embarrassment on her somewhat heavily powdered face. The narrow shoulders of her coat had a most winsome upthrust, and the coat flowed down over a gently elegant figure.

Shingo was puzzled. How had Shuichi guessed that the girl wanted both seats saved? He seemed to have an instinct for such things; but how had he known that the girl would be waiting for someone?

Now that his son had taken the lead, however, Shingo too thought it most evident that the girl had gone to look for her companion.

And why, since she had been sitting by the window, opposite Shingo, was it Shuichi to whom she had spoken? Probably because, as she had stood up, she had found herself facing him; and then again, perhaps Shuichi was for a woman the more approachable of the two.

Shingo looked at his son's profile.

Shuichi was reading the evening paper.

The girl got back onto the train. Clutching the frame of the open door, she looked up and down the platform. Apparently the person with whom she had an appointment had not come. Her light-colored coat, as she returned to her seat, flowed rhythmically from shoulder to hem. It was held together by a large button at the throat. The pockets were well down and forward. She swayed from side to side, one hand in a pocket, as she came down the aisle to her seat. The cut, though somewhat strange, was most becoming.

Sitting down opposite Shuichi this time, she looked repeatedly at the door. It would appear that she had chosen the aisle seat because it offered the better view.

Her handbag still lay on the seat opposite Shingo. It was a sort of flattened cylinder, and had a large clasp.

The diamond earrings were no doubt imitation, but they had a good luster. The wide nose stood out on the firm, regular face, and the mouth was small and well shaped. The thick eyebrows, with a tendency to sweep upwards, had been clipped short. The line of the wide eyes was equally graceful, but disappeared before it reached the corners. The jaw was firm and strong. These various features added up to a face that was in its way beautiful.

There was a certain weariness in the eyes, and Shingo had trouble guessing her age.

The doorway was suddenly crowded. Shingo's eyes and the girl's were on it. Five or six men, apparently on their way home from an excursion, came aboard with large maple branches in their arms.

The dark red of the leaves suggested cold mountain country.

Presently he learned, from the boisterous talk, that the men had been deep in the mountains of Echigo.

"The maples in Shinshu will be their best," he said to Shuichi.

He was thinking less, however, of the wild maples in the mountains of his old home than of the large potted maple, its leaves crimson, among the memorial tablets when Yasuko's sister had died.

Shuichi, of course, had not been born.

He gazed at the red leaves, speaking so vividly of the season.

He came to himself. The father of the girl was seated before him.

So she had been waiting for her father! The thought somehow brought relief to Shingo.

The father had the same wide nose, so similar indeed that the effect was almost comical. The hairlines were identical. The father wore dark-rimmed glasses.

Like strangers, father and daughter neither spoke to nor looked at each other. The father was asleep before they had left the outskirts of Tokyo. The daughter also closed her eyes; and even the eyelashes seemed identical.

Shuichi did not resemble Shingo as closely.

Although waiting for the two to exchange even a remark, Shingo felt somehow envious of this complete indifference.

Theirs was no doubt a peaceful family.

He was therefore startled when, in Yokohama, the girl got off by herself. They had in fact not been father and daughter but complete strangers!

He felt that he had been deceived.

The man opened his eyes slightly as they stopped in Yokohama, and went untidily back to sleep.

Now that the girl had gone the middle-aged man before him seemed untidy to Shingo.

3

Shingo nudged Shuichi with his elbow. "So they weren't father and daughter."

Shuichi did not give as much evidence of interest as Shingo had hoped for.

"You saw them, didn't you?"

Shuichi nodded perfunctorily.

"Very strange."

Shuichi did not seem to think the matter strange at all.

"They did look alike."

"Yes, I suppose they did."

The man was asleep, and the train would have drowned out Shingo's voice; but still it did not seem right to be loudly assessing the man right before one's eyes.

Shingo looked away, feeling guilty even at staring; and as he did so a sadness came over him.

It was at first sadness for the man, and then it came to be directed at Shingo himself.

The train was on the long run between Hodogaya and Totsuka. The autumn sky was darkening.

The man was younger than Shingo, but in his late fifties even so. And the girl—would she perhaps be the age of Kikuko? There had been in her nothing corresponding to the cleanness of Kikuko's eyes.

But how could it be, Shingo wondered, that she was not the man's child?

The more he thought about the problem the more his wonder grew.

There were in the world people so resembling each other that one could only take them for parent and child. There could hardly, however, be large numbers of such people. Probably in all the world there was only the one man to go with the girl, only the one girl to go with the man. Only the one for either of them; and indeed perhaps in all the world there was only one such couple. They lived as strangers, with no suggestion of a bond between them. Perhaps they were even ignorant of each other's existence.

And quite by chance they were aboard the same train. They had come together for the first time, and probably would never meet again. Thirty minutes, in the length of a human life. They had parted without exchanging words. Sitting side by side, they had not looked at each other, and neither could have noticed the resemblance. And they had separated, participants in a miracle of which they had been unaware.

And the only one struck by the strangeness of it all was an outsider.

He wondered whether, accidental witness to it all, he too had partaken of the miracle.

What had it meant, creating a man and woman who looked like father and daughter, and putting them side by side for a half hour in their whole lives, and showing them to Shingo?

There she had sat, knee to knee with a man who could only be her father; and only because the person she had been waiting for had not come.

Was such the way, Shingo could only mutter to himself, with human life?

The man got up in some confusion as the train pulled into Totsuka. Taking his hat from the luggage rack, he dropped it at Shingo's feet. Shingo picked it up for him.

"Thank you."

Without bothering to dust it, he put it on.

"Very odd." Shingo at length felt free to speak. "They were strangers."

"They looked alike, but they weren't gotten up alike."

"Gotten up?"

"The woman paid attention to herself, and the man was a shambles."

"But that's the way it is—girls done up in the best, fathers in rags."

"Their clothes were on two completely different levels."

Shingo had to nod his assent. "The girl got off in Yokohama. And the minute she left it seemed to me too that the man went to pieces."

"He was in pieces from the beginning."

"But it happened in such a hurry. It struck home, somehow. He was a good deal younger than I am."

"Well, there's no doubt about it." Shuichi threw the matter off with a joke. "An old man looks better when he's out with a young girl. How is it with you, Father?"

"You youngsters are envious."

"Nothing of the sort. There's something uncomfortable about a handsome man out with a pretty girl, and you feel sorry for an ugly man when the girl is beautiful. Let's leave the beauties to old people."

But the strangeness of the pair was still with Shingo.

"Maybe they really are father and daughter. Maybe she's a girl he fathered away from home somewhere and left behind. They've never introduced themselves to each other, and don't know they *are* father and child."

Shuichi looked away.

Shingo was a bit startled at his own remark.

Having made what seemed like an innuendo, however, he had to go ahead: "Twenty years from now the same thing may happen to you."

"That was what you were trying to say, was it? Well, I'm not that sort of sentimental fatalist myself. The bullets used to go whistling by my ears, and not a one of them touched me. I may have left behind a child or two in the islands or in China. It's nothing at all, meeting your own bastard and not recognizing it, when you've had bullets whistling by your ear. No threat to your life. And then there's no guarantee that Kinu will have a girl, and if she says it isn't mine that's enough for me."

"Wartime and peacetime are not the same thing."

"But maybe another war is on its way. And maybe the other one is still haunting people like me. Still somewhere inside us." Shuichi spoke with asperity. "There was something a little strange about her, and you were attracted to her, and so you go on with these imaginings of yours. Men always get caught when a woman is just a little different."

"And that's all right, is it? Because a woman is a little different, you get her pregnant and leave her to bring up the child?"

"I don't want it. It's the woman herself."

Shingo fell silent.

"The woman that got off in Yokohama—she's a free agent. Perfectly free."

"Free?"

"She's not married, and she'd come if you called. She may put on airs, but she doesn't have a decent living, and she's tired of the insecurity."

The words upset Shingo deeply. "So that's how far you've fallen," he said.

"Kikuko's free too." There was challenge in Shuichi's tone. "She's not a soldier and she's not a prisoner."

"What do you mean saying that about your own wife? Have you said so to her?"

"Suppose you say it to her yourself."

"You're telling me I should send her away?" Shingo fought to control his voice.

"Not at all." Shuichi too was carefully controlling his voice. "We were saying that the girl who got off in Yokohama was free. Don't you suppose you thought they were father and daughter because she was about Kikuko's age?"

Shingo was taken by surprise. "It was just that if they weren't father and daughter they looked enough alike to make it a miracle."

"It wasn't anything to be all that impressed with."

"It was to me." But now, having had it pointed out that Kikuko had been on his mind, he felt a tightening in the throat.

The men with the maple branches got off in Ofuna.

"Why don't we go to Shinshu to see the maples?" said Shingo, watching the branches move off down the platform. "With Yasuko and Kikuko too."

"I don't have much interest in maple leaves myself."

"I'd like to see the old mountains again. Yasuko says she has dreams that her house is going to pieces."

"It is in bad shape."

"We ought to repair it while there's time."

"The frame is strong, and it's not going to pieces exactly. But if you were to start repairing it—what would be the point?"

"We may want a place to retire. And then you may have to get out of the city again some day yourself."

"I'll stay behind this time and watch the house. Kikuko can go have a look at the old place. She's never seen it."

"How is Kikuko these days?"

"Well, she seems a little bored, now that my affair is over."

Shingo smiled wryly.

4

Once again it was Sunday, and Shuichi seemed to have gone once more to the fish pond.

Lining up a row of cushions that had been airing in the hall, Shingo lay down in the warm autumn sun, his head on his arm.

Teru was sunning herself on the stone step below him.

In the breakfast room Yasuko was reading through the pile of newspapers on her knee, perhaps ten days' worth of them.

When she came on something interesting she would tell Shingo. It happened so often that Shingo's answers tended to be perfunctory.

"I wish you'd stop this business of reading all the newspapers on Sundays," he said, turning over sluggishly.

At the alcove in the parlor, Kikuko was putting together an arrangement of red crow-gourds.

"You found them on the mountain?"

"Yes. They seemed very pretty."

"Are there still some left?"

"Just a few. Five or six."

Three gourds hung from the vine in her hand.

Every morning from the washstand Shingo could see red gourds on the mountain, above the pampas grass. Here inside the parlor they were an even more dazzling red.

Kikuko also came into his range of vision.

There was an indescribable freshness about the line from her jaw to her throat. It was not the product of a single generation, thought Shingo, somehow saddened.

Perhaps because the style of her hair set off the neck and throat, her face seemed a little thin.

Shingo had of course been aware all along of the beauty of that line, and the long, slender throat. Was it that, given the considerable distance and the angle from which he was watching her, it stood out in more beauty than usual?

Perhaps the autumn radiance added something.

That line from jaw to throat spoke first of maidenly freshness. It was beginning to swell a little, however, and that maidenliness would soon disappear.

"Just one more," Yasuko called. "Here's a very interesting one."

"Oh?"

"It's about America. A place called Buffalo, New York. Buffalo. A man had his left ear cut off in an automobile accident, and went to a doctor. The doctor ran off to where the accident happened and found the ear, all dripping blood, and stuck it back on. And it's worked perfectly since."

"They say you can put a finger back on if you do it soon enough."

"Oh?" She read on for a time, and seemed to remember something. "I suppose that's true of husband and wife too. If you put them back together soon enough they'll stick. But it's been too long."

"What do you mean?" said Shingo, not really asking a question.

"Don't you suppose it's that way with Fusako?"

"Aihara's disappeared," answered Shingo lightly, "and we don't know whether he's dead or alive."

"Oh, we could find that out if we tried. But what's to happen?"

"So Granny still has her regrets. Give them up. We sent in the divorce notice long ago."

"I've been good at giving things up since I was a girl. It's just that I have her and the two children right here in front of me, and wonder what's to become of them."

Shingo did not answer.

"Fusako's not the prettiest girl in the world. And suppose she *were* to remarry—it would be really too much for Kikuko to have the two children left on her hands."

"Kikuko and Shuichi would have to live somewhere else. And it would be up to Granny to raise the children."

"I don't think anyone could call me lazy, but how old do you think I am?"

"Do your best and leave what's undone to the gods. Where's Fusako?"

"They've gone to see the Buddha. Children are very strange. Satoko almost got run over once on her way back, and she still loves the place. She's always crying to go there."

"I doubt if it's the Buddha itself that she likes."

"It does seem to be."

"Come, now."

"Don't you suppose Fusako could go back to the country? They might make her their heir."

"They don't need an heir," said Shingo curtly.

Yasuko read her newspapers in silence.

"Mother's ear story reminds me." This time it was Kikuko who spoke. "Do you remember how you once said you'd like to leave your head in a hospital and have it cleaned and restored?"

"We were looking at the sunflowers down the street. I think the need is more pressing now that I find myself forgetting how to tie my tie. Before long I'll be reading the newspaper upside down and not noticing."

"I often think about it, how it would be after you left your head in a hospital."

Shingo looked at her. "Well, it's as if you were leaving your head at a hospital every night for a sleep cure, I suppose. Maybe it's because I'm old, but I'm always having dreams. 'When I am in pain, I have dreams that continue reality.' I seem to remember reading that line in a poem somewhere. Not that my own dreams go on with reality."

Kikuko was surveying her completed arrangement.

Shingo too gazed at the gourds. "Kikuko. Why don't

you and Shuichi go live somewhere else?"

Kikuko looked up in surprise, and came over to him. "I'd be afraid." It was a voice too low for Yasuko to overhear. "I'm afraid of him."

"Do you intend to leave him?"

"If I were to, I'd be able to look after you as I pleased," she said solemnly.

"Your misfortune."

"It's no misfortune when you're doing something you want to do."

Shingo was startled. The remark was like a first expression of ardor. He sensed in it a certain danger.

"You're very diligent in looking after me, but don't you have me confused with Shuichi? I should think it would only drive him farther away."

"There are things about him I don't understand." The white face seemed to be pleading with him. "Sometimes all of a sudden I'm so frightened I don't know what to do."

"I know. He changed after he went to war. Sometimes he seems to behave on purpose so that I myself can't tell what's on his mind. But then if you just stick to him like that ear, all dripping blood, maybe things will come out all right."

Kikuko was gazing at him.

"Has he told you that you are a free agent?"

"No." She looked at him in curiosity. "A free agent?"

"I asked him myself what he meant by saying that about his own wife. I suspect he may have meant partly that you should be freer. I should arrange to let you go free."

"You mean from you yourself?"

"Yes. He said I should tell you you're free."

That moment a sound came from the heavens. To Shingo it was really as if he had heard a sound from the heavens.

Five or six pigeons cut a low diagonal across the garden.

Kikuko also heard them. She went to the edge of the veranda.

"Am I free, then?" she said, tears in her voice, as she watched the pigeons fly off.

The dog Teru left the step to run off across the garden in pursuit of the wings.

5

All seven members of the family were present at dinner.

Fusako and her two children were now members of the family too, no doubt.

"There were only three trout left at the store," said Kikuko. "One of them is for Satoko." She set the three before Shingo, Shuichi, and Satoko.

"Trout are not for children." Fusako put out her hand. "Give it to Grandmother."

"No." Satoko clutched at the dish.

"What big trout," observed Yasuko calmly. "The last of the year, I imagine. I'll just pick away at Grandfather's here, and I don't need any of yours. Kikuko can have some of Shuichi's."

They formed three separate factions. Perhaps they should be in three separate houses.

Satoko's attention was concentrated on the trout.

"Is it good?" asked Fusako, frowning. "But what a messy way to eat." She scooped out the roe and gave it to Kuniko, the younger child. Satoko did not object.

"Roe," muttered Fusako, tearing off one end of the roe in Shingo's trout.

"Back in the old days in the country, Yasuko's sister got me interested in writing *haiku*. There are all sorts of expressions about trout—'autumn trout,' and 'descending trout,' and 'rusty trout.' That sort of thing." Shingo glanced at Yasuko and went on. " 'Descending trout' and 'rusty trout' are trout that have laid their eggs. Worn out, completely exhausted, they are going down to sea."

"Just like me." Fusako's response was immediate. "Not that I was much to look at as a healthy trout."

Shingo pretended not to hear. " 'A trout in the autumn, abandoning itself to the water.' 'Trout swimming down the shallows, not knowing they must die.' That sort of old poem. I imagine they would apply to me."

"To me," said Yasuko. "Do they die when they've laid their eggs and gone down to sea?"

"I believe that's the way it went. Though of course there were occasionally trout that spent the winter in deep pools. They were called 'remaining trout.' "

"Maybe that's the kind of trout I am."

"I don't think I'll be able to stay on," said Fusako.

"But you've put on weight since you came home," said Yasuko, looking at her daughter, "and your color has improved."

"I don't want to put on weight."

"Being at home is like hiding in a deep pool," said Shuichi.

"I don't want to stay all that long. I'd rather go down

to the sea, Satoko." Her voice rose. "You haven't anything there but bones. Stop worrying them."

"Your talk about the trout has spoiled the flavor of the trout," said Yasuko, a quizzical expression on her face.

Fusako looked down, and her mouth was working nervously. Then she gathered herself to bring out the words: "Father. Won't you open a little shop for me? A cosmetics shop, a stationery shop, anything. I don't care what part of town it's in. I don't mind if it's just a street stall. A drinking place."

"You think you'd be able to manage that kind of business?" asked Shuichi in surprise.

"I would. Customers don't come to drink a woman's face. They come to drink sake. Are you comparing me with your pretty wife?"

"That's not what I meant at all."

"Of course she can do it," put in Kikuko, to the surprise of the others. "And if she decides to have a try, I'll ask her to let me help her."

"A very fine plan indeed," said Shuichi.

The dinner table fell silent.

Kikuko alone among them flushed. She was crimson to the ears.

"How about next Sunday?" said Shingo. "I'd been thinking it would be good if we could all go to the country to see the maples."

Yasuko's eyes sparkled.

"Kikuko too. Kikuko hasn't seen our old home."

"I'd love to," said Kikuko.

Shuichi and Fusako sat in perverse silence.

"Who will watch the house?" asked Fusako at length.

"I will," said Shuichi.

"No, I will. But I'd like to have your answer, Father, before you leave."

"I'll let you know my decision," said Shingo. He was thinking of Kinu, said to have opened a small dressmaking shop in Numazu, the child still inside her.

The moment the meal was over Shuichi left the table.

Shingo too got up, rubbing at a cramp in the small of his back. He looked absently into the living room and turned on the light.

"Your gourds are sagging," he called to Kikuko. "They seem to be too heavy."

She apparently could not hear him over the sound of the dishes.

A NOTE ABOUT THE AUTHOR

YASUNARI KAWABATA, winner of the 1968 Nobel Prize for Literature, was one of Japan's most distinguished novelists. He is famous for adding to the once fashionable naturalism imported from France a sensual, more Japanese impressionism. He was born in Osaka in 1899. As a boy, he hoped to become a painter, an inspiration later reflected in his novels. But his first stories were published while he was still in high school, and he decided to become a writer.

He was graduated from Tokyo Imperial University in 1924. His story "The Izu Dancer," first published in 1925, appeared in the ATLANTIC MONTHLY *in 1954. It captures the shy eroticism of adolescence, and thereafter Kawabata devoted his novels largely to aspects of love.* SNOW COUNTRY, *a novel concerning the love affair of a Tokyo snob with a country geisha, was published in English in 1956 and excited much praise.* THOUSAND CRANES *(1959) is a deeply moving story of ill-fated love.*

Kawabata was also a prominent literary critic and discovered and sponsored such remarkable young writers as Yukio Mishima. In 1948 he was appointed chairman of the Japanese Center of the P.E.N. Club. His death by suicide in April 1972 came as a tremendous shock to his admirers both in Japan and abroad.

A NOTE ABOUT THE TRANSLATOR

EDWARD GEORGE SEIDENSTICKER was born in Castle Rock, Colorado, in 1921. He received his B.A. from the University of Colorado, his M.A. from Columbia University, and has done graduate work at Harvard University and Tokyo University. He is currently professor of Japanese at the University of Michigan.

Among the important contemporary Japanese novels Mr. Seidensticker has translated are SNOW COUNTRY *and* THOUSAND CRANES *by Yasunari Kawabata, and* THE MAKIOKA SISTERS *by Junichiro Tanizaki.*

Library of Japanese Literature